His Scandal

Emmeline knew just who held her, and although she struggled, Sir Alexander did not release her. His arm encircled her waist, pulling her up against his body. She had never realized how wide and hard a man's chest could be, and how easily she could be overwhelmed. She should be frightened, but instead excitement shivered through her.

He suddenly stilled, and then whispered, "Emmeline?"

She nodded and tried to pull his hand away from her mouth.

"Do you promise not to cry out?"

She nodded again with great exaggeration. He released her mouth, but not her body, and she put her hands on his chest and tried to push.

"How did you know it was me?" she whispered.

Other AVON ROMANCES

GAYLE CALLEN

His Scandal

AVON BOOKS
An Imprint of HarperCollinsPublishers

This is a work of fiction. Names, characters, places, and incidents are products of the author's imagination or are used fictitiously and are not to be construed as real. Any resemblance to actual events, locales, organizations, or persons, living or dead, is entirely coincidental.

AVON BOOKS
An Imprint of HarperCollins*Publishers*
10 East 53rd Street
New York, New York 10022-5299

Copyright © 2002 by Gayle Kloecker Callen
ISBN: 0-380-82109-5
www.avonromance.com

First Avon Books paperback printing: May 2002

Avon Trademark Reg. U.S. Pat. Off. and in Other Countries, Marca Registrada, Hecho en U.S.A.
HarperCollins ® is a registered trademark of HarperCollins Publishers Inc.

Printed in the U.S.A.

10 9 8 7 6 5 4 3 2 1

This is a story about two sisters,
so I dedicate it to my sister, Connie Weiser,
who when we were young,
listened to my story ideas
as we fell asleep each night.
My thanks for your endless patience and your love.

Prologue

London
September, 1588

At the top of the marble stairs, tall, windowed doors swung open, and the queen's courtiers within the great hall turned to stare, knowing that the moment they'd all waited for had arrived. A petite woman stepped into the hall, flanked by two men, identical in every way, from their black hair to their swarthy skin to their midnight eyes.

Even the orchestra faltered as whispers spread out in a hiss. One of the brothers was Viscount Thornton, newly returned from spying on their enemy, Spain, before the armada had sailed. His heroism had been lauded by Queen Elizabeth, and his bravery had won him the hand of his wife, Lady Roselyn. The crowd surged forward to ingratiate themselves with the new hero, then the tide seemed to flow backward as they all hesitated.

Which one was Lord Thornton—and which was his scandalous brother?

No one wanted to congratulate Sir Alexander, who'd spent almost a year and a half deceiving society when he posed as his brother, spending money that wasn't his, misleading noble maidens with the lure of marrying a viscount. His scandals had shaken London to its core, and were clear proof of who deserved the viscountcy.

Just when the confused murmurs rose like bees buzzing to protect their hive, one of the brothers stepped aside and bowed to the couple on the last stair above the crowd. Concluding the obvious, the courtiers swarmed forward, swallowing up the viscount and his wife.

Alex Thornton was glad for the escape, even though his brother shot him a frown over the heads of his adoring audience. Alex winked and turned away, grabbed the first tankard of ale that floated by on a servant's tray, and drained it quickly.

He hadn't even begun to get drunk when he saw Lord Manvil, who'd been working with him on a bill for the House of Lords.

Alex pushed his way through the crowd, then called, "Manvil! Might I have a moment of your time?"

The man turned from his wife and smiled beneath his huge mustache. "Lord Thornton, welcome back!"

Alex gave a lopsided grin. "You're actually speaking with the knight instead of the viscount. I was wondering if you had some time to discuss that bill we've been—"

Manvil held up a hand. "This is highly improper, Sir Alexander. Such private business among the Lords can no longer be your concern."

Alex widened his eyes, trying not to let this newest slight affect his temper. "But I'm the one who wrote the bill."

"Nevertheless—ah, it is Lord Thornton himself."

Alex turned to find his brother standing behind him, obviously having overheard the humiliating encounter with Lord Manvil. To make matters worse, Spencer was trying to hide his worry and pity.

Alex grinned. "There you go, Manvil, just the man you needed. I'm sure you can bring Spence up on all the details."

"Alex, don't leave us," his brother said. "You've hardly had a chance to familiarize me with all your work. Lord Manvil, I'm sure you see the necessity of—"

"Nonsense," Alex interrupted, backing away. "Manvil can explain the whole thing. I'm done with all this, remember? And 'tis about time, too."

He grabbed another tankard of ale and leered at the maidservant carrying it.

Then he went off to find the first of many maidens he would woo away from their outraged mothers for a dance. By midnight, he had propositioned two married women, one of whom had slapped his face, and the other—well, he'd find out her thoughts later that night in her bedchamber. It was good to be himself again.

Scandal was what he did best, after all.

Chapter 1

London
April, 1589

Alex Thornton was fresh out of new scandals. Standing beside his friend Edmund Blackwell, he sighed as he watched the hall full of glittering couples dancing merrily beneath vaulted ceilings.

It had been eight months since he'd given his twin brother Spencer's identity back to him. Eight months of constantly explaining to disappointed people that he'd only *posed* as the viscount.

Alex had vowed to enjoy his own life again, without the responsibilities of a noble title. He would do as he pleased, drink, gamble himself into oblivion, and find willing young women to enjoy it all with him.

Sad to say, those pleasures had grown almost . . . tiresome of late. Each party blurred into the next. He needed a change, something new to interest him.

"Edmund, are you as bored as I?"

Edmund shrugged, and his gaze surveyed the crowd. "I doubt it."

Of course Edmund wasn't bored—he hadn't grown up among the nobility. He was one of those rare men who'd worked hard since childhood to achieve success, and had been knighted for his efforts.

Alex almost envied him.

"We need to enliven the evening," he continued. "I propose a wager."

Edmund rolled his eyes. "You know you can outdrink me."

"No, something new." He met the bright gaze of a lady and gave her a smile. "We seem to have the attention of several young women this evening."

"Until their mothers see where they're looking," Edmund said dolefully, folding his arms across his chest.

"And *there* is our challenge. I wager that I can get one dewy-eyed innocent to kiss me before you can find one who'll kiss that face of yours."

"A virgin? I'd be beetle-headed to accept such a thing!" Edmund scoffed. "You've stolen kisses from half the girls here."

"Not the challenging ones, I haven't," Alex said. "So to make this interesting, I shall pick out the girl for you, and you shall pick out mine."

A slow grin eased Edmund's deceptively hard face. "I'll wager five sovereigns. But what happens if an angry father decides that one kiss compromises his daughter?"

Alex shrugged. "We have to marry sometime, do we not?"

"As if you would ever be trapped against your will," Edmund said. "Very well. I'll be magnanimous and allow you to choose first."

They turned to look out on the great hall. Couples whirled about, and women were lifted in the air by their partners. Crowds of people talked and ate and laughed. Who to choose for Edmund?

Then he saw her—blond, pretty, and not ranked highly enough to look down upon Edmund, who'd begun manhood as a common soldier. Due to her overly protective family, it would be difficult for Edmund to get even close to her.

Alex cleared his throat and clasped his hands behind his back. "I have the perfect girl. Elizabeth Langston."

Edmund looked doubtful. "Her name is not familiar."

Alex pointed to where she stood alone with her parents, not dancing.

"She is quite beauteous," Edmund said. "But surely you had a specific reason in choosing her?"

"I shall just warn you to beware her father—and her brothers."

Edmund sighed and continued to search the crowd. Finally he displayed a triumphant smile. "Ah, now *there* is a woman who'd be a challenge for you."

"Who?" Alex asked, feeling a pleasant sense of anticipation.

Edmund inclined his head toward the merry dancers. "Lady Blythe Prescott."

The younger daughter of the Marquess of Kent. When the crowd parted he saw her laughing face, her shining hair the color of the finest chocolate from the New World. Though he'd never conversed with her, he had often noticed her loveliness and her musical laugh.

He was almost . . . disappointed.

Oh, she was pretty, but the flirtatious glances she bestowed on every dance partner suggested a woman easily kissed.

Edmund laughed. "Do not be so disgruntled, my friend."

"She will be no challenge. Is there something you are not divulging?" Alex asked, his interest returning as Edmund smirked.

And then he saw another woman, an older, paler imitation of Blythe, approaching the girl while wearing a censorious frown. Blythe gave her partner an apologetic look, slid her arm into the other woman's, and walked away.

"And who is that?" Alex demanded.

Edmund grinned. "That was Lady Emmeline Prescott, Blythe's sister."

"Let me guess—a spinster," Alex said with a groan.

Edmund's smile showed almost every tooth in his head. "I am certainly going to relish taking your money."

"You haven't won yet, my good man. There is not a woman born I can't cajole. It will be easy to elude one sister in pursuit of the other."

Edmund gave him a formal bow. "Then I wish you luck, sir—you'll need it. Shall we begin?" He took himself off without a backward glance.

Alex's gaze returned to the two sisters, now standing together near the banqueting table. Blythe's smile was lively as she listened to her sister's obviously serious words. Emmeline had none of Blythe's vivaciousness, and her dark hair had a reddish tinge to it. Perhaps if she smiled occasionally, she would have ensnared a man by now.

Yet she was the daughter of a marquess— surely men must be lining up at her door, if only for a share of her wealth. So why had she never married?

Hell, he didn't have to care about the sister; he only had to outwit her. And for that to succeed, he had to win the younger sister's cooperation.

So he began to follow Blythe about the room, sending longing glances her way, ready for the moment their eyes would meet.

It came as she was talking to Emmeline, whose back was to Alex. Over Emmeline's shoulder, Blythe glanced up and saw him there, not ten paces away, watching her. He held her gaze and gave her a slow smile tinged with a slight wickedness. It was something he was naturally good at.

Blythe smiled back, and her cheeks pinkened delightfully. She returned her attention to her sister, but she eventually glanced at him again. He inclined his head, and this time her face reddened. He beckoned with one hand—a miscalculation, for her smile faded, and she looked away.

Very well, he had tried the easy method, and was relieved that Blythe would be more challenging. The moment Emmeline left her side, Alex was there, bowing before Blythe. That lovely blush returned to her face.

"Lady Blythe," he murmured, reaching for her fingers and kissing them. When he didn't immediately let go, she disengaged her hand from his.

"Good evening, sir," she said, a reluctant-looking smile on her face. "Have we met?"

"No, my lady, but how can any man not know your name? I am Sir Alexander Thornton, and I would gladly pay a king's ransom to dance with you."

"An exchange of coin is not necessary, Sir Alexander," she said, followed by a spirited laugh. "Dancing is such a joy that I'll gladly indulge you for free."

And then he whirled her out into the crowd.

Lady Emmeline Prescott had once again misplaced her sister. She wanted to stomp her foot in frustration, but even in childhood that had never gotten her her way, especially after her mother had died. Emmeline had learned at an early age that her father expected her to rely on herself, but watching over Blythe tested her very intellect and patience.

Emmeline sighed. Her sister was a good girl, just high-spirited, and seemingly unaware that her dowry and her beauty made her a worthy prize to men.

Surprisingly, a dowry alone did not seem to matter, since Emmeline, a wealthy heiress in her own right, seldom had male callers.

But she preferred not to dwell on what could never be. She had Blythe's happiness and romantic success to worry about. Emmeline was determined that her sister would have the husband she herself never would. She would be a part of Blythe's family, a dear aunt to Blythe's children, and know the peace of seeing her sister happy.

If only she could keep Blythe from mischief, and help her to settle on the perfect man.

Then she saw her sister in the midst of the dancers. Who was she with? Every time Emmeline almost caught a glimpse of the tall, dark-haired man, someone stepped between them. She skirted the edges of the hall, keeping out of the way, until she could finally see the couple.

Her sister's partner bowed as the dance ended. When he straightened, Emmeline felt a jolt of awareness. She had seen him from a distance at court. He was broad-shouldered, with a litheness that made him an excellent dancer. Short black hair framed a face distinguished by olive skin and the only clean-shaven chin in the hall. When he smiled at Blythe, his white teeth were blinding. A pearl earbob dangled from one ear, above a brocade doublet well tailored to his impressive chest and a short cape that hung back from his shoulders. Oh, he was too handsome a man, perhaps even of foreign birth.

Suddenly he looked directly at Emmeline, and she managed to meet his unsettling gaze with a cool nod. He laughed and swept Blythe into the next dance, leaving her to feel strangely thwarted. Which was absurd.

It was easy to discover his identity among her acquaintances. Sir Alexander Thornton, the younger son of Viscount Thornton. She was quickly informed of his half-Spanish heritage and his dubious reputation. Her acquaintances made clear that he was not interested in marriage, that he was a favorite of the queen and actually kept mistresses.

Mistresses!

Sir Alexander was *not* a man Blythe should be trifling with.

Her sister usually reserved her flirting for young men close to her own age, and Emmeline knew a stern warning would only make Blythe do the opposite. Surely there had to be another way to keep Sir Alexander away from her sister.

Just then the man had the gall to meet her gaze over her sister's shoulder and grin at her, leaving her flustered and all the more determined.

Chapter 2

Two days later, Emmeline decided that her worry over Alexander Thornton was unnecessary. Blythe hadn't even mentioned his name, and usually she chattered freely about whichever suitor she favored each week.

It wasn't until a maidservant requested a coach to deliver a letter, that Emmeline's suspicions flared back to life. After discovering that Sir Alexander was the recipient and assuring the maidservant that she herself would see the letter delivered, Emmeline walked purposefully to her sister's chamber.

The room was warm and cozy, hung with tapestries and carpets, and overflowing with fresh flowers from their greenhouse. Blythe turned from her dressing table, and her smile dimmed as Emmeline held up the letter.

"Blythe, dear, you know you are always to tell

me before you begin a—a correspondence with a man not well known to us," she said, drawing up a stool to sit beside her sister.

Blythe sighed. "Sir Alexander is not the sort of man you'd think highly of. But Emmy, he is so . . . intriguing."

Emmeline could easily remember his smile; it was still vivid in her mind. She had to proceed carefully, or else Blythe would do the exact opposite of whatever Emmeline said.

"I would just feel better if I knew more about Sir Alexander," Emmeline continued, leaning forward to touch her sister's hand. "Therefore . . . I will deliver this letter and take stock of him myself." Where had *that* idea come from? Visit a strange man alone? What had gotten into her?

"That is not necessary, Emmy!" Blythe said, her eyes widening.

"Are you concerned for my welfare—or about what Sir Alexander will think?" she asked dryly.

Blythe managed a blush. "I'm always concerned about you! But of course you may see the letter to Alex's household, if it will make you feel better."

"Alex?" Emmeline repeated, leaning back on the stool to study her sister.

"He asked me to call him that," she replied brightly. "Will you go now? It is already past midday."

Emmeline reluctantly smiled. It was difficult to deny her sister anything.

* * *

Emmeline had no difficulty persuading Humphrey, the family coachman, to take her to the Thornton Manor upstream on the Thames. He was bald and round and treated Emmeline and Blythe like his grandchildren.

And most important, she trusted that he would not tell her father the details. Her father took his responsibilities as the Marquess of Kent very seriously, and seldom had time for his daughters. He required weekly reports on Blythe's progress in finding a husband, but other than that, he took little interest in their lives. So long as Emmeline kept his households running smoothly and his younger daughter in check, he was satisfied. She had long since stopped wishing that he could be the father of her fancies, a man who dined with them each evening and asked about their day. Even her brothers, when they were in town, seldom saw such a side to him.

While Humphrey dutifully waited by the coach Emmeline approached the Thornton home, only to be informed by a servant that Sir Alexander was not at home, but that he might be at his lodgings above the Rooster, a tavern in Southwark.

Southwark? she thought, as she turned away from the closing door. Why would a viscount's son take lodgings in a disreputable part of London, when he already had such a lovely home?

"Humphrey," she said as she approached the

carriage and he held the door open, "we need to cross the river to Southwark."

She saw his hesitation, but the sweet old man didn't speak until she was comfortably settled on the upholstered seat.

"Milady," he said, removing his cap to lean his head inside the coach, "let me take the letter for ye."

"I must do this myself," Emmeline said firmly. "This man is wooing Blythe, and I need to take his measure. Know you the Rooster?"

He bobbed his head, his worried expression remaining.

"Then let us go."

He hesitated, nodded, and closed the door.

They journeyed over the London Bridge, with its fine merchant homes and shops. At the end of the bridge, she avoided looking at the rotting heads mounted on pikes high above the gate.

She could not fathom why a nobleman's son would want to live here, in an area rife with gambling and bear-baiting, and what other sports she could only imagine. This did not look good for Sir Alexander, she thought, rubbing her hands together to warm them in the brisk air.

Like Blythe's other flirtations, this one would pass, and her sister would eventually settle on a good, decent man. But until then, Emmeline could not relax her vigilance.

When they reached the tavern, she left the

coach, telling herself that the street did not look so very different from ones in the heart of London. There were cutpurses to be wary of, and there seemed to be more scantily dressed women about, but there were hardworking folk too, who did not have her good fortune.

With a deep breath—and a cough into her handkerchief at the smell of rotting garbage and who knew what else—she looked up into Humphrey's worried face.

"I'll be out shortly." She gave him a confident smile.

"Wait, wait," the old man said, struggling up from the seat. "I'll be goin' with ye, milady."

She knew how his bones stiffened in this cold spring wind, and it made her feel guilty. "No, please sit, dear Humphrey," she said, reaching into the coach for a blanket and handing it up to him. "I will be quick, and if I am not, I give you permission to come after me. But give me some time to know this gentleman, to see what sort of man he is."

Humphrey eyed the dilapidated building behind her, with its faded sign of a rooster, and windows shuttered against the cold. "Milady," he began again, but Emmeline settled her hood over her head, pulled the cloak tight about her, and set foot on the doorstep.

She pushed the old wooden door open, and it was as if another world greeted her. She smelled tobacco smoke and body odors, and perfumes of the sort she'd never encountered before. The gloominess of late afternoon was barely penetrated by wax-dipped rushes, which smoked as they gave off their meager light. Both men and women clustered at the bar or lounged at cracked wooden tables, leaning desultorily into the shadows together. No one noticed her in her plain dark cloak, except a grinning old man with no teeth who reached out to feel her skirts. She rapped his knuckles smartly with her purse and sailed past him, stepping in something slimy, and was thankful for her raised soles.

As she walked forward, turning sideways so that her wide skirts fit between the crowded benches about the long tables, she saw Sir Alexander.

He sat alone, a tankard in his hand, a gleaming white smile on his face as he watched the rest of the men toasting the foundering of the Spanish fleet off the Irish coast. A serving girl poured him the last of her pitcher of ale, then freely kissed his cheek before sauntering away. Emmeline was mildly offended, and her ire deepened as she saw his big hands tossing a pair of dice, as if he merely awaited his next game.

Was this why he rented lodgings above a tavern? Was it too difficult to find pleasure in his games from his family estate on the Strand? She knew he was a younger son, but surely his brother would not deny him a home.

She studied him again, trying to see what her sister saw. His doublet was thrown open, revealing a clean white shirt with a narrow collar. His face was darkened even further by a day's growth of beard, and that, plus their surroundings, made him seem dangerous. Emmeline almost began to regret coming.

No. She lifted her chin and eyed the man coldly. She had promised to deliver the letter, and by God above, she would understand what drove him.

She stopped at his table. He slowly lifted his head and looked up at her with eyes as dark as the secretive corners of this bawdy place. A strange feeling crept over her, heating her skin. It wasn't nervousness, and he certainly did not intimidate her. Then why was she suddenly embarrassed, as if what she felt was somehow—sinful?

Sir Alexander leisurely tipped his head, trying to see beneath her hood. "A good afternoon to you, mistress," he said, his voice coming so slow as to make her believe he was already in his cups.

She wet her lips. "Good day, Sir Alexander. I need a moment of your time."

He shook his head. "You know my name, and have yet to reveal yours."

His gaze followed the line of her cloak as if he could see beneath it.

"Or much of anything else," he added.

Suddenly overwarm, she took a deep, angry

breath, ready to put the insufferable man in his place.

Suddenly his eyes widened. "I'll be just a moment, mistress."

He grabbed her about the waist. With a startled gasp, Emmeline fell against him and pushed at his broad shoulders. How dare he handle her so roughly!

But he wasn't even looking at her. She stilled at the sound of swords being drawn from their scabbards behind her.

"Gentlemen," Sir Alexander said in the same easy voice he'd used with her.

But she felt the tension in every line of his body, in the hand that moved toward his own sword as he turned her about to perch on his knee. She caught her hood about her throat and looked up at two plainly dressed young men, holding their weapons far too close to her.

Sir Alexander slowly moved the knee she sat on away from them, and he dropped his arm loosely about her shoulders. She longed to push him away, but she also wished to leave this horrid place in one piece.

"You are spoiling a man's fun," he said softly. "I hope you have good reason for it."

"We'll choose what you should know," said one of the men. They raised their swords and came forward together.

Sir Alexander put his big palm on the back of Emmeline's head and forced her under the table, where she landed on her hands and knees on the foul, sticky floor boards. In dismay, she tried to sit back on her heels, but she bumped her head on the table. With a soft groan, she stayed in the ridiculous pose and watched the frantic legs of the men as they fought above her. She heard the clash of swords, the encouragement of the crowd, and even a call for bets.

At last the tavern's occupants gave a rousing cheer, and the sound of running feet faded away. She only saw one man's long, booted legs on the other side of the table. She had no doubt of his identity, nor of her own displeasure. When his boots retreated from her line of sight, she tried to back out from beneath the table.

From behind, someone caught her hips and tugged, and she let out a startled shriek as she was lifted high into the air and flung over a strong shoulder. Her breath left her body with a grunt, and her face was pressed into the fine fabric of Sir Alexander's doublet.

"Fresh from my triumph," he called in a loud voice, to the laughter and cheers of his cohorts, "I be about my pleasure now. A good day to all!"

She tried to scream, but could summon no air as she was bounced against his shoulder repeatedly as he ascended a set of stairs. The din faded and she heard him whistling merrily, as if he hadn't just escaped death and kidnapped a noblewoman.

Emmeline heard a door open; she felt the sudden warmth of a chamber and smelled smoke, and the not-unpleasant scent of this man. The spurs on his boots jingled as he walked across the surprisingly spacious floor. Just as she began to pound his back, he lifted her off his shoulder and dropped her onto her back on a bed. She came up on her elbows with an angry cry, and her hood fell back.

Sir Alexander was leaning over, smiling contentedly, and was about to put his hands on either side of her when he saw her face. He froze, and she felt a degree of triumph when he slowly sank back on his haunches and continued to stare at her.

"Well, what do we have here?"

Chapter 3

Alex stared at the woman sprawled angrily across his bed. She was wearing fine garments, and a ridiculous little hat with a feather now sadly bent.

"Obviously you are a cut above the average strumpet," he said, and grinned at the look of outrage on her face. "The garments are very nice—a fair approximation of a lady's wardrobe."

Her mouth moved, but no sound emerged.

"But you're not showing enough of the goods."

He reached for the clasp of her cloak and she slapped him away.

"Very well, we'll handle business matters first. I have ample money—in fact, I'm well endowed in many areas." He gave her a lazy grin, thinking that she would be pleasant to look at if she smiled.

24

She suddenly sat up and with surprising strength, gave him a shove. He fell back on his ass and couldn't help laughing, which seemed to annoy her.

She found her voice. "I, sir, am no woman of loose morals."

"Lovely pronunciation, that. Where did you learn such mimicry?"

She tried to get to her feet, but he came up on his knees to block her. When he saw a touch of fear in her eyes, he leaned back. He was hardly going to harm the wench. The fight had wiped away his drink-induced haze, and he now remembered that she had known his name.

"You seem familiar to me. Have we done this before?" he asked curiously. "And is there a husband involved?"

Perched on his bed, she straightened her skirts, lifted her petite chin in the air, and said firmly, "I am Lady Emmeline Prescott. I am here to deliver a letter to you from my sister—but I am loath to do so, now."

Alex suddenly placed her; she had scowled at him from across the hall every moment he danced with Lady Blythe—the object of his wager with Edmund. He got to his feet and gave her a full courtly bow.

"Forgive me for not recognizing you, Lady Emmeline. We've never been formally introduced."

"Nevertheless, your treatment of any woman should be better than this," she said, rising to her feet.

"Ah, now I have done myself a disservice in your eyes. Forgive a man, for we are the weaker sex, are we not?"

Swiftly he caught her hand and brought it to his lips. Though she was all stiffness and propriety, her fingers trembled in his, her cheeks reddened, and the barest tease of perfume wafted over him. He was intrigued. She was taller than the average female, but her cloak hid everything else. For curiosity's sake alone, he wanted to divest her of it, because he couldn't remember her figure from the party.

But again, there was the wager. "You say you have a letter for me from Lady Blythe?"

"At least you remember her name," Emmeline said dryly.

"How could I forget someone as charming as your sister? She quite captured my interest."

That frown of hers could sear a lesser man. He walked to the fire and rubbed his hands against the chill. Lady Emmeline was obviously out of place in this less-than-elegant chamber. But instead of succumbing to hysterics, she kept herself firmly under control, as if he were merely a naughty schoolboy. Somehow, that offended him.

Emmeline could not believe that she was alone in a tavern's lodgings with a man—a man with few morals who consorted with fallen women, yet flirted with young innocents. Why had she even told him about the letter?

She studied him as boldly as he did her. His head almost brushed the chamber's low ceiling beams, and he seemed as at ease here in South-wark as he'd been at a court party. The heated stare of his dark eyes made her want to cover her-self, as if she did not already wear layers of gar-ments beneath her cloak. For a moment she wondered if he was flirting with her, but she knew he wasn't. He was trying to unnerve her, to play his little-boy game of Dare. Somehow she threat-ened him, and that was a good feeling.

"Sir Alexander, who were those men who ac-costed you?"

He shrugged his wide shoulders. "I know not, my lady. They never spoke a word to me, just fought and ran. They were probably thieves."

He grinned then, as if she should worship his prowess, instead of be perturbed by his casual-ness with such violence.

"This happens often in your world?" she de-manded.

He straightened, and she was glad to see his smile lessen, for it was a potent weapon.

"No, not often. But London is a dangerous city, and unless I wish to remain locked up and as pro-tected as a prince, I will occasionally have trou-ble."

"I do not have trouble," she said coldly. "Are you implying that people like me are isolated?"

"Have you ever been away from safety before?" he asked softly, walking toward her.

Every step he took nearer made her feel strange, not like the reasonable, rational Emmeline. Though she was tall, she had to arch her neck to look up at him.

"No," she answered, "but nor do I sit sewing in a comfortable room all day."

He stopped mere inches from her when she didn't give way. The air was charged with a tension she'd never felt before. When he spoke, his voice was lower, huskier, and it seemed to skitter along her spine.

He said, "Perhaps the danger wasn't to me, but to you."

"I beg your pardon."

"No need for that," he said, lifting a hand. "The brigands simply might have seen the attention you paid me, and wanted you for themselves. I daresay they recognized quality when they saw it."

She inwardly cursed her cheeks for blazing her discomfort. "And I daresay you are trying to distract me from your dangerous way of life."

"Forgive me, I tease you unkindly. You have but come on an errand that can only do me good, while I have no answers that will please you."

She said nothing, caught in a trap of duty and promises.

He waited, and when she did not hand him the letter, he offered her a cushioned chair before the fire, which she refused.

"I only wish to speak to you about Blythe," he said, in a kind voice. "Tell me what flowers she likes, what amusements keep her happy."

How could he think that she would possibly help him? "No, Sir Alexander, you have not proven your worthiness to me."

For a moment, she saw wariness in his eyes, gone so swiftly that she'd surely imagined it.

"I promised I would deliver this letter, but that is all I will do." She handed it to him.

He took it slowly, studying her. "Do you wish to wait for a reply?" he asked softly.

She heard the teasing in his voice. "Of course. But please be quick; I'm certain that my driver is frantic with worry."

As Sir Alexander read the letter, his face betrayed nothing. What had Blythe said? He took a piece of parchment, a quill, and ink from a trunk at the foot of his bed, and sat at a table to write.

Emmeline wanted to pace in the sudden stillness, and forced herself to listen to the crackling of the fire, and the distant sound of voices in the tavern below. She tried to keep her gaze from him, but it was difficult. He was so big and dark and reckless, too handsome, too wild. He was nothing like the man she'd once loved and lost.

He looked up and caught her staring, and she lifted her chin and held his gaze.

Oh, he was arrogant, so sure of himself. Well, he would see she was not a woman to cross. Blythe would be protected, no matter what Emmeline had to do to achieve it.

After blowing away the sand from the ink, Sir Alexander folded his reply, sealed it with wax, and handed it to her. She tucked it safely into her purse and turned to the door.

"Lady Emmeline, shall I show you another way out? There might be talk, should you go through the taproom."

"Consideration, Sir Alexander?"

"For myself as well," he said, standing much too close to her. "After all, my reputation would suffer should you appear to leave too quickly."

"Thank you," she said, looking away, knowing he was secretly laughing at her and not understanding why.

He shut the door behind them, pulled the cloak about his shoulders, and led her to a rear staircase that exited to a surprisingly pleasant courtyard near the stables. They circled around to the front of the tavern, where Humphrey had just hoisted himself out of the driver's seat.

"Lady Emmeline!" he cried, his expression so relieved that guilt rose up to swamp her.

"Forgive me, Humphrey," she said, taking his hands. "Sir Alexander was kind enough to escort me out a back way. The tavern was rather raucous."

But when she turned around, Sir Alexander was gone.

That evening Emmeline stood alone in her bed-chamber, surrounded by the books and maps she so loved, and felt disquieted, restless. This situation with Sir Alexander had upset her ordered world. She wished desperately that she could have read his letter first, but Blythe was not a little girl to be so protected.

And yet . . . they had always shared so much. Surely Blythe was ready to discuss the letter's contents—and the writer.

She slipped out into the dark stone corridor, carrying a candle to lighten the gloom. Crossing to Blythe's door, she knocked softly and entered when her sister bade her to.

Blythe was sitting up in her four-poster bed that was hung with delicate fabrics and decorated with endless pillows. She liked to be amongst pretty things, and the room was indeed pleasant. Her sister had blankets piled in her lap and about her shoulders, and she was holding the letter near a candle on her bedside table.

Blythe smiled up at her. "I cannot thank you enough for bringing this to me, Emmy."

"You must have read it many times by now."

A blush suffused her sister's cheeks. "Of course."

Emmeline hesitated. "Might I read what he wrote?"

"Oh, surely," she said, holding it out.

Emmeline took the letter over by the hearth and sat down in a comfortable chair. She bit her lip as she began reading, but there were no intimacies, nothing improper. Sir Alexander merely wrote of Blythe's beauty and his desire to know her better. His handwriting was as bold and confident as he was. It was a nicely romantic letter, but nothing like what she'd received long ago from her beloved, her poet. The thought of what she'd lost brought a pain to her heart that she immediately swept aside, as always. It was Blythe's turn for romance.

"Isn't he wonderful?" Blythe said with a sigh, falling back amidst her pillows and hugging one to her chest.

If one likes rogues. In her mind Emmeline saw his wicked smile, the way his eyes had skimmed down her body as if penetrating the cloak. And he had thought her a *strumpet*.

She wanted to refuse ever to see Sir Alexander again, but Blythe had to be protected. If Blythe couldn't find the right man for herself, then Emmeline would have to.

Blythe slid to the edge of the bed, her legs dangling beneath her linen night rail. "Tell me about him, Emmy; how he was, what he was doing when he read my letter, how he looked when he wrote back."

Emmeline sighed. "He is a man of the world, dearest. You must realize that you are not the first girl to cast her eyes at him."

"I know! But it is so enjoyable to have the interest of men, now that I'm finally of age."

"Well, he was not at Thornton Manor, but in lodgings he rents above a tavern."

Blythe's lips parted in obvious amazement. "A tavern?"

"He says 'tis sometimes too long a journey home."

She suddenly sat upright. "Wait—does that mean you were in the tavern, too?"

Emmeline reluctantly nodded, and Blythe let out a laugh.

"Oh, Emmy, I wish I could have been there with you. Did he offer to protect you from unsavory sorts?"

"You could say that," she said, realizing that if she told the truth, Blythe might be offended enough to lose this infatuation. Very briefly, she explained the sword fight, and Sir Alexander carrying her up to his room.

Blythe's eyes went wide and she covered her mouth with both hands. "How heroic!"

"Heroic!" Emmeline repeated, dropping the

letter on the bed and getting up to pace. "He thought I was a—a strumpet!"

Her sister only giggled. "But surely he was quick to realize his mistake."

"Yes, because I told him."

"And he was a perfect gentleman after that, wasn't he?"

"Well . . ."

How could she say that while Sir Alexander had played the part of a gentleman, his eyes implied wickedness and his smile spoke of seduction? How it must have amused him to tease a spinster. What lengths would he go to amuse himself even further with her young, innocent sister?

Alex lay alone in bed, the fire crackling in the hearth, the noise of the tavern slowly dying as the night aged. Unable to sleep, he had considered asking Viv, the tavern maid, back to his chambers, but the idea had held no appeal—which baffled him. He had always enjoyed the companionship of women: to tease, to enjoy, to lose himself in. Women had been one of his few solaces when he'd posed as Spencer, when he'd begun to fear he didn't know himself anymore. He'd soon realized that as the viscount, he could no longer converse with his own companions. And he hadn't known Spencer's friends well enough to feel at ease with them, especially since his brother's life could be forfeited if Alex was revealed as a fraud.

But there were always women, a bridge between his old identity and the one he'd been forced to don. It merely took awhile before he'd understood that their interest in him was not what it seemed.

Disjointed thoughts rolled around in his head, and he couldn't understand what made this night different. Surely being attacked by the two strangers was the reason.

If they'd wanted his money, it would have been far easier for them to follow him down a street, hit him over the head and rob him. Instead they'd made a very public challenge, as if they wanted to be recognized for something.

And they'd put the lady Emmeline in danger.

"Hellfire." Alex laughed at himself as he threw an arm over his eyes. Where did that thought come from? But once she invaded his mind, it wasn't easy to forget her.

She was nothing like the women he preferred, confident women at ease with themselves. Oh, she *portrayed* confidence well, but he suspected it didn't run deep. She was a spinster, with an uncertain place in this world, and the knowledge that she would always have to depend on others.

Yet Emmeline was interesting, and reacted so strongly to every subtle taunt he tossed at her. It would be amusing to coax her outrage as he teased her sister. Outwitting Emmeline might even turn out to be more fun than luring a kiss from her flirtatious sister, whose type he knew all too well.

Chapter 4

$\sim\!\infty\!\sim$

The next day, as the waterman rowed the wherry up to the dock at Thornton Manor, Alex felt the usual bitter mood steal over him. It didn't help that he'd again had the feeling that someone had been following him in Southwark. He paid the waterman and walked up the long stone pathway, trying to force away the memories of being the master at Thornton.

He had not expected to like the hard work of running Spencer's many estates scattered throughout England, but had discovered that the land and its upkeep interested him. With attempts at agricultural modernization, he'd affected so many lives for the better. He almost regretted the quiet satisfaction he'd achieved, for its absence disturbed him.

Alex opened up the main door of the house and

stepped inside. Ah well, he had the rest of his life to accomplish something else. He'd get to it . . . eventually. For now he would visit his mother, who was soon to leave for the Isle of Wight for the birth of Spencer and Roselyn's baby.

The hall of the house stretched to the second floor, and somewhere in the distance he could hear the raised voices of servants.

"Madre?" he yelled, knowing it would take too long to search for her.

He heard a gasp from a corridor to his right, and he turned to find a little maidservant steadying a tray filled with goblets and cakes.

"Hello, sweetheart," he said, and enjoyed the maid's blush.

"Lord Thornton—I mean, Sir Alexander," she murmured, bobbing a little curtsy while still balancing the tray.

"You could tell it was me, eh?" he teased.

"Lord Thornton is on the island, sir, but surely ye knew that. Should I tell her ladyship ye're here?"

"Are you heading her way?"

She bobbed again, and her linen cap dipped toward her eyes.

"Then I'll just follow you."

She almost scurried before him, as if he would trample on her heels. When they entered the withdrawing chamber, he came up short.

Sitting on a high-backed bench beside his

mother was Lady Emmeline Prescott, dressed in a dark blue serviceable gown with fine, delicate lace at her throat. She was more than amply curved in all the usual places; in fact, she was downright lush—though he could tell she tried to tame her figure into submission with the usual feminine contraptions.

She glanced up at him; a spark of awareness took him by surprise. He was intrigued to see some of the color leave her face, as if she'd been discovered.

Which could only mean she was there to discover things about him.

As he swept his mother off the seat and into his arms, Emmeline leaned back, as if she were afraid to touch him. He *had* handled her roughly last time, after all.

"Alexander!" his mother said, returning his hug and smiling at him.

He wondered if she would ever stop wearing black in mourning for his father.

"I thought I heard you bellowing in the hall," she continued.

" 'Twas me, I admit, *Madre*. Forgive me for startling your guest."

"This is Lady Emmeline Prescott. Her mother was one of my few dear friends at court. Lady Emmeline, my son Alexander."

"Lady Emmeline," he said, bowing and bringing her hand to his lips. He thought she'd have cool hands, but they were very warm and soft, and ah, that blush did interesting things for her blue-green eyes. "We have met before."

Emmeline's wide, shocked eyes returned to his with alacrity, and he grinned, unable to stop himself from teasing her. Spinster sisters who kept him from winning a wager were a special irritant.

He did not ask her purpose at his home, merely waited and watched her squirm and cast her gaze away from him. He could see her intelligent mind wondering: would he tell his mother that he'd tumbled her onto his bed?

"Of course you would have met," his mother said. "Have you been respectful to the young ladies at these parties you attend?"

"Always, *Madre*," he answered easily.

He wanted to laugh when Emmeline's eyes narrowed, but what could she say when her own behavior had been just as scandalous? He remembered her on her back amidst his blankets, warming his bed.

"And what are you two ladies discussing today?" he asked, seating himself on a heavy wooden chair to Emmeline's right.

She slid her knees to her left to avoid his. When his mother asked her to pass him a goblet of wine, he let his fingers cover hers for a moment too long, but she wouldn't meet his gaze. My, she made things interesting. He was reluctant to admit the last time a woman had intrigued him.

His mother sipped her own wine and smiled at him. "Lady Emmeline has asked me to help her with funds for the orphans. Her mother had always been kind to those in need, and Lady Emmeline has continued her work."

Riotous color stained Emmeline's cheeks. Hmm . . . the righteous lady had kept his mother unaware of her true motives.

He leaned a little closer. "I admit my errand here is not as generous. The queen has forgiven my latest indiscretion, and invited me to court for a weekend revelry. I've come to collect suitable garments."

His mother gave him a stern frown, and for an uncomfortable moment, he remembered the feel of her anger in his childhood, something he had deserved far too often.

"Alexander, Her Majesty can only be so forgiving. When will you cease antagonizing her?"

He shrugged. "The old girl likes it when I antagonize her. And I am the only one who can flatter her the proper way."

Emmeline set down her goblet firmly in the sudden silence. "Lady Thornton, please forgive me for taking up so much of your time. Thank you for considering my request."

She rose in a fluid motion that Alexander was so busy admiring, he needed his mother's warning glance to remember to stand.

"Lady Emmeline," his mother said, "I would

like to correspond with you on this subject. I am leaving for Wight today. I have a grandchild coming into the world," she added proudly.

Alex swore his mother thought this miracle was due to her own manipulations.

"Congratulations to your son and his wife," Emmeline said. "Good day, Lady Thornton." After a curtsy, she turned for the hall.

"Alexander will escort you to your coach."

From behind his mother gave him a shove. He could have laughed—until he saw Emmeline's face, and then a darker mood struck him. He was obviously not good enough for her sister, so perhaps she didn't want to be seen with him, either.

He took her arm a little more tightly than he meant to and pulled her close to his side. Her breasts rose and fell with obvious indignation, and suddenly he wanted to see how far he could push her.

"Lady Emmeline," he murmured, as they left the withdrawing chamber. "Perhaps you'd care to tell me the real reason you visited my home."

"Your mother told you my reasons," she said coolly.

"Come now, surely between us you can admit the truth." He leaned nearer and felt her subtly try to pull away. "You came to discover more about me from my own mother."

"Our mothers were friends, Sir Alexander. I need no other reason than that."

"Did you hope to see me?" He opened the door leading to the gardens down to the Thames.

"Of course not!" she said indignantly. "Wait— my coach is on the other side of the manor."

"It is a lovely day. A stroll will do us good."

Emmeline was breathing so deeply and angrily that her corset was digging into her flesh. Sir Alexander held her elbow, guiding her in the spring sunshine where he wanted her to go. She had too much respect for his mother to yank away from him and run, and he knew she was trapped!

"I did not think to see you here, Sir Alexander," she continued as he drew her past a spraying fountain, "because I would naturally assume you to be in the lodgings you rent. Does your mother know about the Rooster?"

"It is no secret, Lady Emmeline."

She glanced up at him, and saw that he was not looking at her face, but lower. A wave of shame heated her skin. She knew she did not have her sister's fine figure, but that did not give him the right to remind her by staring so critically.

"My mother does not want me to ride home late at night," he said.

She heard the laughter in his voice.

"So she approves of your drinking? And does she know that the Rooster is more dangerous than the streets?"

"I almost think you care about me, Lady Emmeline."

"I care about my sister, and what danger you could bring to her."

"And have you another letter for me from the fair Lady Blythe?"

"No!"

Oh, he was so arrogant he thought every subject was about him! When they came to the end of the stone manor, she pulled sideways and forced him toward the front drive, feeling triumphant at his obvious surprise.

Humphrey waited beside the coach, his cap in hand, his gaze obviously taking in how close they walked together. Emmeline pulled away, and literally stumbled because Sir Alexander let her go so easily.

"Tsk, tsk," he murmured, taking her arm again with his strong hand. "Such clumsiness leads me to wonder if you can dance."

"Oh, I dance very well indeed," she said, lifting her chin. My goodness, what was she thinking by practically challenging him?

When Sir Alexander laughed, she couldn't even look at him for fear he'd see that his low, rumbling voice somehow . . . affected her. She climbed up into the coach, banging the door shut behind her and trying not to imagine dancing in Sir Alexander's strong arms.

Alex thought about ignoring his mother altogether, but knew she'd only follow him to his bedchamber. Instead, he went back into the with-drawing room and smiled at her. She narrowed her eyes at him.

He felt too restless to sit for her probing, and found himself aimlessly walking about the room, running his hand over the carpets decorating the cupboards, pretending to admire the tapestries on the wall. He ended up at the lead-paned window that overlooked the gardens, almost wishing he'd taken Lady Emmeline deeper into the foliage, hidden away. What would she have done?

His mother cleared her throat. "Lady Emmeline is a lovely *señorita*."

"I am actually interested in her sister, Lady Blythe," he said, not turning around.

She hesitated. "Oh. The younger one, eh?"

He glanced over his shoulder at her and smiled. "Don't you want me to marry as Spence has? Don't you want more grandbabies?"

"You are interested in marrying this girl?"

"No. Just interested in kissing her."

Lady Thornton groaned and covered her face with her hands. "My son, it is difficult to know what to do with you. Your father would have known."

Alex felt his smile dim. "No, he looked to you for that, didn't he? It was always easier for him to talk to my brother." The sadness in his own voice amazed him. His father had been dead over two years, and still some part of him grieved for the lost opportunities.

His mother rose to her feet and reached out her hands toward him. "Alexander, you always misunderstood your father. He would have been so proud of your work for the queen. Spencer's mission succeeded in large part because of you."

He shook his head and changed the subject. "So you go to Wight, I hear."

"How could I miss the birth of my first grandchild? You could join me."

"I'll let you convey my good wishes. I have too many things to do here."

"What things?" she asked skeptically.

She had good reason. It wasn't as if he had done anything recently except attend parties and other amusements. It was his choice, wasn't it?

His mother tried again. "You have not journeyed to Cumberland since Spencer returned," she said softly.

"Most of those estates are his," he said, unable to keep the warning note from his voice.

"Not all. Every day I can tell how the bailiffs miss you and regret that you could not finish the plans you'd begun."

"It is Spencer's responsibility now. He would not welcome my intrusion."

"But he asked you to manage his northern estates. You have not given him an answer."

Alex kept his back to her until he could manage

an amused smile. "I already told you that I cannot be the servant where I was once the master. Besides, I want the opposite of what Spence wants. I always have."

He didn't confess that he had no idea what that was.

Emmeline strolled uncomfortably through their gardens with Blythe while she relayed the story of her visit to Thornton Manor. Every blossoming vine reminded her of the Thornton gardens, and how it had felt to have Sir Alexander's hand on her arm, their shoulders brushing, her skirts folding around his legs. She almost couldn't look at Blythe, so embarrassed was she by her reaction to a man her sister flirted with.

Blythe leaned against her and giggled. "Emmy, what indiscretion do you think Alex could have committed that would so irritate our queen?"

"It couldn't have been much, if his mother knows about it, and the queen so easily forgives him."

"If he is to be at Whitehall for the weekend festivities, that means he can be one of my dance partners again! Isn't it wonderful that we were invited, too?"

Wonderful? Not if she had to spend all of her time keeping Sir Alexander and Blythe apart.

Chapter 5

In the grand chamber at the palace of White-hall, the light from thousands of candles glittered from the jewel-studded gowns of the nobility's finest ladies. Even the men shone, as the queen wanted it. Course upon course of elaborate food, from roast peacocks decorated with their own feathers to venison pasties, waited to be served, while laughing crowds danced about.

He knew the queen wished him to dance with her, that she enjoyed partnering with him. But he avoided her, and watched the entrances for the sisters Prescott.

Earlier that day, Edmund Blackwell had laughed when he'd asked how Alex's pursuit of Blythe's sweet kiss was progressing. Somehow he'd known about Emmeline coming to the Rooster, and even that she'd visited Thornton

Manor. And Edmund had boasted that his own kiss was surely at hand.

Alex leaned against a marble pillar and scowled, draining his second tankard of ale. He did not like to lose; he would have to concentrate more on kissing Lady Blythe.

Then the sisters entered the hall, and after a cursory glance at the lovely Blythe, he found himself studying Emmeline. Almost like a mother, she hung back and allowed Blythe the grand entrance. Where Blythe's corset showed off a hint of breasts above her square neckline, Emmeline was once again swathed in dull red brocade up to her throat, with a lace ruff collar nestling her chin. Why was she trying to hide her voluptuous figure? And the color of the gown did absolutely nothing for the unique shade of her hair.

Unique shade of her hair? he thought in disgust, as he allowed a maidservant to refill his tankard. *Hellfire.* She was only a stubborn challenge to be overcome.

He watched Blythe search the crowd, and when their gazes met, he raised his tankard to her and bowed. He grinned as he saw Emmeline's frown directed at him, and he strode toward them.

Old Bess herself sat on a golden throne beneath a canopy raised on a dais above the crowd. Perhaps she would not be too offended if he danced with Blythe. The queen loved to dance, and many a time he'd partnered her, showing her off to the crowd as if she were still a young woman. She certainly danced like one.

Before he could reach the sisters, another man approached Blythe, and she was gone, off in a wild dance before the queen's amused regard. Emmeline smiled triumphantly at him.

Alex should have taken offense, since he hated to be bested. But . . . he'd never seen her smile, and it lit up a face she seemed to try to conceal from the world. She had lovely high cheekbones, and eyes that never seemed the same color twice. He stared at her lips, and imagined them against his. He could almost feel the slide of her innocent tongue.

Why did the mystery of her draw him?

Annoyed with himself, he was glad when Blythe returned from her dance, breathless and laughing. He slid his arm under hers. "Shall we dance, my lady?"

She nodded and waved to her sister as he pulled her away. Alex refused to turn back and look at Emmeline. Minutes later, when he drew a laughing Blythe out of the dance for a moment's talk, Emmeline was nearby, the chaperone who kept a proper distance, guarding her sister's virtue.

All he wanted was a kiss, by God, but he'd never win the wager with Emmeline watching over them so closely.

He sighed and turned back to Blythe, who suddenly seemed . . . so young.

"You dance beautifully," he said in so soft a voice she was forced to lean nearer.

"You are too kind, Sir—Alex. My sister taught me."

He wanted to groan aloud. There Emmeline was again, in conversation, if not in sight.

Blythe giggled, an unexpectedly annoying sound.

"I've never seen your sister dance," he said.

"She is a lovely dancer, quite graceful. She just doesn't dance in public anymore, not since—"

She stopped, and Alex was appalled to find *himself* the one leaning forward, hanging on the girl's every word. "Not since . . ." he prodded.

But she shook her head. "'Tis a personal thing, Alex."

"Are you sure you do not wish to tell me?" he murmured.

Blythe giggled again, and he found his gaze lifting until he saw Emmeline standing against the tapestry-covered wall not ten yards away. She wasn't close enough to hear what they said, but he could swear she was blushing again. Then an older woman drew her away.

Blythe glanced over her shoulder. "When I was younger, a man wanted to marry her once," she said in a rush, as if someone might stop her. "But he was only a poet, a tutor, and beneath her. Since then, no one has asked her to dance."

Alex felt a coldness move through him. Why had he thought Emmeline was different from the others? She was just like every other woman he'd pursued when he'd been the viscount. Only a title and circumstance mattered.

For a moment, it seemed that he was once again at the queen's celebration of the defeat of the Spanish armada. His brother was in attendance, and both of them were relieved to be alive, after having spent a few days in the Tower of London contemplating charges of treason.

He had approached Spencer, who was the center of a group of admirers. Good old Spencer had pulled him into the circle, claiming he could not have spied for the Crown without Alex's help.

But Alex remembered the vivid feeling of being dismissed. One after another, Spencer's friends tried to insist they'd known all along something wasn't right, that Alex had behaved too scandalously to be Spencer. When Alex had had enough, he'd tried to draw away Lady Margaret, the woman he'd been most enamored of, only to have her look back at Spencer longingly. She'd pulled away, claiming their being together wasn't seemly. Yet she hadn't minded when he'd taken her out into the dark garden for stolen kisses only a week before.

He'd still been the viscount then.

But he'd been too stubborn to see the truth all around him. When women weren't pretending to be away from home when he visited, they literally discussed marriageable noblemen in front of him—because he was no longer in consideration. He was the younger son, not the heir, and they had been quick to forget their association with him.

And Emmeline was the same.

Yet there was still something about her that drew him—surely only the mystery of her, why she hadn't found another man to marry. With Blythe, he thought only of a stolen kiss; with Emmeline he thought of stolen passion, hot flesh against hot flesh in the night. He wanted to peel away each garment and reveal everything about her, to prove she was no better—nor worse—than any other woman.

Emmeline finally managed to disengage herself from the baroness and her elderly friends, careful not to hurt their feelings. They had lost husbands, and she would never have one, so she might soon be sitting in their circles regularly.

But she could not leave Blythe alone too long with Sir Alexander. She found them dancing again, and breathed deeply with relief. He lifted her sister high in the air several times, and each time she laughed gaily. Then another man swept Blythe away, and she seemed just as happy.

Emmeline's gaze followed Sir Alexander as he

danced with another woman. He was richly dressed in a black satin doublet embroidered with tiny diamonds. His short black hair brushed his high collar, and another diamond dangled from one ear. Beneath the doublet he wore striped, padded breeches loose about his thighs. He seemed every bit the nobleman beneath the rakish tilt to his hat, and every bit dangerous. She could not blame Blythe for her flirtation, although she didn't understand her own strange reaction to him.

Though he was gifted with words, he was not a poet. He did not speak of education or politics, as she so enjoyed. He obviously cajoled women with his eyes and his voice—and she grudgingly admitted that he was very good at what he did. Even she felt distracted and dazed every time he turned those dark eyes solely on her.

When Blythe returned to her side, Emmeline smiled at her sister's out-of-breath laughter.

"Oh, Emmy, I am so happy that I am old enough to attend the queen's court!" She gave Emmeline a hug and pulled her onto a padded bench.

"You are doing Father proud," Emmeline murmured.

"He's not here, is he?" Blythe asked quickly.

"No, dear, he went to Nottingham on business." Their father seldom attended any party or court function, leaving Blythe's care in Emmeline's hands.

"I am greatly relieved, since I was dancing with far too many men than must be good for me. And I don't want his anger to ruin this magical night." She heaved a melodramatic sigh. "I could not believe Lord Seabrook noticed me! And we danced!"

Good, her first words were not of Sir Alexander. "Lord Seabrook will someday inherit his father's dukedom," Emmeline said reasonably. "His interest can only be flattering to you. And he is close to your own age," she added.

The girl grinned. "I can't even hold that against him."

Emmeline should have known that the following sennight passed too smoothly. She spent each day with the servants, organizing a massive cleaning for her father's expected return. Extra bakers were hired for the many special desserts he needed when he entertained. Blythe visited with friends or agreed to Emmeline's occasional tutoring, but never once did she mention suitors.

Emmeline should have asked.

The day their father returned began as any other. Without even sending a messenger home, he and his entourage arrived in many coaches. Emmeline ordered the servants to begin unpacking, and then she met him in his withdrawing chamber to present him with the correspondence that had accumulated in his absence.

Her father was a big man, like her older brothers, although he'd grown stout as he aged. He was balding on top, and seemed to make up for it with a well-trimmed gray beard. His eyes, too, were a piercing gray, as if he could see right through to whatever she was hiding. Emmeline had long since come to terms with her ambivalence toward her father. He fed her, clothed her, allowed her to be tutored—but he did not love her.

While her father looked through his papers, she waited, looking out the windows toward the gardens and thinking of the approach of summer.

Without glancing up, he finally said, "Blythe has been introduced to all the important families?"

"Yes, Father."

"Are suitable young men paying court to her?"

"Yes, Father." In her mind she saw Alexander Thornton, and knew he was not the kind of man her father meant.

"Any serious suitors?"

"It is early yet."

He looked up and studied her intently, and Emmeline forced herself not to fidget.

"Very well. Let us go over your estate accounts."

She smothered a groan and seated herself across from his desk. Hours passed before she could escape. Once she had, she only wanted to retreat to her bedchamber and lie down with a cold cloth to soothe her aching head.

But when she reached the second floor, Blythe stuck her tousled head out into the corridor and looked both ways.

"Did I hear Father arrive?" she asked in a frantic whisper.

"He's here," Emmeline said. "Wear your newest gown today. He likes to see you looking your best."

But Blythe grabbed her arm and dragged her into her own bedchamber. "Emmy!" she wailed and fell back on the bed.

Emmeline folded her arms over her chest and watched her sister disapprovingly. The girl was still so young. "That is not the best reaction to this news."

She lifted her head up. "But I don't know what I shall do!"

"About what?"

"I have made . . . plans tonight."

Emmeline's head began to pound harder and she steadied herself by gripping the bedpost. "What do you mean? You'd best explain everything, because I shall only find out in the end."

The girl sat up with a long-suffering sigh. "Twice this week I have exchanged letters with Alex, and he's coming to meet me tonight, to walk in the gardens."

"Blythe! Have I taught you no better than this? You cannot go wandering off with any man who takes your fancy; it could be dangerous."

Blythe smiled and shook her head. "He's not dangerous, Emmy. Our mothers knew each other; our fathers respected each other. Alex would never hurt me."

"Then why do you think he wants to be alone with you?"

"But it was my idea! How else will I learn to be alone with a man if I don't try it?"

Emmeline threw up her hands and began to pace. "Maybe he just made you *think* it was your idea. Regardless, you can't go out there tonight; Father will expect you to sing for him after supper. If he has guests, it will be an even longer evening."

"I know, I know," Blythe said, rubbing her hands up and down her arms.

"Can you send Sir Alexander a message?"

"'Tis too late! He already said he'd meet me at the stables at nine of the clock, but that he would be about town during the day."

"Calm yourself, dearest." Emmeline sighed, leaning forward to take her sister's hands. "I will intercept Sir Alexander."

"But I could not ask that of you! Father will wonder where you are."

Knowing she would not be missed after supper, Emmeline smiled at her sister's naïveté.

"I will claim illness after eating," she said, putting a hand to her head. "And it will not be far from the truth. I will lie down now, while you prepare yourself for Father and his guests. Everything will be all right."

Blythe stood up to hug her, and Emmeline felt how fragile her sister was. After a slight hesitation, she whispered, "Does this man mean so much to you, then?"

Blythe laughed. "No more than any other. But I do enjoy flirting with him."

Supper that evening was formal, with many courses of pheasant and lamb and trout, as well as several types of wine. Emmeline did not have to lie when she said she felt unwell. She left Blythe with their father and his guests, Lord Seabrook and his father, the Duke of Stokesford. How her father had known just the right suitor to invite, Emmeline would never know.

As she returned to her chamber for her cloak, she told herself not to dwell on the fact that her father had never invited men home to meet *her*. She knew it would be far easier for him to marry off Blythe, with her radiant beauty and agreeable disposition.

The mansion was so large that Emmeline had no difficulty eluding servants on her way outside, and the light of the half-moon guided her down the gravel paths to the stables. The familiar evening sounds of her home made her spirit ease. She could hear the boats on the Thames, their owners calling to one another across the water. Insects buzzed and chirped within the garden. Though a cold breeze ruffled her cloak and slid beneath her hood, she was thankful for the coolness on her flushed face.

She did not like lying to her father, liked even less how disappointed Sir Alexander would be to see her instead of Blythe. What had their correspondance this week said?

When she reached the stables, she avoided the warm room at the front used by the grooms, horse trainers and stable boys. As she passed close to the wall, she could hear their laughter, and knew there would be cards and dice aplenty.

She slipped in between the stalls, reaching out to pet one horse after another, shushing their neighs and murmuring to them.

Suddenly, she bumped into what she had thought was a shadow. She gave a startled cry, and the "shadow" reached out to grab her, putting a hand over her mouth.

Chapter 6

~~~oⓈo~~~

Emmeline knew just who held her, and although she struggled, Sir Alexander did not release her. His arm encircled her waist, pulling her up against his body. She had never realized how wide and hard a man's chest could be, and how easily she could be overwhelmed. She should be frightened, but instead excitement shivered through her.

He suddenly stilled, then whispered, "Emmeline?"

She nodded and tried to pull his hand away from her mouth.

"Do you promise not to cry out?"

She nodded again with great exaggeration. He released her mouth, but not her body, and she put her hands on his chest and tried to push.

"How did you know it was me?" she whispered.

61

She felt his hand sliding down her back to her waist. "You feel very different from Blythe."

She gave him a hard kick in the shin and he let her go.

"Ow! I promise I have only held your sister as we danced, if that is what worries you."

She shivered as the wind blew her hood back onto her shoulders.

When she lifted her hands to it, he said quietly, "Leave it, if you don't mind. I like to see who I'm talking to."

"We have nothing to discuss," Emmeline whispered, fearing discovery. She could still hear the laughter of her father's grooms, scant yards away. "Our father has returned home suddenly, and Blythe could not leave."

"But you could?"

She heard his doubts—good. "Blythe has a lovely singing voice, and she often entertains Father's guests."

"You left your visitors for me?"

Even by the moonlight that filtered into the stables she could see his amused smile, and it made her want to force some humility into him.

"For Blythe," she countered coolly. "My sister sends her regrets. She does not always understand the proprieties of what she does. *You* should know better."

She turned to leave and felt his hand clasp her shoulder. Just that one point of contact between them warmed her, and she remembered how it felt to be held against his body. Deep inside, she was embarrassed to realize she wanted to know such a feeling again.

He was too scandalous, touching her as if he had a right to!

"Are you scolding me, Emmeline?" There was open laughter in his voice now.

She whirled to face him. "I know this meeting was my sister's idea, but I resent your agreeing to it. She is young, and does not think through the consequences of her actions."

"She is not much younger than you," he said mildly, folding his arms over his chest.

"Seven years, sir. I have practically raised her, and will not see her abused."

"Abused? *I* feel abused at your implications. I am but a poor suitor, helpless before the beauty of the Prescott sisters."

Emmeline smothered the beginnings of a smile. He was too charming. It was probably easy for his mother to spoil him.

"Do not bother using your charms on me, Sir Alexander."

"Alex," he replied, stepping closer.

She looked up at him, as dark as the night except for the white of his teeth. "Sir Alexander."

"Too formal. Even the queen does not call me that."

"And what does she call you?" she heard herself ask, some part of her curiously eager for the answer.

"The best dance partner in all England," he replied brightly.

She rolled her eyes.

"And since your sister enjoys dancing, I do not see the harm in allowing me to partner her. Blythe knows her own mind."

"And as you can see, her mind clearly told her not to come out and meet you this evening."

"And the next words out of your mouth would be, 'because she has sense'?"

Alex liked the quirk in her lips when she hid her smile.

Her sense of superiority should grate on him. He should remind himself that she preferred men her noble equal, not second sons like him. She was the daughter of a marquess, related to royalty—

Yet a sadness lingered about her faintly, as if he looked hard enough, he could see the reason why. But always he turned his head too quickly and her sadness darted back into the mysterious shadows around her.

"Blythe does have good sense," Emmeline replied. "She also has the sense not to anger our father."

"Ah," he murmured, leaning against the rail of a stall. The horse behind him nickered and bumped its nose insistently against his back.

"And why is it all right for *you* to risk his wrath by seeing me?"

A little frown line marred the smooth perfection of her forehead. "Of course I do not wish to flout my father's rules. I should not be here, either."

"Yet you are."

"Just out of consideration that you came all this way for nothing."

Was that all she felt, he wondered, even as he remembered the tremors of her soft body against his. "That's hardly nothing," he said. "You do admirably well for a man's evening. Surely you've been told that by many a suitor."

He immediately regretted his words as a formal stiffness drew up her impressive height. In the gloom of the stables, her eyes glittered.

"You mock me, sir. I am beyond marriage, beyond a man's interest. And there was never much interest to begin with."

When she whirled away and clutched the wooden rail of the opposite stall, Alex realized she regretted revealing her pain. He thought again of the man she'd rejected, wishing he knew more of the story. Why was she sad, when she only had herself to blame?

Was there a different Emmeline beneath her cool capability—an unsure, vulnerable woman?

He turned away from her and absently petted the horse's neck. He did not want to know. He only wanted to care about his pleasure; not worry about everyone else, as he'd begun to do when posing as the viscount. But it crept back on him insidiously, this need he'd never had before to take care of people. He still remembered the overwhelming feeling of awe he'd had the first time he realized a decision he'd made had enriched someone's life. It wasn't his appearance as the viscount that had mattered, but the knowledge that he'd shared. It had made him want to educate himself on the newest inventions to ease a workman's labor. But it had all been for nothing when people found out the truth, that it was not Spencer but he who had shared his advice. Though they tried to hide it, he knew the bailiffs of the estates went back to examine every decision he'd made.

Suddenly Alex heard the slowly rising voices of men in the garden as they approached the stables. With his luck, it could only be the marquess himself. Before he could even make a decision about how to protect Emmeline, she pushed him aside, unlatched the gate of the stall and dragged him inside with her.

She shoved him into the corner closest to the interior of the stables, then surprisingly covered his mouth with her hand. Did she think he did not understand the need for silence?

My, she was amusing—and strong, too. He quite liked the way she leaned against him. He almost felt . . . forced, a novel and intriguing sensation. Her head was turned aside as she listened to the voices now within the stable itself. He heard the invasion of the groomsmen, saw the eerie shadows of oil lamps in procession.

Should he be wary of being caught alone with a rich virgin who'd given up on a husband? Perhaps she did this deliberately, to ensnare him.

But no, she was too honest, too forthright. And, he thought with a touch of bitterness, she could have someone better than him.

But for now, there were many ways to provoke a reaction from the proper Emmeline. Very deliberately, he licked her palm.

She yanked her hand away with a stifled gasp, then promptly covered her own mouth, eyes wide with horror.

A man's voice boomed just on the other side of the wall. "Wait until you see the stallion I just purchased, Stokesford. He'd been smuggled in from Spain."

The horse inside their stall had given up sniffing them for food, and now leaned his head out. Was their luck so poor that *this* was the horse the marquess wanted to display?

But the party kept on moving down the stables, and the flickering light went with them. He could feel Emmeline sag against him with relief. What lovely breasts she had, so full and proud. He rested his hands on her waist, barely resisting the urge to slide them up her sides and cup her full-ness. He breathed in her scent, and thought about how her hair would feel against his face.

He suddenly realized he was becoming oddly aroused by this spinster guardian. She was nothing like the open, sensual women he usually preferred.

But perhaps that was the true challenge. Her lush body contradicted all the formal restraint of her manner. Every quirk of her lips implied something hidden, something worth seeking out.

He leaned over her very slowly, feeling the first tickle of stray strands of hair, then the brush of softest silk against his cheek. He could not miss the way she quickly inhaled. Yet she didn't move away, though he felt her tremble.

Oh, he wanted more of her.

But there was the wager, and Blythe—whom he could barely picture in his mind.

The voices drifted away, and darkness curled itself around them once more, as he heard the restless movement of the horses. Emmeline remained still except for the occasional shiver. He wanted to enfold her in his embrace, but she would only fight him.

Instead he took her hand and pulled her out of the stall.

"They could return!" she hissed, using all her strength to tug at him.

He gripped her harder, not knowing what he meant to do, but only enjoying it. "We cannot talk here. Follow me."

He left the stables and moved out deeper into the gardens, where rose vines climbed trellises and blocked part of the starlit sky. Only when the path opened up again to circle a gurgling fountain, did he stop to face her. Her breath came rapidly, and one long curl had come loose against her cheek.

He released her and she withdrew her hands back into the armor of her cloak.

"This was unnecessary, Sir Alexander. We have nothing left to say to one another."

"But I was so enjoying our conversation." He stepped nearer and was rewarded when she held her ground. He admired her courage, which only made him more puzzled about the men in her life. "So, tell me why you had so few suitors. It makes no sense to me."

"You mock me, sir. Surely you can see that I am not the ideal of beauty."

"What?" He tried not to laugh because he knew how serious she was. "There is only one ideal? Then I should have been disappointed that the women with whom I've been . . . well acquainted have all been so different. Who told you such nonsense?"

He saw her bite her lip, sensed that she once

again regretted her impulsiveness. Her silence
was eloquent, sad, and he wanted to lighten her
mood.

"Then a jealous woman must have said so. Any
woman who would berate your figure must be as
flat as a Yorkshire moor."

She gave a choked little snort, then her shoulders shook with laughter. "My—my aunt."

"Don't give the old crone another thought. That
can't be the reason you're not married."

"I had a suitor once." He heard the defensive-
ness in her voice.

Immediately he regretted the turn of the conversation. He didn't want to hurt her—nor did he
want to hear about her ideal man, one whom she
considered her equal. But it seemed he'd opened a
floodgate.

"He was a gentle, intellectual man, a poet."

Her voice went all soft and dreamy with re-
membrance and pain, and Alex wanted to scoff,
for how many poets were amongst the men of his
class?

But he remained silent, and thought he was a
fool for respecting a pain she had caused herself
by refusing this "wonder" of a man.

"A poet, eh?" he said, keeping his tone light. "I
am very good at poetry." He sprawled leisurely
on a bench beside the fountain.

Emmeline told herself to leave, that he would

not dare follow her. But she had foolishly opened up herself to this man, and now she was trapped, morbidly fascinated that he did not mock or insult her.

Why *didn't* she leave? Why could she not forget the way he had felt when she'd pushed him against the stable wall? His body was so different from hers, hard where hers was soft, confident where she was unsure.

"*You* are a poet?" she heard herself say.

He clutched a hand to his heart. "You doubt me? Fa, how you wound me, my lady. Night and day, only pretty words occupy my mind."

She knew he was teasing her. "Then surely you could give me a small performance."

"Now?"

"Now."

"No longer in such a hurry to leave me?" he responded in a low voice, rising and walking toward her, the dark mystery of the night enveloping him like a cloak.

He did *not* intrigue her, and she would not allow herself to be intimidated.

"You are changing the subject. Show me proof." She blushed with embarrassment at so obvious a challenge.

He cleared his throat and struck a pose, one hand on his hip, the other raised to the sky.

She held back a giggle.

"My lady," he began slowly, "is like the moon, calling to me with mystery, clothing herself in dark garments that glitter with diamonds."

She felt a little catch in her breath, and her knees went weak at the deep currents of his voice. He was a sorcerer, an actor, and he would enthrall her if she were not careful.

He lowered his voice and drew nearer, and still she could not move away.

"I am but the earth, ever apart from her, a mortal to her goddess, mud to her dark seas, dirt to her glow, an ant to her flower—"

"An ant?" she interrupted, almost happy to be amused rather than experience the puzzling emotions she'd first felt with his words. "Surely I have never heard a poet compare himself to an ant."

He shook his head solemnly. "Only talented poets understand the implications."

"I thought the point of poets was to *explain* things with words."

"I'll leave such judgments to the critics, my lady, as I bid you good night. Shall I walk you back to your house? And if it is dark inside, I could walk you to your room."

Oh, he was too amusing—and for a moment, she wished their meeting didn't have to end. "No, that will be quite enough for one evening, Sir Alexander."

"Call me Alex. And does that mean there will be other evenings?"

Shaking her head, she turned and hurried away.

Emmeline was wearing her night rail and dressing gown when there was a sudden knock on her door. The latch lifted and Blythe peered inside.

"Emmy? Might I come in?"

She gave her sister a tired smile. "Of course you can. Come tell me all about Lord Seabrook."

Blythe took Emmeline's hands and pulled her to sit down on the bed. "There is nothing much to say, for our fathers never left us alone, although I did enjoy the intriguing looks he gave me. But I can wait no longer—tell me what happened!"

"Nothing much," Emmeline said with a sigh, unable to meet her gaze.

"Nothing? But Father took the duke and his son out to the stables! I tried to stop them, but Father kept insisting that he'd had enough singing for one evening."

Emmeline smiled and squeezed her sister's hands. "I guess even your beautiful voice can't keep a man away from horses."

"Can I assume Father didn't find Alex?"

"You assume correctly. Not that it wasn't close." She regretted the last sentence immediately.

"Close? What do you mean?"

"I . . . I had to pull Sir Alexander into a stall to hide."

Blythe's blue eyes widened. "Oh my goodness! Was he offended?"

"Of course not. Naturally Sir Alexander did not wish to be found, either."

"Then he might have had to marry you," she said, wearing an impish smile.

Emmeline's mouth suddenly went dry as a hot summer day. Marriage to a man like that? Forever knowing that he'd been *forced* to marry her? Even spinsterhood was a better option.

"I certainly would not let such a thing happen," Emmeline said in a tight voice. "I could never hurt you like that."

"Dearest Emmy, your happiness could not harm me. Losing one suitor of many would be a small price to pay."

"It is of no consequence, because we were not discovered. We were able to leave the stable unseen."

Blythe nodded, then caught her lip between her teeth. "Was Alex angry that I did not come to meet him?"

"Of course not. He understood that our father had newly returned and wanted your company."

After a quick kiss to Emmeline's cheek, Blythe walked to the door. "Thank you, Emmy. I will return the favor the moment you ask."

"You will waylay strange men in the stables for me?"

Blythe giggled as she opened the door, looked carefully both ways down the corridor, then closed it behind her.

Soon Emmeline lay in bed watching the patterns cast by the fire across the beamed ceiling. But she could only remain still so long. She rolled over on her side and punched the pillow into a new position. After a moment, she groaned and rolled onto her stomach, but still her rambling thoughts would not allow sleep to claim her.

Every time she closed her eyes, she remembered Alex's cheek against her hair, his body pressed to hers. He was so large that he made her feel delicate.

She pulled the coverlet over her head. What could he have been thinking? Surely he was just making sport of her.

But when she was with him, she felt like the only woman alive. Truly, he was gifted with this unique ability to make a woman feel like the focus of his every thought.

But he focused on *every* woman, not just her.

Emmeline covered her face with her hands. Why did he have to be intelligent? Why was there so much more beneath the surface he showed everyone? He intrigued her, and that wasn't good.

She thought again of the poem he'd created so

quickly. She wanted to giggle—she wanted to sigh at such talent being lost on a man who could not appreciate it except for its ability to seduce women.

Clifford had known the true beauty of poetry. Clifford had never abused its power.

But Emmeline had been forced to send him away.

Chapter 7

Three days later, Alex stood before the entrance to the grand London home of the Marquess of Kent. Columns rose high above him, and carved stone flanked the massive doors. Tall windows let in the light.

He had to court Blythe for a kiss, which meant visiting her.

Then why did his evening with Emmeline spring immediately to mind?

He could admit to curiosity. He wanted to face her in the light of day, and see if her customary serenity could be upset by memories of their time together.

Or did he mock himself? Was it he who wanted to forget the sensations he'd felt as he held her lush body? He remembered the brief taste of her flesh, the brush of her hair against his skin. Such simple things with other women—but downright erotic with Emmeline.

He lifted the doorknocker and let it fall. The door opened immediately, as if the liveried manservant's only duty was to welcome guests.

"I have come to call on Lady Blythe. Is she at home?"

The servant bowed as Alex stepped in. Stone walls rose high above him, covered with paintings and tapestries, and clean rushes were strewn across the floor.

"Might I ask your name, my lord?"

"Sir Alexander Thornton."

"Please wait in the front parlor while I inquire, my lord."

While Alex was seated on the low-backed settle, Lord Kent entered the front hall, where two servants adjusted his cloak and handed him his hat. He stared into the parlor at Alex, who promptly rose to his feet and gave his best court bow.

"You are—?" said Lord Kent brusquely.

"Sir Alexander Thornton, my lord."

"You are here to see Blythe?"

Why was Blythe the immediate assumption? "Yes, my lord."

Kent sent one of the servants away with a message for Blythe. Then he leaned forward on his decorative cane, but still did not enter the room. "Your father was Viscount Thornton?"

"He was."

"A good man."

"Thank you, my lord."

"I hope your brother can do half as well. A pity he's married."

Alex felt the heat of anger rise in his face, but before he could decide on the best retort, Emmeline appeared at her father's side and peered into the parlor.

Her eyes widened, and Alex thought that she paled a bit, as if she feared he was discussing her with her father. He calmed himself and managed a bow in her direction.

"Lady Emmeline."

As she looked back and forth between the two of them, Lord Kent gave his elder daughter a nod as if she were a servant.

"Keep Thornton company until Blythe arrives. Mind you, he's not to stay long. Lord Seabrook has asked to attend your sister today."

Of course Lord Seabrook, the heir to a duchy, would be a far more fitting suitor than a mere knight, Alex thought with disdain.

The marquess left the mansion, followed by a trail of servants. A moment later, Alex and Emmeline were alone, though still in two separate rooms. She looked at the front door for a moment, but Alex saw not even wistfulness cross her features. She controlled every emotion—or thought she did. He began to wonder if only he could bring out her impulsiveness.

He was no longer shocked that her father used her to amuse her sister's suitor; instead, he would take advantage of it. She was not wearing a ruff about her neck, and he could see the long line of her throat, the delicate width of her shoulders, the creamy skin that disappeared into the square neckline of her tan gown. Serviceable, plain garments, but they framed her uncovered auburn hair like a jewel.

"My lady."

Emmeline barely controlled a shiver at the deep, smooth tone of Alex's voice. She could not imagine what it would be like to be the sole recipient of his attention, to be the constant focus of a gaze so direct, so dark with a secret knowledge she didn't possess.

She was tempted to leave him alone—especially after their evening together three nights before—but she could not be so rude. She had to sit with him like an elderly aunt, because her father had ordered it.

Lifting her chin, she entered the parlor and walked toward Alex. He had remained standing, and a shaft of sunlight from the high mullioned windows seemed to glow about him, reflecting off the shining emerald satins and brocades of his garments.

And then he smiled at her, and his teeth flashed

like the diamond dangling from his ear. It was a knowing, secretive smile, and she knew that her blush must rival the hue of her hair.

She sat down opposite him on a cushioned bench before the hearth. "Good day, Sir Alexander."

He shook his head as he settled his long arm on the back of the wooden settle. "I thought we had settled that issue. Call me Alex."

"'Twould be highly improper, sir." Goodness, now she even *sounded* like an elderly aunt!

"Improper? Nothing is improper between two friends. You did save my life the other night."

"Save your life?" she repeated.

"Of course. Had you not used your own body to shove me into that stall, your father might very well have fed me to the swans."

She controlled the smile that threatened to erupt. "Come, sir, my father is not a barbarian. He would have understood my explanations."

"Would he? His daughter, out alone with a man?"

His deep voice and wicked eyes made her wonder what could happen out alone with him—not that she wanted to find out.

The truly sad thing was that her father would have been angry with *her*, not with Alex. Though her father had allowed her education, and trusted her judgment just as well as the steward of his estates, her judgment with men was ever faulty in her father's eyes. Not that she'd had much chance to test his theory.

Just then, Blythe stepped into the room, and Emmeline could only smile her fondness at her radiant sister, who glittered in white and silver like a ray of moonlight. And she knew just what Blythe was thinking—Sir Alexander and Lord Seabrook were both coming to visit her. Two flirtations in one day, for a girl new to having a man's attention, was a heady thing. Emmeline was happy for her—but she felt a flash of guilt as Alex kissed the back of Blythe's hand. Her guilt would never leave her, for she could not tell her sister the truth—that she'd felt something when Alex had touched her, that his tongue on her palm burned her, that his chest pressed to hers made her ache in places she'd never imagined.

Was he even now making Blythe feel the same things?

Emmeline turned to go sit in a corner of the room to work on her embroidery, when Alex said, "Lady Emmeline, come, do not sit alone. What more could a man want than the attention of two such lovely sisters?"

Blythe smiled. "Surely you can work here with us, by the warmth of the fire."

With a nod, Emmeline sat down on a stool near her sister, then dropped her gaze to the canvas in her lap. There was an uncomfortable silence for a moment, but soon Alex's ready voice relaxed her.

"Lady Blythe, I enjoyed dancing with you, very much. Whoever tutored you was clearly the best in London."

Emmeline gripped the canvas, waiting.

Blythe giggled. "I already told you, Alex, 'twas my sister, because she teaches me everything."

Emmeline could not stop her gaze from rising to Alex. He was watching her quietly, an amused smile lifting his generous lips. His eyes roamed down from her face, and it was as if he spoke, telling her he would dance with her soon. She shivered.

Why were her thoughts so fanciful? she wondered wildly, as she looked back at her canvas. She would never dance with him. No man asked her anymore, not in years. It was as if they had all suddenly decided at one particular party that she was unworthy. She remembered it as if it were yesterday, the humiliation and loneliness. She'd never known why, and always wondered if they'd heard about Clifford.

"Your sister must be an excellent dancer," Alex said, and she could hear the amusement and promise in his voice.

Emmeline was mortified at his flirting, and wished desperately that he would not do so in front of Blythe. But her sister began to ask Alex about his friends, his travels, and the conversation moved on to safer topics.

Safer in one way, perhaps. Her curiosity about him was dangerous, yet she could not stop listening. Though he told Blythe many amusing stories about the people who moved through his life, Emmeline could tell instinctively that he had only Edmund Blackwell for a true friend. Why? Alex was so amusing and interesting, and even kind in his own way. He'd defended her figure, she remembered with a blush, making her aunt's comments about her lack of beauty seem petty rather than hurtful.

"You have a brother, too, don't you?" Blythe asked.

Perhaps only Emmeline sensed the sudden tension in the room. She looked up to find Alex regarding her sister almost warily. If she were Blythe, she would move on to another subject.

"Your brother?" Blythe prodded.

"Yes, my brother Spencer became the viscount after our father died."

Blythe gave the smallest frown, as if she expected more. "And . . . ?"

Emmeline wanted to poke her sister, but that would have been too obvious. Instead she bit her lip and watched Alex from beneath her brows.

"And?" he echoed softly.

"Are you not twins?"

"Yes." He leaned forward, piercing Blythe with his gaze.

Emmeline held her breath, fascinated despite herself. Why was he so upset, but trying not to show it?

"Identical twins?"

"Yes."

Emmeline almost gaped as she imagined another man looking exactly like him. She couldn't summon indignation when Blythe merrily continued her inquisition.

"How fascinating, Alex! Are you so alike that you were able to fool people when you were younger?"

Now his smile had the slightest twinge of bitterness. "Yes."

He stood up, towering over the sisters. "Lady Blythe, surely I am a dull conversation piece compared to yourself."

And without Blythe even knowing she'd been manipulated, Alex started to ask questions about her interests.

But Emmeline was more curious than ever, and she could not help narrowing her eyes as she watched him.

At the sound of creaking wood, Alex came abruptly awake. He lay in his bed above the tavern, knowing it was the middle of the night by the absolute silence below. He wiped a hand over his face, feeling dull-witted from an evening spent drinking and gambling. Still, there was an edge of tension, something that felt wrong.

Just when he turned to see if the fire had gone out, he heard a rustle of garments. He quickly came up on his elbows, then immediately rolled off the bed onto the floor. By the dim firelight, he saw that two men were attacking him. They tried to grab for his arms, and Alex punched one in the face, then reached for his sword, propped next to the bed. With a triumphant yell, he scrambled to his feet and faced them with his blade, only to find the door wide open and his assailants gone.

He ran into the torchlit corridor and down the stairs into the taproom, but they'd had too much of a lead. He lowered his sword, then closed the outer door. He heard a stirring behind him, and whirled with his blade aloft, but it was only Viv, the tavern maid, lifting her head from her pallet before the hearth.

She gave him a dreamy smile and pushed herself to a sitting position. "Milord, I knew ye'd change yer mind. And ye don't need a sword to make me come with ye."

As he lowered his weapon, he suddenly realized why she had gotten the wrong idea. In his haste, he'd neglected to don his clothing.

He grinned at her. "Sorry, Viv, but I'm not needing companionship this night."

She looked down his body in puzzlement, then shrugged and burrowed back under her blanket.

Alex ducked into Edmund's chamber, but his bed hadn't been slept in. He must have found his own companionship for the night.

Alex knew he couldn't sleep now, so he went back to his room to dress. He wondered if these were the same two men who'd attacked him a fortnight before. He hadn't seen their faces clearly, but he'd wager that it had been them. As he buttoned up his doublet, he glanced to the table beside his bed, then cursed.

His pouch of coins was gone.

Alex searched the floor, beneath the bed, even in his trunk. The small stash of sovereigns he kept hidden was still there, but growing ever smaller. He'd patronized almost every moneylender in London, and his credit was fast running out. Soon it would mean a journey to his Cumberland estate for more money, something he'd been avoiding. The trip was long, arduous, and boring. The last couple weeks, life had become more interesting because of the Prescott sisters—and not just Blythe alone. He would have to make do for a while on the money he had left.

And he would somehow have to find out why these men were his enemies. Summoning a justice of the peace would be useless, because there were no witnesses, and the thieves had already fled.

But they'd be back, and he would be ready for them.

Two days passed as Alex concentrated on finding his enemies. He looked over his shoulder constantly, and found himself awakening at the sound of every rat scurrying behind the walls.

Finally he realized that he was ignoring Blythe and allowing Edmund free reign in their wager. He would merely wait for his enemies to show themselves again. Meanwhile, he had to find a way to be alone with Blythe, without spending much pocket money.

Lady Morley gave him the perfect opportunity by inviting him to an outdoor party being held at her country home the next afternoon. He well knew Lady Morley's reasons for inviting him: she had a marriageable daughter, and her other suitors would look better beside him and whatever scandalous behavior he could create for her guests.

He could start the first small scandal by inviting guests of his own: the Prescott sisters. Oh, he would try to invite only Blythe. But if Emmeline found out, she would also come; he was counting on that. She was much more amusing than her sister. He hired a boy to take an invitation to Blythe, then sat back and waited for curiosity to do its work.

*   *   *

When Emmeline heard about the invitation from Alex, she could only fume. Could he possibly have known her schedule? It was the one afternoon a week when the council on exploration met at Whitehall, and she so enjoyed observing their meetings.

Worse yet, the fine weather had yet to ripen, and they would freeze!

Blythe kept insisting that a few maidservants were all she needed to accompany her, but Emmeline knew Alex could outwit any of them with a wink of his eye and a slow grin. No, she would have to attend this silly gathering, for she could not dissuade Blythe, who thought it perfectly wonderful to be invited somewhere by a man.

Emmeline told herself she was *not* averse to the outing because of Alex himself. She knew she could control her proclivity to watch him; she would pretend she didn't feel . . . unsettled when he was too near.

Yet when she stood in the arched doorway of her home and watched him ride his black gelding toward them, her breath caught, and her heart began a strange rhythm. Under the bright blue sky of an unusually warm spring day, he was so handsome in a sleeveless leather jerkin over a brilliant white shirt. His breeches were striped red and black, and he wore high black leather boots up to his knees. Why did she imagine that he smiled at her before he looked at Blythe?

Emmeline turned away and mounted her own horse sidesaddle. Then she allowed Blythe to ride in the lead at Alex's side, while she rode behind with their groomsman. The roads were not so heavily traveled on the outskirts of London, where farmers' fields still competed with the building of mansions along the Thames. Soon the houses were few, and they even rode past a village green with a duck pond in the center.

She tried to enjoy the lovely day and the serenity of the ride, but she kept straining to hear what Alex and Blythe were discussing. She only caught occasional words, while she watched his broad gestures and the uninhibited way he laughed. For a moment, she felt absurd and small-minded worrying about Blythe's future with such a man.

But her sister was an innocent, and who knew what Alex's true purposes were? He was a scoundrel, as everyone made sure to tell her.

Lady Morley's home nestled between two small hills in the valley, and was made of a light, pretty stone, with high windows along every wall. It glittered like a jewel in the sun, and Emmeline shaded her eyes to see it better. Alex guided his horse along the gravel path that led to the rear of the estate.

As Emmeline rode up to Blythe's side, she couldn't help the little gasp of pleasure that escaped her. It reminded her of her father's gardens in Kent, which she missed terribly. Lady Morley's gardens were really a park, with orchards and a kitchen garden in the distance, and ornamental flowers and trees scattered around a fishpond. In the distance more ponds were connected by footbridges. And everywhere a green hue was returning to the earth, and primroses and daffodils gave new color.

It took Emmeline a moment to realize that Alex was speaking to her. With a start, she tore her gaze away from the peaceful garden, and saw that Blythe's horse was trotting forward as she waved to friends. The groomsman followed her, as Emmeline had instructed him, and she was left behind with Alex.

Chapter 8

Alex was staring at her, and his expression seemed to soften.

"Beautiful, isn't it?" he said in a low voice.

He wasn't looking at the garden, which made Emmeline uncomfortable. Bother her face for so easily blushing.

"It is lovely and so peaceful," she replied cautiously. "It was good of you to invite Blythe. As you can see, she already feels at home here."

Alex glanced briefly to where small colorful pavilions had been set up to give the ladies shade. But again his gaze returned to her, and there was a moment of silence that seemed too long.

"Aye, your sister has friends everywhere, does she not?"

Emmeline smiled. "Sometimes it seems that way."

"But not you."

Her amusement died as she glanced at him sharply, but he was not mocking her, just studying her with an intensity that made her uncomfortable. "I have friends."

"Yes, but well chosen and small in number, I think. No, do not ruffle your feathers, young swan. Sometimes I think we have much in common."

"Young swan?" was all she could manage, as she tried to imagine having anything in common with such a scandalous man.

"The beginnings of a poem, I think," he said.

He suddenly grinned at her in that carefree manner so much a part of him. It was as if another man had appeared for a moment, then was gone. She scoffed at herself for such fanciful notions.

"Oh, not another poem, Sir Alexander."

"I told you that words always toss about in my mind." He leaned over and suddenly chucked her under the chin. "Do call me Alex."

With a tap of his heels, he set his horse trotting away from her.

The reaction of the other guests to his arrival was not what she would have expected. As usual there were young girls who fanned themselves a bit too much when he bent over their hands, but there were also barely tolerant stares. As she rode closer, Emmeline even heard Lady Morley thanking him for inviting the Prescott sisters. It was then that she realized Alex himself had invited them, without informing their hostess.

She wished she could disappear, but suddenly a man rode up beside her, and slowed his horse's pace to match hers.

"Lady Emmeline," he said respectfully, in a deep voice that was almost a growl.

She smiled, knowing he seemed familiar. "Sir, have we been introduced?"

"I am Sir Edmund Blackwell, a friend of Alex's." He returned her smile, and suddenly the sheer size and breadth of him seemed less menacing. He was not the most handsome man she'd ever seen, but there was a friendliness in his face that put her at ease.

"Ah yes," she replied, "I think I saw you with him at a party a fortnight or so ago."

He dipped his head in acknowledgment. "Come, allow me to escort you to the gathering. And perhaps you could introduce me to your sister."

Riding up with Sir Edmund, she politely smiled at all in attendance, then dismounted to stand beside her sister. As grooms led the horses away to pasture, Alex's friend remained at her side, obviously waiting.

Emmeline touched Blythe's arm. "Blythe, allow me to present a friend of Sir Alexander. Sir Edmund Blackwell, this is my sister, Lady Blythe."

Sir Edmund's courtly bow rivaled that of his friend. Perhaps Alex would be foiled by yet another man dancing attendance on Blythe. When

Emmeline glanced at Alex, his eyes were narrowed as he studied his friend.

Little benches and stools were scattered about the lawn for the ladies' ease of sitting with their wide gowns. The men either stood or sprawled on blankets. The first course of their meal, an assortment of fine white breads, was served on little plates, and wine liberally refilled in every goblet. Emmeline sat on a bench beside her sister, who seemed wide-eyed with excitement as she ate.

Blythe delicately nibbled a pastry and leaned nearer to Emmeline. "What do you think of Alex's friend?"

"Dearest, we've only just met."

"Sir Edmund is very different to look at, is he not? Rather like an old-fashioned knight in my favorite stories. Where do you think he's from?"

Emmeline could only shrug, and allow her gaze to linger on Alex and his friend, who conversed in low tones a little apart from everyone else, polite smiles on their faces.

Alex's jaw hurt from gritting his teeth. "You know you were not invited here, Edmund."

Edmund laughed softly. "Neither were the lovely Prescott sisters, but that didn't stop you from bringing them. I'm sure Lady Morley thinks I'm just the next assault in your rudeness campaign."

"Why did you come? I have not seen you much

these last days, and when I have, you've seemed preoccupied."

"Then I guess you have not noticed Elizabeth," Edmund replied, and his voice lost some of its gaiety.

Alex glanced at the circle of young ladies and finally saw Lady Elizabeth Langston. She looked their way briefly, and pointedly turned her back.

"Are you in danger of losing this wager?" he asked, allowing only a hint of triumph in his voice.

"Not at all," Edmund said.

Alex could tell he had to force a smile.

"Besides accompanying Elizabeth, I could not resist checking on your progress. I see you've not managed to shake the spinster sister."

"Do not call her that," Alex said without thinking.

"Call her what?" Edmund asked, looking far too amused and speculative. "A spinster? Is that not what she is?"

Alex's hesitation was brief as he struggled for the right tone. "She might hear you and be offended. That will hardly do my quest good."

"I think the point *is* not to do your quest any good at all, my dear fellow. Enjoy the afternoon."

Edmund strolled away, but not toward Lady Elizabeth. Still curious, Alex watched him go.

Just when Emmeline thought she could not eat another bite of such delicious fare, Lady Morley asked the musicians playing beneath the nearby trees to begin a galliard. With glad cries, the young people abandoned their elders and became swept up in the lively dance. Alex appeared before them and reached for Blythe's hand, winking at Emmeline as he took her sister away.

Emmeline grudgingly admitted they were a handsome pair. It seemed almost decadent to be dancing so openly under the sun. Her toes tapped in the grass, and her head nodded to the lively music. Once again, she noticed what a fine dancer Alex was, how his lean, muscular body moved with grace. He partnered Blythe well, and it was easy to forget he only amused himself for the moment.

When the dance ended, people called for more, and suddenly Emmeline found her own hand grasped in a much larger, warmer one. She looked up to see Alex leaning over her, his face in shadow due to the blinding sun above him. He filled every part of her vision; her breath seemed to catch in her throat.

"Now, didn't I promise you this would be a glorious day?" he asked, and tugged on her hand.

She tried to pull away. "Sir Alexander, please, I do not dance."

"You mean you have not danced recently," he said as he brought her to her feet. He didn't release her hand, and her fingers tingled against the heat of his skin.

Blythe was beside them, laughing and pushing

Emmeline farther out onto the lawn. "Go with him, Emmy! 'Tis such fun!"

Alex's arm came about her waist as he drew her forward, and she saw the stares and the whispers travel in a circle about them. She knew he had imbibed far too much of the potent wine, and his behavior was surely proof. She must be scarlet with embarrassment, but that did not stop her from noticing how good a man's arm felt about her, and how she could feel his long fingers splayed at her ribs. It had been so long.

"She calls you Emmy?" he said softly into her ear.

His lips grazed her skin, and gooseflesh shivered across her arms.

"A pet name only," she said as Alex's arm came across the front of her body so they could pivot about one another. She was almost afraid to breathe because her breasts might touch him.

"Enjoy the day, Emmeline. Put your arm about me like a good girl."

"Do not scold me as if I were a child!"

But reluctantly, she settled her arm across his body and held onto his waist only a moment before the Italian Pazzemeno began. He suddenly whirled her about, and her feet remembered the steps. Soon they were advancing side by side in a solemn march toward the trees, then gliding effortlessly as if across a polished floor.

Emmeline's breath came in gasps, and she felt

like laughing at the sheer joy of moving so freely. She knew what was coming next, but she could not prepare herself for the feel of Alex's hands sliding up her ribs, nor the sudden sensation of weightlessness as he effortlessly lifted her into the air. This time she did laugh aloud, and he grinned up at her for a suspended moment, until the dance required him to set her down.

What was she thinking? How could she so freely have given into the pleasure of the dance? She couldn't meet Alex's gaze, knowing he was only amusing himself.

"Look at me," he whispered.

She heard the laughter in his voice. It made her stiffen and lift her face to his, even as they whirled about each other. His black eyes were as warm as twilight at the end of a summer day, full of pleasure—but it did not seem at her expense. As the trees whirled behind his head, and the sun flickered in his dark hair, she stared back at him, biting her lip to keep from smiling. But devil that he was, he knew and was pleased with himself.

It was over too quickly, and he was soon leading her back to the bench.

"Blythe was right," he said softly. "You are a wonderful dancer."

"Thank you," she murmured, feeling overheated and overwrought by the sensations his touch invoked inside her.

Blythe flung herself onto the seat and hugged

her. "You were incredible! Did you not see that, Alex?"

"Yes, I did," he replied almost gravely.

Emmeline wanted to cover her face in mortification. What was wrong with her? She was here to protect her sister, not fall victim to every kindness from a man who couldn't possibly mean it.

While Alex partnered Blythe again, Emmeline desperately tried to regain her composure. Just when she thought she could watch the dancing without feeling all hot and unsettled, she realized she could no longer see Blythe.

Or Alex.

A nerve-rattling feeling clenched her stomach and she stood up quickly. Walking the perimeter of the dancers, she searched for them, but they had vanished. She spun in a slow circle, gazing at the orchard and the arbor tunnel of newly sprouting vines.

"Can I help you?"

She turned to find Sir Edmund staring down at her with kind, even sympathetic eyes.

"Have you seen my sister?"

He nodded toward the horses. "She and Alex went for a ride. They made no secret of their leave-taking."

They wouldn't have needed to, because Alex had flustered her so successfully. Had that been his plan?

"I must find them." She strode toward her

horse. "Was my groom accompanying them?"

"No. Isn't that the fellow over there with the other servants? Would you like me to accompany you?" Edmund asked, walking beside her.

"No." After glaring at her shame-faced servant, she looked about for a mounting stool.

"Allow me."

Suddenly Sir Edmund's big hands were on her waist, and he lifted her up into the saddle. Giving him a brief nod, she kicked her mare into a gallop.

As the gardens fell away behind her and the meadows took on a wilder, more natural appearance, all Emmeline could think about was how much wine Alex had imbibed, and how she had failed to keep her sister safe. If anything happened, she could only blame herself.

As she rounded a corner of the riding trail, she saw their two horses left to graze in the grass. She flung herself from the saddle and marched past the animals, only to draw up in shock at what she saw.

On the bank of a little stream, in the shade of draping willow trees, Alex and Blythe stood in each other's arms, staring at one another.

Emmeline could make no sound, so heartsick was she. She leaned against a tree and watched Alex smile at her sister, a girl barely out of childhood, who didn't know what a man was capable of.

And then Alex looked up and saw her.

Chapter 9

Alex froze when he saw Emmeline, her eyes wide and anguished as she clutched the tree. Something inside him almost snapped with pain. He didn't want to be affected by her, but he was. He was luring away her little sister for no good reason, at the same time as he flirted shamelessly with Emmeline herself.

And his conscience began to roar back to life.

He released Blythe, who looked up at him so innocently.

"Your sister just arrived," he said.

The girl didn't look guilty, just turned a smile on Emmeline. "She must be upset I didn't tell her where I was going. I'll go speak with her. But don't worry," she added in a lower voice. "I won't tell her about our wonderful kiss just yet."

Alex wanted to wince as he watched Blythe run

to her sister, catch her by the arm, and draw her toward the horses.

Their kiss.

He could hardly call it one. Blythe's tightly closed lips had touched his for a brief moment, and he hadn't even wanted to make it last longer. He had felt nothing, not even the arousal of holding a beautiful woman in his arms.

All he could think about was Emmeline, and how it would feel to hold her in his arms, with her mouth beneath his.

Could he not control his own thoughts anymore? he wondered darkly. Even his dreams were dwelling on her with startling regularity. Afterward, he awoke aroused and perspiring and unsatisfied.

Now he watched Emmeline help her sister into the saddle, then she stepped on a rotting log to mount her own horse with graceful athleticism. She glanced at him only briefly, and in her eyes he saw anger and the promise of retaliation, not the hurt he thought he'd glimpsed a moment before.

As the two sisters rode away, Blythe looked back and waved for him to follow. He mounted his own horse, no longer so eager for the rest of the afternoon.

When he returned to Lady Morley's garden, the first thing he did after dismounting was drain a goblet of wine and ask for another. He told himself not to look for Emmeline. He had done nothing to be ashamed of. Men were bound to kiss her beautiful sister; why shouldn't he be the first? Why couldn't Emmeline understand harmless flirtation for what it was? He had spent his life flirting with women—he certainly wasn't going to stop now.

Emmeline watched Alex swallow another mouthful of wine and shook her head in disgust. She stood beside Blythe, who was chatting with a friend. It was obvious Blythe was waiting for the perfect moment to tell her what had happened with Alex.

Just what she wanted to hear: her sister's romantic moment with a drunken libertine.

Too soon, Blythe drew her beneath a vine-covered arbor and leaned close.

"Emmy, I'm so sorry I didn't tell you where I was going."

Emmeline looked into her sister's sincere eyes and worried that some day Blythe would be hurt by a man—maybe this one. "'Twas a foolish thing to do. You don't know Sir Alexander well, nor do you know his motives."

"We're becoming acquainted," Blythe said in obvious delight. "That's a good motive."

"And what about Lord Seabrook?"

"I'm becoming friends with him, too."

"Make friendships while other people are around you, Blythe. Until you know these men well, you can't trust them alone. You can't trust the situations they might lead you into—like today."

"Oh, it was a glorious ride, and such a peaceful place for my first kiss from a gentleman!"

"What?"

Emmeline buried her bewildered hurt, beneath an anger the likes of which she'd never felt before.

"Oh, Emmy, he kisses divinely! I wonder how Lord Seabrook kisses?"

"What else did Sir Alexander do to you?" she demanded, gripping her sister's hand in urgency.

"Nothing," Blythe replied in a puzzled voice. "He's always been a gentleman."

"Perhaps so, but it is best not to push gentlemanly manners too far," she warned, trying not to sound as angry as she felt. "Please promise me you'll never again go off with a man alone. You are an heiress, and many a man would kidnap you for the chance to marry such wealth."

She laughed. "Oh, Emmy, he does not want or need my money. He comes from a powerful family in his own right."

"Do you see many women lining up to marry him?" Emmeline couldn't believe how cold and cruel she sounded.

Blythe cupped Emmeline's cheek in her hand. "You are just saying these things to scare me, and I appreciate your devotion. But look out there— does Alex look like a man who lacks female friendship?"

Emmeline turned her head, and across the lawn

she could see that the dancing had resumed. Alex was in the thick of it, moving with an abandon that seemed forced. Couldn't Blythe see that?

They returned to the gathering, and Emmeline allowed her to go off with her friends to the bridges between the ponds. Emmeline seated herself on a stool beside Lady Morley, who held court as if she were the queen herself. More and more Emmeline was one of the elders, sitting off to the side while the young people danced.

"He looks so like his brother 'tis uncanny."

Emmeline could not help listening to the conversation going on a few feet away from her. The speaker was an older woman she hadn't met before, whose nose was so high in the air that it was amazing a bug had not flown in.

"But he's *not* like his brother," cautioned a younger woman whose perpetual frown already marred her brow. "Do you remember that dreadful statue he presented to Her Majesty?"

Emmeline held her breath, fascinated despite herself.

"Yes, young lady, I do, though we should not be discussing it. Imagine sending a naked statue of oneself to your Queen!"

Emmeline was so busy choking down a horrified laugh that she almost missed their next words.

The young woman leaned closer to her companion, and Emmeline unashamedly leaned nearer as well.

"Tell me truly, Lady Boxworth, did it honestly have wings, like an angel?"

"Or the very devil himself," Lady Boxworth intoned. "After displaying it rather vulgarly, the Queen gave it back to him. I understand he uses it to decorate his brother's home."

The two women turned to look at Alex, and Emmeline did the same. Oh, how she wished she'd known that the statue was at Thornton Manor, because she surely would have looked for it.

When Emmeline realized how improper her thoughts were becoming, she fanned herself vigorously to disguise her blush.

To make everything worse, Alex came over to the ladies and flopped down on his side on a blanket, propping his head in his hand. Those dark eyes were alive with such mischief that Emmeline braced herself for the worst as she allowed her anger to simmer. Even worse, his fingers casually rubbed the lace on her hem, and she could feel every tug of the material across her knees and up to her waist. Appalled, she wondered if anyone could see. She wanted to kick him, or step on those groping fingers, but such behavior would only call more attention to his antics.

Soon the other gentlemen joined them, and as the sun began to wane, Alex said, "Ladies, I fear we have not much time left of our lovely afternoon."

Blythe came to sit beside him, holding her skirts down with her arms.

"What amusements can we poor gentlemen provide you?" he continued.

Emmeline straightened with sudden inspiration. "Sir Alexander, I have heard you say more than once that you are a gifted poet. I am certain we'd all enjoy hearing your work."

Though the smile never left his face, Alex's gaze was riveted to hers, and she barely withheld her own smile of glee. Ah, what a wicked repayment for treating her sister so lightly.

Sir Edmund choked on his tankard of ale. "Poetry?" he managed to say, before succumbing to a coughing fit.

There were titters of laughter, and even Blythe grinned. Alex slowly sat up, every muscle rippling into the next like the stretching of a wild wolf. Emmeline caught her breath, refusing to do the sensible thing and back down.

"Ah, Lady Emmeline, I would not want to make anyone uncomfortable with my deepest feelings."

"Sir Alexander," she replied sweetly, "you do us a grave injustice if you believe we would not appreciate your thoughts."

She could not believe her own nerve, and she knew some of the women would be looking at her in a new light. She usually said little at parties, except to her few friends. But something about Alex brought out her daring, and she relished the heady power of it.

"Very well, I accept your challenge," he said.

"Challenge? Whatever do you mean?"

"You of all people know how private poetry is."

She felt the sting as if slapped. How dare he allude to something she'd said in private!

"But I will gladly bare my soul to entertain you, Lady Emmeline."

She thought of what else he'd bared before the whole court, and willed herself not to blush again.

"Thou young swan, be ever true," he began, leaning back on his hands as if the impromptu crafting of words came easily to him.

Blushing, Emmeline hoped no one had overheard him calling her a swan earlier.

"Thy flock of chicks needs all thy mothering. Temper thy . . . temper when one does stray."

When his audience laughed, he shrugged. Emmeline pinned him with a narrow-eyed stare.

"For the black swan's wiles cannot be denied."

Emmeline watched the ladies titter and the men laugh, while her insides seethed at the subtle challenge. Alex stood up to bow, but she was not so easily vanquished. The black swan had better be careful, or he would find himself roasting on a spit.

* * *

A short while later, Alex stood beside Edmund, watching the ladies say their good-byes.

Edmund gave a low laugh. " 'The black swan'?"

Alex shrugged, his gaze on Emmeline, who was proudly watching Blythe curtsy to the noble-women. He didn't know many women who gladly gave center stage to another, even their sisters. "I was desperate. Could you not tell?"

"Oh, I could tell. So is the nest you're disturbing sundered yet?"

Alex didn't even hesitate. "No, it is a difficult challenge that you've given me, Edmund."

Such a virginal kiss didn't count, and he wasn't ready to be done with the Prescott sisters. "The Lady Emmeline interrupted us. Did you have something to do with that?"

"After I saw you leave, I could not lie to her concerning your whereabouts, could I?"

Alex clapped him on the shoulder. "Never you, Edmund. Would you like to accompany us back to London?"

"You don't mind my interference?"

"Lady Emmeline is plenty of interference all by herself, so you're welcome to come with us—unless you have business with Lady Elizabeth."

Edmund's face remained impassive. "I'm biding my time with that one," he said shortly. "So thank you, I accept your offer."

Once their horses were guided onto the narrow lane, Edmund somehow managed to ride ahead with Blythe, leaving Alex alone in the middle as Emmeline stubbornly rode beside her groom. Alex slowed down until Emmeline had no choice but to ride beside him, or risk leaving Blythe with yet another man.

Emmeline's face was coolly fixed forward on her sister, who was laughing at something Edmund said. Alex couldn't help studying Emmeline in her simple gown, so devoid of the ornamentation other women reveled in. Again he wondered if she wanted everyone to see only the shining light that was Blythe.

"My lady, you have crushed this poet's spirit."

He saw her lips twitch, but she only glanced at him before turning her gaze back to the village in the distance. The dusk of shadows had begun to darken the fields, and the descending sun was at their backs.

"I could not crush such a monumental conceit as yours, Sir Alexander."

"You challenged me to poetry, yet you made no comment about all my hard work."

"But, sir, you have disappointed me. I thought you might be able to embrace subtlety, and it is such a cruel blow to be confronted with the truth."

"What truth, my lady?" he asked, enjoying their sparring.

"That you are not even capable of *pretending* competence."

He laughed. "One cannot master everything, Emmeline. At least I try."

He could tell she stiffened by the way her horse tossed its head and pranced.

"And what do you mean by that?"

"I don't settle for only the many things I'm good at. I take risks. I attempt to fly, which swans are usually good at. But perhaps you know something different. Does the Marquess of Kent clip his swans' wings?"

Alex felt a strange sadness as Emmeline glared at him, blinking furiously.

Her fingers gripped the pommel as she leaned toward him. "Cease stretching your wings. My sister will not be treated as your next conquest."

"I don't wish to conquer her," he said simply.

She didn't answer, only tapped the horse's flanks with her heels and rode ahead of him.

That evening, Emmeline's father asked Blythe to sing again for his guests. Emmeline accompanied her on the spinet, and along with the gathered noblemen, watched how Blythe's beauty seemed to glow. Part of what made her sister so special was that she had no idea how wonderful such innocence was; it was simply a part of her. With the paneled parlor as her backdrop, Blythe stood confidently.

Too confident, too fearless—and Emmeline had encouraged it.

The scene by the stream unfolded again in Emmeline's mind, and she saw her fearless, curious sister in Alex Thornton's arms.

Emmeline knew she herself was at fault, that she had failed to teach Blythe proper caution. Was it too late? Would her sister only learn by taking one risk too many?

She couldn't allow that to happen. And she needed a stronger approach. Alex was a scoundrel and she had to prove it, even if it meant cataloguing his every sin.

It was time to show him that *she* would be the winner in their battle—and she had the perfect plan.

Chapter 10

Emmeline had thought her plan to spy on Alex and record his behavior was brilliant—until it was time to carry it out. It took two days even to find an opportunity to sneak out of the manor.

The only people usually on the street were commoners, but it seemed too risky to dress as a maidservant, and be at the mercy of every passing man.

When she thought of disguising herself as a boy, she felt a shiver of unease, followed by a mounting excitement.

It was easy to shuffle through the supply of servants' garments to find a pair of breeches and a loose shirt. When she was dressed, she added a doublet to hide the curves that would mark her as a woman, and high boots to disguise her legs. She tucked her hair up beneath a round woolen cap.

When she was safely out the door she broke

into a run through the garden, enjoying the freedom from her gown and the promise of a sunny day for her adventure. At the Thames, she hired a wherry boat to take her to Southwark.

Surely she would find Alex abed at the Rooster. The sun still hid behind the buildings as she tried to walk with a confident swagger from the dock to the tavern. More than once she had to fling herself into a doorway to keep from being run over by a fast-moving coach. She was deciding how to watch both entrances to the building, when the front door began to swing open. Ducking aside, she glanced over her shoulder and stared with surprise at Alex's back as he strode away. He tossed his short cape back from his shoulders; the spurs on his long boots jingled. He looked awake and ready for the day, and a whistle trailed behind him.

Why had she thought him the type to be grumpy and ill from the effects of drinking? She had expected that to be the first fault on her list.

No matter. The day was young, and Alex was certainly capable of every kind of scandal, both large and small. She would have plenty of things to warn Blythe about.

The first place he visited was Paris Garden, only a few streets away from the Rooster. She knew what went on there—bear-baiting—and she repressed a shudder.

But as the crowd gathered, and she had to stand on the tips of her toes to see Alex's dark hair and broad shoulders, she was determined to follow him.

All sizes of men closed about her, from hunched, toothless old grandfathers to eager youths much younger than she. She was elbowed and pushed along a path she hadn't chosen, and the sudden roar of cheering men rose like a wave. After losing sight of Alex, she could only trot along to keep from being trampled. She dreaded that someone would notice she was a woman.

They went into a tunnel beneath the building, and Emmeline paid a penny. Soon she was standing beneath the gallery, with large men blocking her view of the sunlit pit. While a pack of dogs snarled, every roar of the bear made her wince as she imagined what was being done to the poor thing.

"Here now, lad," said a gruff voice behind her. "Can ye not see?"

She looked over her shoulder to find an older man squinting down at her, his tanned face etched with white lines at his eyes and around his mouth.

"I don't need to see, sir," she said, remembering to deepen her voice. "I'm looking for my friend."

"So he brings ye to the bear-baiting and leaves you for a doxy, right?"

"Well, no—"

"Worry not, lad, me boys here can make sure ye

have a grand old time. Who has another pint of beer for me new friend here?"

Emmeline's eyes widened. "Sir, you are too kind, but—"

"The name's Robbie, lad."

Someone thrust a tankard of beer at her, and as it sloshed all over her hands, everyone laughed.

"Now lad," Robbie continued, "we can tell ye be taking a holiday from the manor to be with us common folk—"

She glanced nervously at the many curious faces peering down at her. Why had she spoken so formally?

"—but no need for fear. Ye're among friends. Drink up!"

A couple of the boys cheered as she took a cautious sip, and then another. She'd had beer before, and though this was hardly the best she'd sampled, it did quench her thirst.

"Come on, it'll put hair on your chin!" Robbie said with a laugh.

He put his big hand on her back and pushed her between two much taller men, whose elbows grazed her shoulders. She was pressed against a wooden balustrade, and she clutched the tankard to her chest to keep from spilling it. She could see a muddy pit encircled by three levels of galleries, all crowded with boisterous patrons. There were even women hanging on the arms of their men. Taking another sip of beer, she laughed as she realized she could have dressed plainly and come as herself.

The bear roared again, and her gaze was reluctantly drawn to the pit. A brown bear with scars about his muzzle and through his fur was chained from his iron collar to a stake in the very center of the pit. Circled by a pack of growling mastiffs, the poor bear didn't know which way to turn.

Emmeline gasped when the first dog finally leapt at him. With a roar, the bear caught him in a bone-crushing hug. Feeling queasy, she turned away and took another swallow of beer. She knew the bear wouldn't be allowed to die, for he was worth much to his handlers. But as for the dogs . . . she didn't want to speculate. She sipped her beer and lifted her gaze to the gallery above her.

She suddenly saw Alex. He was standing with a group of men, not even watching the bear-baiting. There was money passing between him and another man—could he be gambling? Absently drinking her beer and studying him, she remembered how he had questioned the quietness of her life. Of course she took risks! What would he think if he saw her now?

Robbie swung a beefy arm about her shoulder. "Ye done with that one yet, lad?"

"Not quite, sir."

"Drink it down! Me boy Matt wants to race ye."

"Race?" she echoed. The youth had to be several years younger than she was, for he was thin and gawky, with ears too large for his head. He clutched a tankard between two hands.

"Sure, drinkin's something all me boys are good at. Here's another pint."

She found herself gripping two tankards.

Though she wasn't afraid, for they seemed a nice sort, her stomach felt uneasy, and her head a bit light. She really didn't want to drink any more beer.

Alex leaned his elbows against the balustrade and munched the lamb pasty he'd just purchased, fighting a feeling of boredom. Bear-baiting was not his first choice in entertainment—in fact, it was near the bottom. But his dwindling supply of money was keeping his entertainment simple.

He took another bite of the pie and let his gaze wander over the crowd. Down below he heard raucous cheering, and watched with interest as a boy was being urged to drink by a circle of half-drunken revelers.

Alex's smile slowly faded, and a strange sense of tension tightened his muscles. The boy looked about him, then up at the gallery Alex was standing in. Their gazes locked, and Alex saw blue-green eyes rimmed with a heavy fringe of lashes no boy would have.

Emmeline.

What the hell was she doing at Paris Gardens dressed as a boy? And why was his first reaction on seeing her an immediate tightening of his groin and the memory of her well-curved body held against his?

Dropping the pie, he ran for the back of the gallery and pushed past several men on the stairs. It was more crowded at the bottom of the stands, and he had to force his way through until he reached the circle of men gathered around Emmeline.

"Excuse me," he said loudly, elbowing two of them aside. "Emmett, why did you run off?"

He almost laughed at the sight of Lady Emmeline Prescott with a cap pulled low over her forehead, and a pint of beer in each hand. She gave him a nervous smile as he scowled and shook his head.

"Em, you promised that if I brought you today, you'd remain at my side."

She grinned, and he realized she was already befuddled from the beer.

"But Alex—" she began in a dangerously normal voice.

"Not another word." He hoped she understood the warning. "I see you've not finished the beer these kind gentlemen purchased for you. Certainly I've taught you better manners than that."

Slowly her eyes widened, and she looked from him down to the beer and back to him. He could have sworn she gulped before obediently bringing the first tankard to her lips. It only took her a few gulps to drain the contents, and as a cheer rose around her, she blearily grinned.

Straightening almost in defiance, Emmeline started on the next beer. Alex let her have a few swallows before his conscience got the best of him.

Taking the tankard from her hand, he said, "I guess that's enough for today, Em. How do you feel?"

She shrugged, and to his surprise, her gaze dropped almost speculatively down his body. Pleasure stole over him like a warm summer rain until he remembered that they had an audience, drunken though it was. He took her by the shoulders and turned her toward the entertainment. He sipped her beer, and found himself contemplating drinking from the same spot her mouth had touched. Damn, his thoughts were getting away from him.

Emmeline was looking at him out of the corner of her eye. Feeling uncomfortably aware of the men all around them, Alex for once wished a woman wasn't staring at him so blatantly.

She suddenly took the tankard out of his hand and swallowed a gulp before he managed to pull it away. Her eyes were full of amusement as she licked the last drop from her lower lip. All sensation seemed to pool in his groin. He couldn't look away from the slow, knowing smile that spread across her face. Innocent that she was, she couldn't possibly understand what she was doing.

"Gentlemen, thank you for taking care of my brother," Alex abruptly said. "He can be a handful, as I'm sure you've discovered."

"He's a good lad, that he is," said one of the men cheerfully.

"Thanks, Robbie," Emmeline replied through a grin.

Alex wanted to groan. How could they not know she was a woman? Her doublet was sagging down one shoulder, and soon the thin shirt she wore would reveal her charms. The tantalizing thought gripped him with a dark eroticism. Or had she bound her breasts?

He shook himself back to reality.

"I thank you, too, Robbie," Alex said, handing the tankard over, "for taking care of my brother. Good day to you."

He gripped Emmeline's elbow and pulled her away from the pit. When they reached the grounds outside the entrance, he continued to drag her along.

"You can let go of me now."

"I don't think I shall." He managed to frown down at her. "You're drunk enough to be a danger to yourself."

"I am not inebriated, I assure you," she said, pulling away and straightening her doublet.

"You *must* have been drunk to even think of

coming here dressed like that. This is a dangerous place for a woman alone."

"But I've got you to guard me, don't I?" Grinning, she leaned against his arm.

As Alex felt the insistent pressure of her breasts, perspiration broke out above his lip. When he gave her a little push upright, she stumbled and staggered ahead of him.

"So why *are* you here?" he asked.

She didn't answer. He stayed behind her just to watch her hips sway, then realized what this might look like to other men.

Suddenly her feet went out from under her, and he caught her from behind, his arms beneath hers, his hands overflowing with her breasts. His palms burned as he felt her pointed nipples. With perfect aim, her backside landed against his hips, and his erection went from a possibility to a certainty.

He stood her upright so fast she almost went face-first into a ditch. He grabbed her elbow and steered her across a little river of sewage, trying not to breathe in the odor.

"Where are we going?" she demanded.

"Down to the river. I'm going to make sure you arrive safely home." He leaned nearer and whispered, "Unless you wish to return to my lodgings. I live nearby, you know."

"I know."

Though her voice had a huskiness that intrigued him, she also sounded guilty, and he tried to read the truth in her face. Had she been to the Rooster today? Was she *following* him?

For a moment, he desperately wanted to take her to his chamber, because from the look on her face, she wouldn't refuse.

Desperation? he thought suddenly. Was that what Emmeline Prescott had reduced him to? No, he would have none of it.

He escorted her through an alley to the river's edge, then tossed a sovereign to a waterman standing near his boat. The man gaped into his hand and back at Alex.

"Let me borrow the wherry," Alex said, helping Emmeline in and stepping down beside her. The craft almost capsized as she sat back heavily on the wooden bench. "I need to take the lad across while I speak to him alone. I promise to return this to you within the hour."

The man fisted his hand about the coin and bobbed his head. "Aye, guv'nor."

Alex settled down between the oars as the man gave them a push away from the dock. He began to row slowly, watching Emmeline. Their knees practically touched, and her gaze was almost a caress. He had to think of something besides the unfulfilled passion gnawing a hole in his gut.

She *had* been following him, he reminded himself. Why?

He knew she probably wouldn't answer such a

direct question, so he let the rocking of the boat and the cry of the gulls relax her. Gradually they pulled away from the city traffic as they headed upstream.

Emmeline swayed, then straightened stiffly. Her gaze narrowed on him, and when she spoke, her words were cautious and slurred. "You obviously know you are sinfully handsome."

"I beg your pardon?"

She rolled her eyes. "Now you sound like *me*."

He could barely keep from gaping. She reached out to touch his hand when it neared her as he rowed. He pulled back hard on the oars, cursing their lack of privacy.

"There's another bench behind you," he said. "Why not lean back?"

She hesitated, then glanced over her shoulder. With a sigh, she leaned back on her elbows and lifted her face to the sun. The cap fell off and her auburn hair tumbled down her back. Alex felt a hitch in his breathing as he watched the sun highlight the red in her curls. The pace of his rowing slowed.

How could she not understand how truly beautiful she was?

He studied her face, devoid of the paint so many women used to whiten their skin. She glowed with health and a touch of the sun. Her nose was pert and her lips the perfect fullness for kisses. Leisurely his gaze traced a path down the long elegance of her throat. With her elbows back and the doublet gaping, the shirt was tight across her breasts, which she had not bound.

His throat went painfully dry as he stared at her dusky nipples thrusting against the white fabric. She was laid out like a feast before him, her legs spread apart, the line of her throat begging for his kisses. He imagined finding a tree at the water's edge, its branches drooping to trail in the water and form a natural bower. He would row beneath, and the leaves would close over them like bed curtains. In the dim coolness he would rise above her, then settle between her thighs. He'd start with her magnificent breasts, suckling them to hard points until the damp shirt was transparent.

"You're not rowing," Emmeline said.

Alex gave a start and glanced about them, noticing that the city had given way to the sloping lawns leading up to the mansions along the Thames. Hellfire, he'd almost come in his breeches at the idea of merely touching spinster Emmeline Prescott.

It wasn't as if he would take advantage of a drunk virgin anyway, he thought as he adjusted his breeches. He picked up the pace of his rowing.

Unable to help himself, his eyes were drawn again to her relaxed body. He couldn't stop thinking about what her breasts would look like in a damp shirt. Mischievously cupping a hand-ful of water, he splashed her chest. He thought she would jump up indignantly, but she only laughed, and he ogled the spreading wetness as it enveloped one breast and practically revealed her nipple. It tightened into a little point and he almost groaned.

She slowly lifted her head and smiled at him, a womanly smile full of promise and passion. Alex told himself she was unaware of what she was doing, but she might as well have kicked him in the stomach, for the effect was just as profound.

He watched the slide of her hair along her arms and neck as she slowly let her head fall back again.

She licked her lips and spoke. "I still remember your tongue on my hand."

He stared at her and his voice became hoarse. "What are you talking about?"

"That night—in the stables. Your tongue touched my palm when I was trying to keep you quiet."

"Yes. I . . . remember."

"I would have thought such a thing to be loathsome."

"Was it?"

She laughed. "Not at all."

"Might I do it again?" he asked softly, seeing Kent Hall slide ever closer and wishing he could stop time. "I long to taste other parts of you, as well."

She looked wide-eyed at him and he could see a shiver move through her. She made him feel so unlike himself. Where was his easy control?

The wherry bumped against the stairs leading

up to Kent Hall. Emmeline was the first to look away, and as she stood up, almost capsized them. Alex grasped her waist. Her hands dropped to his shoulders and they stared at one another a moment too long. When he let his thumbs rub across her stomach, she leaned over him, her hair a curtain about them. Would she actually kiss him? But her eyes went wide and she broke away to climb out of the boat.

"Thank you," she called over her shoulder as she disappeared up into the garden.

Alex dropped his head to his chest, then gripped the oars and rowed as fast as he could away from Emmeline Prescott.

Emmeline slammed the door to her chamber and leaned back against it, breathing heavily. Her head ached—from the sun, she was certain—and her mind was racing a thousand ways at once.

The day had not gone at all as she'd expected, though she could put Alex's gambling on her list of his shortcomings. She should feel embarrassed to be caught and escorted home by him—but she wasn't. Even though the details of her wherry ride home seemed rather vague, she still felt like she'd won a contest of sorts.

And she wasn't going to stop proving to herself—and Blythe—that Alex was not a suitable suitor.

Chapter 11

Alex thought for certain that Emmeline was cured of her curiosity, but he was mistaken. When he took in a play at the Curtain with a young woman he frequently escorted, there was Emmeline in the balcony across the theater, her narrow-eyed gaze taking in everything he did.

Alex only smiled at her, bowed his head, and then threw an arm about his companion. Emmeline nodded once in challenge, then left, as if him seeing her was all that mattered.

What was her game?

Even an afternoon spent fencing with Edmund at the Queen's tiltyard could not keep him free of Emmeline. He felt her gaze before he saw her. He parried Edmund's blade aside, then shielded his eyes as he searched the balconies at Whitehall. He saw her then, standing alone at a railing just above, watching him. He swept his hand before him and bowed low.

Was that a glimpse of a smile? What did she hope to achieve by following him?

But still she didn't go away, so he turned back to Edmund and gave her the show he was capable of. Edmund stumbled back a few paces, eyes wide. He glanced between Alex and Emmeline speculatively, then brought his sword up and attacked. Steel met steel and rang repeatedly through the tiltyard. Soon Alex's breathing became labored, and his arm felt afire. He had never beaten Edmund before, for Edmund had raised himself up from poverty through mercenary work, and his body was massive because of it. Alex was good enough to survive a duel, but Edmund was good enough to survive a war.

Inside Alex's focused mind he and Edmund were youths again. Edmund had been the best friend of his childhood, a poor laundrywoman's boy who'd never shown fear of his masters, only belligerence and stubbornness. After a fight, the two had become fast friends, and as they'd aged, Alex had insisted Edmund be his squire, instead of the noble boy who fostered with the Thorntons. Side by side they'd learned and trained, until Edmund had left to make his own way in the world.

Suddenly with Emmeline watching, Alex was determined to hold his own.

And Edmund knew it. With a grin, he increased

the tempo, increased the power of his sword thrust. From somewhere Alex thought he heard the sounds of men cheering, the call of bets.

Emmeline gripped the balustrade so hard that the stone scraped her palms. The skill and grace Alex displayed were mesmerizing. She could tell that Edmund would soon triumph by sheer size alone, but Alex was crafty and intelligent, as she already knew.

With a sudden flurry of motion, Alex drove hard at Edmund, who stumbled back and tripped. As he landed on his backside, Alex knocked his sword away, threw back his head, and laughed.

Then he turned and looked up at her, as did all the soldiers in the tiltyard. She was on display, conspicuous beneath the glare of the sun. But it didn't seem to matter. All she could do was stare at Alex, who wore a sleeveless leather jerkin that bared muscular arms the likes of which she'd never seen displayed. She'd been held tightly in those arms, pressed against that body he now used like a weapon. She felt overheated and over-wrought, and very aware that he was a man and she a woman, because his eyes told her so.

Suddenly he dropped the sword and came toward the palace.

With a gasp, Emmeline drew back from the edge of the balcony and fumbled for the door handle. She knew he was coming to her.

All week she'd followed him, taking notes on

his behavior, telling herself she would use it all against him somehow. Yet she'd said nothing to her sister so far, even as she'd watched Blythe open Alex's letters, or set his gifts next to all the others she'd been sent by various admirers.

All Emmeline had accomplished was to make Alex suspicious, and now he was coming for her.

A little thrill shot through her as she ran through a dimly lit parlor set aside for the Queen's ladies. Thankfully, no one was about to see her haste. She went out into the corridor, where there were enough people that she was forced to slow to a walk.

"Lady Emmeline," Alex called in a loud voice, "might I have a word with you?"

She glanced over her shoulder and saw him at the far end of the wide corridor. She picked up her pace, knowing none of these important courtiers would know who she was. No one would care that she was ignoring Alex—except Alex.

She turned down the next hall, then ducked through a door leading to one of the queen's private gardens. A sudden brisk breeze made her shiver as she pressed her ear to the door. When the handle shook, she gasped and tried to hold the door closed with her body.

"Emmeline!"

His voice was low, intimidating. She could not fight him on strength alone, so she lifted her skirts and ran, knowing the paths that circled the elaborate marble sculpture almost as well as her own gardens. She heard the door slam open, then closed. Her breath came rapidly in her chest, she was almost gasping—but she wanted to laugh, to fling her arms wide at the exhilaration of the chase.

"Emmeline!"

He was close now, just on the other side of the statue. She skirted a pear tree, then ducked through a vine tunnel, which was ripe with the new greenery of spring. She just knew there was a door through the wall somewhere. Queen Elizabeth liked to have more than one exit, in case her life was in peril.

Emmeline came out of the tunnel and saw the door across a patch of blossoming flowers. She had taken one step away from the gravel path, when suddenly Alex caught her arm, spinning her about.

With a cry she tripped and fell backward, tangling her legs with his and landing amidst the daffodils. He came down on top of her.

The weight and pressure of his long body felt dangerously intriguing, touching her in all the places that burned. Wide-eyed, she stared up into his shadowed face. He wore a small smile but said nothing, just used his lazy, dark gaze to roam her face and settle on her mouth.

Emmeline was stunned by how delicious sin could feel. No man had ever touched her like this, and she felt the first inkling of uneasiness. Alex wielded a special kind of power, making her feel like she was the only woman in his mind—at least, for that moment.

The sensation was . . . overpowering.

Every breath she took pressed her breasts even harder against his broad chest. Her hands shook where they touched his hot, bare arms that had just performed feats of incredible strength and skill. Even though all their clothes separated them, she could feel his thigh between hers, resting against her.

Her mouth was suddenly so dry that she had to lick her lips, and she discovered with astonished wonder that this somehow affected him, because he tensed against her.

It was up to her to stop this. She had to master her emotions, fight him, force him off her.

But all she could manage was, "Alex, you should stand up."

"I should, should I?" he murmured, his laughing gaze sweeping her face.

"I mean you must."

He lifted himself up the slightest bit, and his gaze continued from her face to her neck to her chest.

"You're very comfortable, Emmeline."

She sucked in a breath, then wanted to groan because it only made her ridiculously large chest look bigger. And he was staring at it!

She slapped at his shoulder. "Please, Alex, stop looking—there!"

"Where?"

"You know! My—my—"

"Your breasts?" he murmured.

She sucked in a breath. "It is improper for you to say such things."

"But 'tis the truth. I'm looking at your breasts."

A blush burned her cheeks.

"And they're surely a lovely sight. Shall I describe how they make me feel?"

With a gasp, she covered her breasts with her hands. A groan rumbled through his chest, vibrating deep within her.

"Maybe I don't have to describe what I'm feeling," he whispered, leaning down over her. "Can't you tell?"

He slowly ground his hips into hers, and she felt something long and hard and dangerous. She gaped at him in shock, so embarrassed that she felt suddenly warm and wet between her thighs. What was the matter with her?

Alex lowered himself even farther, until their mouths were dangerously close. She saw nothing but his face; her world was the strength of his body, and she was frightened because it felt so right.

"Don't I even deserve a kiss for all you've put me through?" he murmured.

"A kiss!"

She pushed against his chest, and he rolled to his side almost too easily. She scrambled up and away from him, brushing down her skirts, feeling for leaves in her hair.

"No kiss?" he asked in mock sadness.

She meant to give him her best glare, but he suddenly rolled onto his back in the yellow daffodils, folding his bare arms behind his head as if she'd just left him in bed.

Oh my lord. A wild, wicked side of her wanted to lie back down with him. What was he doing to her—no, what was she allowing to happen?

"Why the sudden blush?" Alex asked.

"Was not your—your—groping enough of a reason?"

He looked so relaxed, stretched out at her feet, as if he was not nearly as affected as she was. She whirled and stalked away, but he quickly rose and appeared at her side.

"Emmeline, surely I deserve to know why you've been following me."

"Is it not obvious?" she retorted.

"Have you been reporting my activities back to your sister?"

She caught her breath and looked away. "Not . . . everything."

"And what does that mean?" he asked, tugging on her arm and pulling her to a stop.

How could she explain? She hadn't told her sister all the truth, not because of Alex, but because of her own unusual behavior. Every decision she'd made where he was concerned turned out wrong. Even if she told Blythe that she'd been following Alex for Blythe's protection, was it true? Or was it only her own curiosity, the fact that she was enjoying his scandalousness too much?

She'd become a different person somehow, a woman who truly understood how much she was missing, what she'd never have in her life. And it hurt.

"I have to go, Sir Alexander," she said formally, trying desperately to push her foolish emotions aside.

"It's Alex," he whispered, reaching to cup her cheek. For once he wasn't smiling, and he looked more intense and handsome than she could have imagined.

For her own sanity, she broke away from him and ran.

Alex watched her go, then remained alone in the garden, trying to remember the wager, Blythe, anything instead of the beguiling sight of a flustered Emmeline. Strands of her hair had come loose to tumble temptingly down her cheeks and neck. Why hadn't he touched them when Emmeline had lain beneath him?

Because her hair wasn't what he'd been thinking about then. With a sudden overwhelming need, he'd wanted to lift her skirts and settle himself between her soft thighs. He'd wanted to kiss every part of her skin, smell every scent, until she blushed for him alone.

The thought of that damned wager made him sigh with regret. Unless . . . would Edmund agree to modify it? Surely a spinster was just as much of a challenge as a girl *guarded* by a spinster?

Then he remembered the way her expressive eyes had dimmed when he'd asked if she were reporting his activities to Blythe. Did she truly think him so unworthy?

Gritting his teeth, he strode back through the corridors of Whitehall until he reached the tiltyard. He found Edmund straddling a bench, a dipper of water in his hand. Alex took the dipper, slurped the last of the water, picked up his sword, and went out into the center of the yard.

Edmund stared at him.

Alex lifted his sword. "We weren't finished, were we?"

Edmund walked toward him, his weapon dangling from one hand. "What happened with Lady Emmeline?"

"Nothing," he said, raising his sword. "Let's have at it."

But Edmund only circled him slowly, his eyes thoughtful. "Did she tell you why she's been following you?"

"I've always known why." Alex thrust forward.

Edmund parried, then stumbled back as Alex

came at him again. "Since when has practice become serious to you?"

Alex only answered with his sword.

Emmeline's father decided to celebrate his homecoming with an "event." He wanted to have a masque, with actors performing for his guests, and she hoped planning it would make her forget the thoughts of Alex that constantly crept into her mind.

But she wasn't successful. Every moment that she wasn't focused on the party, she thought of him and remembered their solitary moments in the garden like some secret dream she had never thought could come true. She'd felt every part of his body against hers, and the dark, simmering passion of it all would not leave her. She didn't know how she would face him again, for she could barely face Blythe—or even herself in the mirror.

He'd wanted to kiss her! Over and over she wondered what it would have felt like, and guiltily wished he'd done it. The shame of being dangerously attracted to her sister's suitor was all mixed up with the excitement and dread. During the week before the masque, he had twice visited Blythe, and Emmeline made sure she was busy elsewhere. Oh, she was careful to keep a servant in the room with them, but she herself stayed far away.

How could she look him in the eyes? Certainly all she would remember was his body on hers. Her face would give her away, especially to Blythe, who might want answers Emmeline couldn't give.

The sooner she got Alex Thornton out of their lives, the better. She personally oversaw the guest list, inviting every eligible man in London. Surely there were other men who would appeal to her sister.

Though it had rained all week, the night of the masque was clear and moonlit. The gardens seemed to shimmer with moisture and the promise of summer's heat. On impulse, Emmeline had allowed Blythe to set up a pavilion for the masked drama, rather than hold it indoors. All week she'd been close to changing her mind, but as the beauty of that Saturday night unfolded, she was thankful. Her father actually commended her efforts before he disappeared into his withdrawing chamber with the other older gentlemen.

The guests hummed about her in droves, the food was devoured and praised, even the actors' performances drew hearty laughter and applause. Though Emmeline was in the center of it all, she felt alone, removed from everyone. The week's efforts had culminated in a success—but all she felt was tiredness.

Even as she watched approvingly while the young men gathered about her sister, she thought of Alex. She didn't want him here—yet she did. Once, she had seen him standing beneath a cluster of lanterns as he watched one man after another dance with Blythe. He didn't seem sad, so much as . . . alone. He made no effort to dance with Blythe himself, as far as Emmeline could tell.

Could he finally be realizing that Blythe was wrong for him? Or was he just bored and ready to move on to another young woman?

Emmeline watched her father approach Blythe, while a young man trailed him. There were introductions made and shy smiles exchanged, and her father's approving nod.

Tears stung Emmeline's eyes. But her hard work would be worth it if Blythe could be happy all of her days.

Turning away, Emmeline hugged her cloak about her shoulders and followed a torchlit path. The breeze was cool off the river, and the sweet smells of budding flowers calmed her. She wound deeper into the garden, until even the voices of her guests faded. Nothing but lapping water and peace. She sniffed and wiped away a foolish tear.

"Blythe!"

Emmeline gave a start at the sound of Alex's voice.

From around the bend of hedges, she heard him call again. "Blythe, you know your sister wouldn't want you to run off by yourself."

He was coming. Emmeline looked about almost frantically, but the Thames was before her and Alex close behind. She kept her back to him, wishing she knew what to say, how to explain the reasons for her actions.

She heard his heavy sigh, then stiffened when he caught her elbow.

"Blythe, let me take you back—" He turned her about, then froze, his hands gripping her upper arms. For what seemed like an endless moment they stared at each other, again caught alone in a garden, but this time with the magic of moonlight.

She tried desperately to sound unaffected. "Alex," she said, nodding her head.

He didn't let her go, just watched her with an unreadable expression.

She felt her throat go dry, her heart beat strangely, but still he didn't release her. "Is it your turn to follow *me* through a garden?" she asked in a husky voice unlike her own.

He bent his head even nearer. "I'm glad I did."

She could feel his warm breath on her face, felt his hands slide down her back to her waist. She couldn't seem to get enough air, didn't know what to do with her own trembling hands. What was he doing? What could he be thinking?

Then he caught her hard against him, and she only had time for a gasp before he touched her lips with his.

Chapter 12

Emmeline felt frozen with shock and the rush of such confusing emotions that she was overwhelmed. Alex Thornton was kissing her, his lips moving so gently, so lightly, that she wanted to groan with the tantalizing promise of it all.

Then he lifted her up on her toes, pressing every part of them together. Through her gown, she could feel that hard part of him again, and her restraint vanished with this sure knowledge that he desired her.

"Emmeline," he said hoarsely against her mouth.

Then his tongue slid along her lips and she gasped. Only one man had ever kissed her, but it had been chaste and sweet—not like this. Not like he had to go on kissing her or die.

Her hands were caught between them and she

pressed them flat to his chest, feeling the strength
and hardness of his body, the tautness as he leaned
over her.

"Let me taste you," he murmured, and the vi-
bration of his mouth on hers made her moan.

"You already are," she whispered back.

She could tell he smiled, could feel every part of
him. He slanted his head and his mouth took hers
harder, until she helplessly parted her lips and let
him do as he willed.

He invaded her mouth like he'd invaded her
life and dreams, swiftly, forcefully. His tongue
claimed hers and she shuddered, letting him press
her even harder to his hips. His hands cupped her
buttocks, and she shamefully wished there were
no layers of garments between them.

She moaned, reveling in the wildness of his
mouth on her lips, on her cheek, on her throat. She
arched back, secure in his embrace, giving him
freely whatever he wanted to kiss as she plunged
her hands into the softness of his hair.

He murmured her name against her throat,
then against the barely revealed curve of her
breast. She wanted more; she wanted to disappear
with him into the dark, to—

And then she heard laughter.

They came apart so fast that Emmeline had to
grab hold of tree trunk not to fall.

Alex straightened his garments as he looked
over his shoulder. "I don't see anyone coming."

"I hear them!" She covered her mouth with her hands and waited, trying desperately to invent a fabrication for why she would be out in the dark with a known scoundrel. She looked into the trees, out across the dark Thames, anywhere but at him. Oh God, what had she done? What *would* she have done, if they hadn't been interrupted?

Then the voices drifted away, and they were alone again. She burned with a humiliation she'd never felt before. This couldn't go on; he had to get out of their lives, out of her thoughts.

"Alex." She winced at how uneven her voice sounded. "I have to tell you something, something important. And I want you to listen very carefully."

By moonlight he looked amused, but his intense eyes never left her.

"Emmeline, what just happened was—"

"No! Do not speak of it; just listen to me. I don't mean to offend you, but you have to understand that you are not the man for Blythe."

One of his eyebrows rose, but she was desperate to get the words out now—because otherwise she might remain silent just so that she could occasionally see him, even if only from afar.

"Allow me to finish. Blythe wants marriage and children. She needs a steady man, one who will provide for her."

His smile never diminished, and she hated feeling that he laughed at her.

"My dear Emmeline, I have no plans to marry."

"Well, that settles that," she said in a rush.

"But that doesn't mean I can't enjoy myself, and provide some enjoyment in return."

Her cheeks heated again, and she was grateful for the night. "You must understand that that isn't what I wish for my sister."

"Or yourself?" he asked softly.

When he reached for her, she stepped away.

"I have to return. They'll be looking for me."

"Blythe will, but I'm not so certain about your father."

"Don't!" she warned coldly. "Don't speak about things you don't understand." She turned away, drew her cloak tighter, and began to walk as quickly as possible.

Alex walked slowly up the path, whistling softly. As he approached the lights of the party and the sounds of guests enjoying themselves, he tried to analyze what he was feeling—something he hated to do. He'd never lost control of himself like that, especially not in someone else's home. But in those few moments when he'd held her against him, nothing else had mattered, not even the dangerous excitement of impropriety.

Kissing Emmeline was more exhilarating than even he had imagined—and he could imagine a lot. There was a hunger inside her, a passion she denied, probably because she hadn't known it existed.

But now *he* knew, and just the thought made him hard again.

When he finally had himself under control by thinking about crop management rather than Emmeline, he left the dark garden paths and returned to the party. Blythe was making a speech, thanking her father for the evening. But her true thanks were reserved for her sister, whom she drew forward despite Emmeline's protests.

Emmeline was blushing prettily as she hugged her sister. She curtsied to applause, but Alex thought she looked uncomfortable, that she forced her pleasure for her sister alone. He knew her well enough to know exactly what she was thinking: *I just kissed your suitor!*

Alex didn't feel guilty. Blythe was led off to dance by Seabrook, while Emmeline did the hard work of keeping the masque running smoothly. Blythe would easily find someone better than Alex to marry. But Emmeline—

His thought stopped as he watched her speak with the servants, and he felt something in his gut tighten. Emmeline seemed to always be in the background, making everything run smoothly for everyone else. Even he, who'd wanted to visit her during the week, had pretended it was Blythe he meant to see. He was positive no one had danced with Emmeline tonight.

Alex stepped forward to right that wrong, then halted. She wouldn't welcome an offer to dance from him now. So he stood in the shadows and watched her.

It was another hour before Emmeline felt like she might make it through the evening after all. She had calmed her mind by returning to her duties, and now Alex's kiss was just another memory, best forgotten. She was grateful he did not come near her—yet depressed at the same time. She needed a distraction.

And got it in the form of Maxwell Willoughby, a baron and cousin to an earl. They met at the refreshment table, and Emmeline found him charming and gentle, so thoughtful in his speech. He had a blond English handsomeness that seemed refreshingly safe. He wasn't very tall, or very broad, not threatening in any way.

He might be perfect for Blythe. After all, Blythe would tire quickly of Lord Seabrook when she realized all he truly loved to talk about were his horses.

Emmeline allowed Lord Willoughby to pour her a wine punch, then asked, "Lord Willoughby, do you live in London?"

"Only occasionally, my lady. I spend most of the year at my estate in Sussex."

Not too far away; that was good. "And what most occupies your mind there?"

His eyes widened a bit, but he had the grace to laugh pleasantly. "Do not allow me to start on my passion, Lady Emmeline. I might bore you."

"Never, my lord!"

"Very well. I am endeavoring to grow wine grapes. It is such a shame to import wine, when here in England we have the finest soil, if only we could figure how best to use it."

"So you study for this interest of yours?"

"Oh, yes. And I travel each year to the best vineyards in France."

This was even better. Blythe had always talked about wanting to see the world. As he talked longer, Emmeline was charmed by his fascination with his project, his good-natured intelligence, and his love of reading.

When Blythe came over to speak with her, Emmeline tried to control her excitement.

"Blythe, dearest, I'd like you to meet Lord Willoughby. My lord, this is my sister, the Lady Blythe."

Lord Willoughby's eyes widened as he beheld her sister, and he bowed quite charmingly. Smiling with excitement, Emmeline looked back and forth between them. But . . . Lord Willoughby remained silent, though his posture spoke interest and attention.

After a moment, Blythe said, "How nice to meet you, my lord," and reached out her hand.

Emmeline looked at Lord Willoughby and waited. He licked his lips once, and just as Emmeline was tempted to give him a subtle kick in the ankle, he wiped his palm on his breeches, took Blythe's hand, and bowed over it.

"Lady B-Blythe," he murmured. "A p-pleasure."

Emmeline wanted to gape at him. Where had this stuttering, unsure young man come from? He had been so pleasant and confident with her. She tried to bring up his estate, surely a good topic. But he seemed to have nothing to say, and could only stare at Blythe.

Blythe managed to escape when Lord Seabrook asked her to dance. She shot a sympathetic smile at Emmeline and whirled away.

Emmeline was speechless. She watched her sister for a moment, then turned to Lord Willoughby, whose face now glowed a dull red.

"I muddled that, didn't I?" he murmured, and shook his head in obvious disgust.

"I don't understand what just happened."

"Lady Emmeline, forgive me. This always happens. Whenever I try to impress a beautiful woman, I cannot think of a thing to say."

"You had no problem conversing with me."

"But you're different, my lady. You're easy to talk to, and you seem interested in what I have to say. A woman like your sister—why would she be interested in someone like me, when she has

Lord Seabrook dancing attendance on her?"

Though Emmeline felt frustrated, she wasn't going to let Lord Willoughby off this easily. He was too nice a man, and she wanted her sister to see that. There had to be something she could do.

When Alex finished a dance with Lady Morley, he escorted her to the benches, then turned to look for Emmeline again.

She was talking to a man.

Frowning, Alex walked slowly towards them, keeping to the shadows beneath the overhang of the trees. He eventually recognized Maxwell Willoughby, a decent fellow, if a bit shy. They were talking rather animatedly, then Emmeline laughed and shook her head in a fond way.

Had she finally found her next poet?

Alex folded his arms across his chest, and a wave of blackness enveloped his mind, a sudden surge of jealousy that took him totally unaware.

The women he usually surrounded himself with were but pale imitations of Emmeline's vibrancy and intelligence, yet she remained ignorant of her own attributes. Now she was trying to replace one weak man with another, as if she didn't deserve better.

And suddenly Alex knew he wanted better for her, that somehow he wanted her to move ahead with her life, and leave her past mistakes behind. And he was just the man to show her the way.

Late that night, Emmeline stood behind Blythe and brushed out her hair. Usually a maidservant did the task, but Emmeline felt a need to be close to her sister. She knew it was out of guilt, but felt she could make it up to Blythe by introducing her to the perfect man. If only Lord Willoughby had cooperated.

In the mirror she watched Blythe's eyes blink slowly, heavily. "It's time for you to sleep," she murmured.

Blythe shook her head and sat up straighter. "Oh no! My head is still buzzing with memories of our wonderful party. I would so like to be more a part of the preparations next time, so I can some-day do what you do."

Emmeline smiled. "That would be wonderful." She completed a few more strokes, then asked, "So whom did you dance with this evening?"

She sighed. "So many men that I feel blessed! Lord Seabrook was especially generous with his time, and even Alex's friend Sir Edmund showed that for such a big man, he is quite graceful."

"I didn't see you dance with Sir Edmund," Emmeline said cautiously, trying not to frown.

"He didn't arrive until late in the evening."

"Oh. What about Lord Willoughby?"

"Who?" Blythe asked, once again blinking slowly.

"Lord Willoughby, the young man I introduced you to at the refreshment table."

"Oh him! He seemed . . . nice, I guess. He didn't ask me to dance."

Emmeline already knew that, and she wanted to groan at the man's shyness.

"But Alex did."

When she heard his name, she accidentally pulled the brush too hard and Blythe gasped.

"Oh, dearest, forgive me!" she said, upset that her hands started to shake, that her mind immediately took her to the dark garden, and Alex's arms around her, his mouth on hers. "What did Alex do?"

"He danced with me," she repeated, giving Emmeline a puzzled look.

"Oh. I'm surprised he managed to find the time to attend our little party. He has been so busy of late."

"He has?" Blythe said after a big yawn. "How do you know?"

"I have seen him . . . about." Oh, why had she started this conversation?

"Where?"

Emmeline softened her strokes and lowered her voice, to put Blythe to sleep. "I saw him at a play, when I went with the queen's ladies."

"On the day that my head ached so?"

"Yes." She hesitated, then blurted out, "He was with a lovely young lady."

Blythe only nodded. "He told me about her. She's married, and her husband dislikes plays, so Alex takes her."

Was that *all* Alex did with her? Emmeline couldn't help wondering, and she realized that she was jealous of a woman she didn't even know. She began to brush again, slower, slower, as Blythe's eyelids drooped.

She whispered, "Come dearest, go to bed now. You've had a long evening."

Eyes practically closed, Blythe kissed her cheek and crawled under the covers. Emmeline returned to her own bedchamber, but sleep would not come easily—not with Alex tormenting her mind, reminding her of everything she would never have.

Alex's shadow had returned. Once again he could not shake the feeling he was being followed, nor the frustration of being unable to catch the scoundrel. If he owed somebody money, why didn't they just ask for it? At least the creditors hounded him openly. It had been damned difficult getting used to no longer having his brother's money to spend, and maybe in a drunken state he'd wagered something he shouldn't have.

In a brief moment of clarity, Alex wondered

what the hell he was doing with his life. All he had to do was go back to his estates in Cumberland. The work he'd been doing as viscount could be applied to his own land. There, he was their master, whom his steward had no choice but to listen to. He could gain their respect, if he wanted to try.

But when he'd lost the viscountcy, when he'd returned to being Alex Thornton, drunken scoundrel, none of it seemed so important. He couldn't go back until he'd exorcised this restlessness inside him, until he'd proven—

Proven *what*?

That he was still Alex? That pretending to be Spencer for a year and a half had not changed him in some fundamental way?

So, he would continue to live his life the way he wanted, determined not to let these hidden cowards affect him. Let them *try* to capture him, if they wanted.

They tried again on his return home from a night of cards and gambling at a friend's house. He was riding his horse through the muddy streets by moonlight and the occasional lantern hung outside a shop.

He heard the jingle of horses nearby. He pulled up on the reins and stopped. So did the sound from the other horses. A feeling of menace stole over him, and he looked over his shoulder. He had his sword with him, but they might have firearms.

He had deliberately taken the road leading past the high walls surrounding Emmeline's estate. He had meant to look upon it and think of her kiss, and his next plans for her. Now, in the shadows where the walls met at a corner, he reached up and caught the top of the gritty wall, letting the horse slide out from under him. He pulled himself up and over, then dropped to the ground and held still. He heard no outcry, only the jingle of spurs as horses passed by.

Alex leaned back against the wall and released his breath in a sigh. Across the neat rows of a kitchen garden loomed Kent Hall, massive and regal, jutting with turrets and tall windows in every wing.

Somewhere in there Emmeline slept.

Well, he had to do *something* until he was certain he'd eluded pursuit. It had only been a few months since he'd snuck into a woman's house. He hoped he wasn't out of practice.

He approached the mansion, then moved from window to window on the ground floor. It wasn't long before he found one unlatched. Pushing it open, he slid his legs inside and dropped to the floor.

Chapter 13

❧❦❧

Emmeline couldn't sleep. Through her mind ran thoughts of how to make Blythe and Maxwell comfortable with each other. She discarded plan after plan and still had nothing.

And then there was Alex, and what to do about him. In the few days since the masque, he had not come to call, nor sent a letter to Blythe. Emmeline wondered if it bothered Blythe.

Was her sister awake? She got up and looked across the dark hall, but saw no light beneath the door.

Suddenly, she heard a sound from somewhere else in the house, and it echoed softly and died away. Who could be awake at this time of night? She quietly opened Blythe's door, and found her sister fast asleep.

Returning to her room, Emmeline shrugged

into her dressing gown and tied it about her waist. She took the candleholder from her bedside table and walked out into the dark hall.

The candle wrapped her in its glow, but made it hard to see anything else. She went down the front staircase very carefully, the cold marble numbing her bare feet.

Light glowed from the parlor, as if the servants had put wood on the fire before they'd gone to bed. But only the kitchen fire was supposed to be left—

She saw the silhouette of a crouching man before the hearth and frowned, her unease blossoming. He didn't look like any of her people . . .

Then he rose up, and seeing that he was a stranger, she gave a startled cry and dropped the candle.

"Emmeline!"

Alex Thornton rushed toward her. She shuddered with relief and leaned against the doorframe, watching rather dazedly as he picked up the now unlit candle.

He scuffed his foot across the spot on the floor. "I don't think it did any damage," he said, looking back up at her.

He had the gall to grin. She could easily have slapped his face, but then his gaze roved down her body, and his smile faded. Remembering vividly how it felt to be held in his strong arms, she stiffened and pulled the dressing gown even tighter at her waist. He seemed to choke as he turned back toward the fire.

"What are you doing here?" she demanded as she followed him, her voice low.

"Passing the time."

"You cannot possibly make me believe that Blythe *knew*—"

"No, of course not," he said, holding up a hand as he turned to face her. "I didn't intend to stop in, but it seemed the best alternative."

"Alternative to what?" Emmeline rested her fists on her hips and glared up at him as if being alone in the night with him did not do strange, wicked things to her insides.

"To being accosted by criminals out in the street. I was being followed, and I had to go somewhere, didn't I?"

He busied himself at a small table, and she realized with disbelief that he was pouring himself a goblet of wine.

"Is that my father's?" she asked faintly.

He lifted it toward her in a silent toast, took a sip, then sighed with obvious pleasure. "I assumed he wouldn't mind. Can I pour you some?"

"No. Just—just tell me why you were being followed."

He shrugged. "Thievery, I guess."

"Like that evening I came to the tavern?"

He nodded, looking very much at ease in the flickering firelight in someone else's home. She had to think about something else.

"Do you think the incidents are related?"

He glanced at her sharply. "Smart girl."

"What do they want?"

"They already stole most of my money, yet still they come. It makes entertaining myself rather difficult."

"But . . . surely you have more money. Your family is wealthy, is it not?"

She watched his profile as he stared unseeingly into the fire.

"I won't borrow from my brother," he said in a low voice. Then he turned and grinned at her. "And it's such a long journey to my own estates. Unless you'd like to keep me company?"

He was teasing her, and she hated how flustered he could make her feel. "How long do you mean to hide here? What if someone sees you?"

He poured himself more wine. Then, holding her gaze, he sank down in a large chair beside the fire, his knees spread, his body loose and languorous as he smiled at her. She caught her breath, unable to stop staring as heat seemed to blossom inside her body in embarrassing places. She remembered his lips on hers, his tongue thrusting inside with a boldness that had nearly made her swoon. Would he try to kiss her again—goodness, did she want him to? Never had she thought the element of danger about a man would intrigue her.

She closed her eyes and braced her hands on the mantel.

Alex's mouth went dry when Emmeline leaned before the fire. Her dressing gown was so thin and fine that he could see the luscious curves of her body, even her nipples where they strained against the fabric. He was overwhelmed with the urge to take her clothes from her, to lay her down on a carpet before the fire, and show her what she did to a man.

"Emmeline." He had to clear his throat to continue.

She turned her head and he tried not to watch the fall of her heavy hair where it slid against her body.

"Don't ask me to leave," he whispered. "And please, don't stand like that."

"Like what?"

She turned toward him and words failed him as he remembered the arousing passion of her kiss. How could she not know how alluring she was? "You're wearing little, love. I'm only a man, you know."

She seemed puzzled, then her face flamed as she once again pulled her dressing gown tight. Did she truly have no idea how she pushed up her generous breasts when she did that?

"Don't be cruel, Alex," she said in a low voice. "I wouldn't have believed it of you."

"Cruel?" He leaned forward to take her hands in his. "I am only saying the truth. If your poet would have seen you like this, he would not have allowed you to turn him away."

He felt the tension in her hands, and saw a sudden sheen of tears sparkle in her eyes. "I didn't *want* to turn him away. I didn't care that he was only a tutor. But my father did. He forbade me to marry him."

For a moment, it was as if every truth Alex had ever known shook itself into a new place. She hadn't rejected her suitor because he was unworthy of her? *Her father* had denied her happiness?

Unable to deal with his own sudden confusion, he resorted to what he did best. Standing up, he reached out to cup her cheek. She didn't move, only stared at him, her lips parted, her eyes shining.

"So you had a suitor," he murmured, letting his fingers brush over her soft skin. "Did he ever touch you like this?"

Emmeline couldn't even remember her poet's name. She could form no rational thought at all as he stroked her cheek, and down her neck.

She swallowed and tried to sound affronted, but only managed breathlessness. "No, he was a gentleman."

With his hand behind her neck, he pulled her slowly forward. "But if this man truly loved you, he would have *needed* to caress your skin, to smell your hair."

Her breasts touched his body first, then her hips, and she wore so little it was as if her skin was alive with new sensations. Her nipples hardened to sensitive nubs against his chest; her belly tightened when he pressed the hard evidence of his desire against her. He brushed her hair back over her shoulder, then bent and pressed his mouth beneath her ear.

It was all too much.

Emmeline fought tears as she whispered, "If he never loved me, then I don't have a single precious memory to carry into spinsterhood. Don't take that away from me."

His tongue licked a path to her collarbone as his hands pulled her even closer against him. "I can give you such memories."

His deep voice rumbled against her chest. His hands were sliding from her waist and up her stomach. Though it was one of the most difficult things she'd ever done, she caught and held them just below her breasts.

"You do not love me. You're pursuing my sister."

"I don't love her, either."

She felt the tension in his hands as if he would break free and do as he wished with her. To her embarrassment, she wanted to let him. She wanted to feel what it was like to be desired by a man, to know the heady sensations of passion she'd only just begun to glimpse. But then she'd only be his mistress.

She shoved him and he stumbled back.

"Go home to your tavern, Alex. I'm sure you can find other women who don't mind that you're not in love with them."

He caught her arm. "Do you want me to be in love with you?"

Pain knifed through her. "No! Nor do I want intimacies that mean nothing to you but easing your lust."

"Em, you can't believe—"

"Do not tell me what to believe! Do you see that window over there? Go out it!"

"But Em—" he began.

He smiled with such amusement that she wanted to pound her fists against him, to shake him into realizing what he'd done here this night.

"Go home, Alex!"

He stared at her for a moment, then shook his head as he donned his cloak. "Don't worry for me, love. I'm sure those angry villains have gone away."

"I *won't* worry."

When he had his legs over the windowsill, she was tempted to give him a push. Instead she watched him drop out of sight, then slammed the window shut and locked it.

She put her shaking hands over her mouth and began to cry as her memories of Clifford faded even further. Had she been lying to herself?

Was it truly only Alex who had ever made her

feel wanted and alive? If so, then she was doomed, for although he desired her, he made no secret of the fact that he enjoyed many women in the same way.

Emmeline had to forget her own woes and concentrate on Blythe's newest hope for a suitor. Lord Willoughby was a sweet man, and surely once he and Blythe were together more often, his tongue would loosen. She invited him to play cards with her and Blythe, but the scheme fell apart. Once again, he talked to her freely, but when Blythe made an appearance he was tongue-tied, and could barely bring himself to ask for the next card.

To make matters worse, Blythe had overheard him speaking so easily to Emmeline, and tried to convince Emmeline that Lord Willoughby really liked *her*.

But Emmeline wouldn't give up. She vowed that when they attended the Duke of Stokesford's dinner party on Thursday, she would make sure Lord Willoughby and Blythe were alone together. She would remain nearby, but how else would her sister see that he was intrigued with her?

Her plans were frustrated by Blythe, who developed a cough and a fever. Emmeline had to send their regrets with an explanation. Little did she know how her "explanation" would be received. The afternoon after the dinner party, four of Blythe's friends arrived, full of sympathy and comfort—and sweets. Emmeline had her hands full entertaining the girls, while trying to keep Blythe in her room.

She was serving a tray of tarts to the ladies in the parlor when the manservant announced Maxwell Willoughby. He walked in carrying an armful of flowers that practically hid his concerned face.

"How is Blythe?" he asked quickly.

Emmeline smiled. "She is fine, my lord. How good of you to inquire after her. But she's not seeing visitors today."

"Please, call me Maxwell. Without your sister, life must seem dull. I thought I could keep you company, and perhaps catch a glimpse of Blythe from afar. I even brought her wine from my estate."

He turned sideways, and she saw a bottle tucked beneath his arm. Emmeline stepped aside so he could join her other visitors, and as she did so, she saw the servant showing another man in— Alex Thornton.

He walked in carrying two roses, and it was as if excitement suddenly sizzled through the room. The four ladies gasped and giggled. Maxwell visibly drooped. And Emmeline felt her face redden and her body react with betraying pleasure.

She reminded herself that he was here to see Blythe.

But then he stopped beside Maxwell, who peered up at him through the flowers.

"Good afternoon, Lady Emmeline. When I heard about your sister's precarious health, I had to come see for myself." He held out the two roses. "One for Blythe, and one for her doting sister, who has had the added burden of playing the nurse." He glanced over Emmeline's shoulder and smiled at Blythe's friends. "And hostess as well, I see. It is a good thing I arrived to help you."

"Help me?" she repeated, her teeth clenched.

"Why, of course. Allow me to amuse the ladies while you see to Willoughby's flowers."

He sent her a positively wicked grin, then walked into the midst of four scandalized girls. Emmeline was certain they were counting their blessings that their mothers weren't there to keep them away from the notorious knight. She stood beside Maxwell and watched Alex sit between two girls on the settle, then spread his long arms on the wooden back behind them.

Rolling her eyes, Emmeline turned back to Maxwell, who looked about as wilted as his flowers would soon be.

"Maxwell, let me find a vase."

He gave her a grateful smile. "Thank you. I guess many of us had the same idea, eh?"

"It was very kind of both of you, I'm sure," she murmured, beckoning to the maidservant standing near the door. She gave instructions to the girl, handed her the flowers, and watched her go. Emmeline wished she could go, too. She'd planned to relax with a new book while Blythe slept.

Perhaps, as he'd suggested, Alex could do her entertaining for her. She watched in dismay at how easily he charmed the young ladies. He even included Maxwell, who sat rather awkwardly in their midst, with little to say. If only Maxwell had a small portion of the confidence Alex had, she was certain Blythe would be interested in him. She wondered if there was any way to teach such a thing.

Within the next half-hour, she fended off a visit from a bored Blythe, served the ladies wine punch, and spoke quiet words of encouragement to Maxwell. Alex continued to interrupt, obviously including them in his circle of admirers. As if he needed any more, she thought, smiling grudgingly.

"Lady Emmeline," he finally said, "come to the window, please; I have something to show you. I know how interested in horseflesh you are. The rest of you sweet ladies will have to question Lord Willoughby about his winery. He grows his own grapes, you know."

As Alex took her arm and led her away, she looked over her shoulder apologetically at Maxwell, whose eyes had gone wide as all four lovely women turned to look at him.

At the window she shook off Alex's hand, but

didn't look into his face. "That was hardly necessary. Where is your horse, so I can return to my guests?"

"Actually, you can't see him from here," he said.

The amusement in his voice made her groan and turn to leave, until he caught her hand.

"Lady Emmeline, is it so horrible that I'd like a moment alone with you?"

"Alex, this is not the time—"

"Won't you even look at me? Turning cowardly so soon?"

He already knew her too well, she thought, lifting her gaze to the challenge. He stared down at her with those dark, knowing eyes, as the sun glistened in his black hair. Where their hands touched, heat blossomed.

"It is hardly cowardly to return to my guests," she said.

"You are working much too hard, Emmeline."

"And you had to come and give me even more to do?"

"I?"

He was so good at pretending innocence. Yet she didn't remove her hand from his.

"How could I be a bother?" he continued. "I've been *helping* you. I've been amusing those silly young girls with my outlandish stories, refilling their goblets—"

"Practically feeding them with your own fingers, weren't you?" she said, knowing that her smile was no longer hidden.

"You noticed! All my hard work is not going to waste."

Emmeline sighed and shook her head. "Go home, Alex. You won't see Blythe today."

"Perhaps I didn't come to see her," he said in a lower voice.

She stared at him, trying to remove her hand even as he held her tighter. "These games don't help, so cease them. I've already told you that your pursuit of Blythe is useless. Please don't make me involve my brothers."

"Why, Em, have you reached a situation you cannot handle alone?"

"I didn't mean—"

"No, no, please, I understand. Your brothers have long been gone from London, haven't they?"

He touched a sore point with her. "It's been a year since we've seen them."

"Then by all means, summon them. You don't need me as an excuse. But you might not want to mention my name to your eldest brother."

"John?"

"That's the one."

Emmeline narrowed her eyes. "Do you know my brothers?"

"Oh yes, all three. Studied with them, even. But

I was forced to play a joke upon John, and I fear he has yet to forgive me."

"A joke?" Whatever sort of joke could *anyone* pull on John? He prided himself on knowing the character of every man he dealt with, and would not tolerate fools.

But then, Alex was hardly a fool, and she wondered why he liked to pretend so. As they stared at one another, she vaguely heard a raised voice.

"I do believe you're . . . wanted, Lady Emmeline," he murmured, his thumbs rubbing circles on the backs of her hands. His gaze dropped to her lips, and a shock traveled through her.

Chapter 14

Alex knew people might be watching them, and didn't care—but Emmeline would. Though he could easily lose himself in her blue-green eyes, he released her and looked toward the front hall.

Edmund stood there, watching beneath raised eyebrows. Alex frowned at him.

The servant stood hesitantly beside Edmund. "Lady Emmeline? Sir Edmund Blackwell comes to visit."

Alex watched her stride away from him, and he knew a puzzling need to pull her back, to keep her at his side.

"Sir Edmund," Emmeline said. "How good of you to see to Blythe's welfare."

"My lady, your sister is such a gentle soul. It grieves me to know that she suffers."

She led him toward her other guests. "Grieve no more, Sir Edmund, for Blythe is recovering quite well. Come, allow me to introduce you to her friends."

Afterward when Edmund finally glanced his way, Alex motioned him over with a nod, and he brought a goblet with him.

"Fine wine," Edmund said. "Willoughby made it, you know."

Alex only shrugged, finding he didn't wish to taste the stuff. He knew Willoughby's game. He watched Emmeline lean over to speak to the man, who laughed as he answered.

Something curled tighter inside him with a tinge of unfamiliar pain, and he needed to ignore it. "So what are you doing here, Blackwell?"

"Blackwell, is it?" Edmund's amusement was palpable. "From that dark look on your face, I'd say you need me."

"I don't need you except for your good company at the bar."

"Then Lady Emmeline needs me."

Alex rounded on him. "What?"

Edmund laughed. "I like her. I want to make sure you treat her well in this quest for her sister's kiss. But then maybe she's suitably preoccupied with someone else."

He raised his glass in toast toward Willoughby, and Alex felt the need to hit someone. "He's pursuing Lady Blythe."

"So certain, are you?"

"Yes. He's my competition." He took Edmund's goblet and drained it. "The stuff's bitter, is it not?"

"I thought it quite good. Willoughby might be on to something."

"I have something better to talk about." He turned his back to Emmeline and her guests, as if he were looking out the window. "I need a favor."

"You have only to ask."

Alex glanced at him and smiled. "You haven't heard it yet, old friend." When Edmund only shrugged, he continued, "I'm short on money since the robbery."

"I know. Your creditors have begun to question even me."

"I need a fresh infusion, which means a trip to Cumberland. And I can't leave London right now. Would you be willing to take the journey for me, as you've done so ably before?"

Alex knew it was ridiculous to ask Edmund to leave in the middle of their wager, he was as competitive as Alex himself.

But Alex just couldn't bring himself to leave town, not when things were going so well with Emmeline. Each day was more interesting than the last, and the wager had paled in comparison.

"I'll go," Edmund said quietly.

Alex stared at him. "I was certain you would refuse. There *is* the wager."

"There is."

Was he imagining it, or did Edmund look pale? "We could call it a draw."

"And why would you want to do that, old friend?"

Alex shrugged, even as he looked at Emmeline. She laughed in response to something Willoughby said, and he watched her fine figure as she leaned back in the chair. She wore lighter colors this day, and she seemed as young and carefree as the girls she entertained. Did Willoughby bring about such ease in her?

"Is it Lady Emmeline?" Edmund asked.

"She is . . . more of a challenge, I admit."

"Very well. We'll discuss the wager when I return. I'll be off to pack. Come soon and write out a letter to your steward for me."

"You're going now?" he asked curiously. "You just arrived."

Edmund didn't meet his eyes. "I see no reason to wait. You can explain my departure to the ladies. I'll see you at the tavern."

As Edmund walked away, Alex stared after him, feeling uneasy. It wasn't like his friend to abandon a challenge, especially one involving money. Edmund had been distracted lately, hardly himself. What was going on?

He glanced at Emmeline as she approached, and felt something ease inside him.

"Your friend left rather abruptly," she said.

"I know. He asked me to beg your forgiveness."

"He had a pressing errand, I take it?"

"I guess so," Alex said speculatively. Then he smiled down at her. "But I don't. I could keep you amused for the rest of the afternoon."

She sighed, and suddenly he saw her weariness.

"Ah, we are a burden," he said, before she could answer. "I'll take all your guests away and let you rest."

Scrutinizing him, she asked, "You would do that?"

"I would—and I can. Just watch me."

"Ever one for a challenge, aren't you?"

"Makes a dull life interesting."

Her regard intensified. "Your life is so dull, then? Perhaps parties do not satisfy you, after all."

He leaned down toward her, inhaling the sweet scent of her, enjoying the way her breath caught in a soft gasp. "The parties are only a preliminary, love. It's what comes later, in the dark of the night, that makes it all worthwhile. I *have* offered to be your guide in such pleasures."

For a brief moment, he savored the memory of a firelit night in this parlor, when he held her tightly to him. He knew she felt it, too, this awareness, this need.

He thought for certain she would blush to her toes and leave him, but Emmeline was obviously made of sterner stuff. She lifted her chin and eyed him with a cool superiority.

" 'Tis a shame that only in darkness do you feel at ease. Why is that? What is wrong with showing the world the real Alex Thornton?"

"You think I hide myself?"

"Do you?"

He touched her chin. "You'll just have to find out, Em. Now, off I go to amuse your guests."

He was true to his word. Within minutes, he was taking all the ladies—and Maxwell—out for a walk in the parks of her father's estate. Emmeline sat before the fire with her book, enjoying the solitude. Only when she noticed how dark it was getting did she realize Alex must have made sure they all left without returning to the house.

She was grateful.

Though Emmeline and Blythe planned to attend festivities at Whitehall at the end of next week, Emmeline wanted to bring Blythe and Maxwell together sooner. She just had to find a way that didn't seem obvious.

Alex presented her with an opportunity when he invited her and Blythe to attend a country fair with him at the nearby village of Islington on Saturday.

In Emmeline's bedchamber that night, Blythe held up his letter. "Oh, do say we can go, Emmy! Father will be away, and the last fair we attended was in Kent, ages ago!"

Emmeline deliberately hesitated, then hoped

God forgave her the lie she uttered. "Dearest, I already invited Lord Willoughby to dinner that afternoon."

"He may join us! I'm sure Alex won't mind."

Emmeline did not particularly care if Alex minded; she felt no guilt at all for changing the guest list of his little outing.

She pulled her dressing gown even tighter and decided to ask the question that had been haunting her. "Dearest, has Sir Alexander tried to kiss you again?"

"Not at all."

Emmeline let out the breath she'd been holding. "Does this bother you?"

"Not really," she said, and shot her a saucy grin even as she dabbed Emmeline's perfume at her wrist. "In fact, I'm looking forward to kissing Lord Seabrook, just to see the difference."

Emmeline almost gaped at her, unable to voice a sisterly warning. She couldn't imagine even caring about another man's kiss after having experienced Alex's. And the fact that Blythe seemed unaffected lightened her heart.

Saturday morn, Emmeline dressed with special care. Around her waist she wore a rolled hip pad, which flared her skirts wide, but would be comfortable when she was riding. She chose a sky-blue linen gown that she'd embroidered herself with vines and flowers rather than jewels. She rejoiced in the newness of springtime and had a sense of anticipation that she didn't understand but didn't question, either.

When the maid was finished dressing her hair and perched a small brimmed hat on top, Emmeline felt ready for adventure, for fun. She and Blythe had their mares brought around from the stables, while they waited on marble benches under the bright sun.

Blythe regarded her thoughtfully for a moment, wearing a fond smile. "Emmy, you look very lovely today."

"So do you, dearest," she replied, squeezing her sister's hand.

"Is there a particular reason, I wonder?"

"What?"

Blythe shook her head. "Pay me no consequence. I have fanciful imaginings, 'tis all. I just want you to be happy."

Maxwell arrived first. He was expressing his thanks for the invitation to Emmeline, and shyly managing to greet Blythe without stuttering, when Alex rode up on his magnificent black gelding. Emmeline withheld a smile when he pulled up short on seeing Maxwell. He shot her a narrow-eyed glance.

"A good morn to you, Sir Alexander," she said, feeling like giggling. Ah, foiling his plans brought a cheer to her heart.

Alex nodded back as he dismounted. "Lady

Emmeline, Lady Blythe, your beauty surely rivals this fine English day." He nodded at Maxwell, his smile still evident. "Lord Willoughby, glad I am that you're joining us."

They clasped hands.

"Please, call me Maxwell. No need for formalities here."

"Then I'm Alex. Shall we be off, ladies?"

When Emmeline stepped up on the bench to mount her horse, she turned to find Alex before her. She looked down at him crossly. "You're between me and my horse, sir."

"I'm going to put you *on* your horse," he said, clasping her about the waist with his big hands.

She had time only for a squeak of surprise before she found herself set gently on her sidesaddle, as if she were light as cotton. His hands remained a moment too long and she implored him with her eyes.

"Please, Alex," she whispered. "They'll see."

He sighed and stepped back. "Mustn't have old Willoughby notice you're a woman."

"What does *that* mean?"

He shook his head as he turned away. Emmeline looked up to find Blythe already mounted, with Maxwell smiling blissfully up at her. She felt a moment of disquiet, as she hoped she was not setting Maxwell up for disappointment.

The men were soon mounted and leading the way into the heart of London. As the streets grew crowded, and the upper stories of timbered buildings jutted out over their heads, the gentlemen split up. Maxwell fell back to Emmeline's side, leaving Alex with Blythe.

Before an hour had passed, they joined the traffic of the northern road. The city fell behind them, the air smelled clean, and on both sides of them hedgerows divided the rolling farm fields, where the spring planting had begun. By midmorning they reached Islington, a small village overflowing with London folk out for a day of leisure.

Emmeline knew she should be enjoying the sights as they approached the village green, where booths roofed with green boughs crowded against one another. But she couldn't stop watching Alex and Blythe riding before her, pushed so close together by the crowd that their knees bumped. Why couldn't Maxwell be at her sister's side, impressing her as he so easily impressed Emmeline?

She had to admit that there was a secret place inside her that wished Alex were at *her* side, flashing his wicked grin, letting his gaze tell her what naughtiness he was thinking.

Alex soon led them out of the village green to a tavern. When Emmeline gave him a pointed stare, he laughed.

"Lady Emmeline, I know the owner, and I'm sure he'll keep our horses in his stables for the day."

"Do you know the owner of every tavern?" she asked sweetly.

Blythe hid her smile behind her hand.

Alex dismounted and stood at Emmeline's knee. "Only the best. Now do come down, and let's see what the day brings."

He grabbed her about the waist and lifted her down. Her skirts rustled against his garments, and her feet landed between his. She was off-balance, and he caught her arms and held her still, where she could feel the brush of his body. Flustered and refusing to look him in the eye, she stepped away, grateful that at least Maxwell was left to assist Blythe. She heard Alex chuckle.

With her sister at her side and the men behind, Emmeline walked into the crowd roaming the village green. She felt like a young girl again, overwhelmed with the excitement of watching the jugglers and the acrobats perform. A little monkey danced for coins, and there was even a lumbering bear on a chain. The taverns spilled out laughing people, and everywhere were cries for "Fresh tarts!" and "Boiled eels!" and "Ribbons for the ladies!"

Alex presented them each with the latter, and Emmeline thanked him, then tied hers in a bow at her waist. She looked up to find Maxwell watching her despondently.

"Is something wrong?" she asked him.

He glanced after Blythe, who now walked between tables of cloth from exotic countries with Alex trailing behind her. "Why do I never think of things like this?"

"Maxwell, it doesn't mean anything. Alex only does this to make women like him. It is not true generosity."

"I think it is. He could make Blythe like him without purchasing anything at all. And he even bought some for you, whom he's not pursuing."

But she knew Alex had selfish reasons for plying her with gifts, and was not impressed.

"Just relax and enjoy the day, Maxwell. Blythe is here with you. You just have to talk to her."

She looked up to find Blythe walking toward her swiftly, a worried frown on her face. Her sister looked back once over her shoulder, then drew Emmeline away from Maxwell and Alex and spoke in a low, hurried voice.

"Emmy, I wish I didn't have to tell you this, but you need to know so that you're not shocked."

"Slow down, dearest. Whatever do you think could shock me?"

"Oh, I don't know what he's doing here!" Blythe said, twisting her fingers together. "Didn't he used to live in London?"

"Who, Blythe? Just tell me who you've seen."

She bit her lip, then gripped Emmeline's hands in her own. "Oh, Emmy, 'tis Clifford Roswald."

Even after all these years, she felt a shiver of regret for the life she once thought she'd have with Clifford. "It's all right, dearest," she said absently.

She hadn't seen him in seven years, since she'd told him that her father wouldn't allow her to marry him. Though the pain had dulled with time, she didn't want to see the sadness in his eyes again. She wished she could go home, but it would be a cowardly thing to do. And how could she deny Maxwell and Blythe the opportunity to know one another better?

"Emmy, there's something else I haven't told you."

She forced herself to smile. "Yes?"

"His wife is with him."

"Oh."

"And his children."

"I see. What a kind father, to bring his family to the fair." She didn't want to see his wife or children—the children that could have been hers. She had known that someday she would face Clifford again—but perhaps this time she could avoid him.

Emmeline squared her shoulders and looked up to search the crowd. The first person she saw was Alex, watching her with narrowed eyes from only a few paces away. What had he overheard?

Chapter 15

Alex had heard everything. He kept his expression carefully blank, but inside, he pitied Emmeline. She had been denied what she obviously thought was her only chance at happiness. More than ever, she needed him to show her that she was a desirable woman, that she could someday find a good man.

But not Maxwell Willoughby. He was all wrong for her.

Alex turned to look where Blythe was pointing. A small family stood in the shade of a tree. The man, obviously Clifford Roswald, was plainly dressed and gentle of expression. He held a young child in his arms and talked to his wife. The woman was pregnant, and two more children spun a hoop in the dirt. Though they were wearing the simple garments of farmers, they seemed well fed and happy.

Alex glanced at Emmeline, whose lips were pressed in a thin line. He saw the stiffness of her posture and knew she was trying her best to pretend it meant nothing to her. But if he allowed her to walk away from this, she'd never understand that Roswald was happy with his wife and family, that this was the life he'd been meant to live—that Roswald and Emmeline weren't meant to be together.

He walked over to the Prescott sisters, swallowed a mouthful of beer, and asked, "Who's that?"

Emmeline was visibly startled. "Who?"

"The family you two are whispering about."

Blythe looked at them with the wide eyes of a wounded doe.

Emmeline smiled at her sister. "I'll deal with Alex. Take Maxwell to the puppet show you've been eyeing."

"Are you certain?"

"Just go, dearest."

Alex stood at Emmeline's side and watched Blythe walk away, Maxwell trailing hesitantly behind her. Alex shook his head. The boy was hopeless. Surely Emmeline couldn't prefer someone like *him*.

"You overheard everything, didn't you?" she asked.

He nodded.

"Then there's nothing to discuss."

He slung an arm about her shoulders and she stiffened. "There's plenty to discuss. So this is the tutor? He looks like a farmer now."

"A gentleman farmer."

"Don't be defensive, love. Farming is a noble profession, and after all, I'm almost a farmer myself."

"Oh, that's amusing," she scoffed.

" 'Tis true. I oversee my own farmland. I simply employ men to do the actual labor."

"As if you'd ever do such physical work."

Now it was Alex's turn to feel defensive. He brushed his fingers down her cheek and she stiffened. "Do you doubt that I've worked my own fields? These are calluses you feel, my lady. If you touched other parts of me, you could feel my hard-earned strength."

She blushed in that lovely way she had. "Alex, stop! You have no interest in farming. And it looks like Clifford had taken a very active interest, for his family looks healthy."

"And happy," he murmured near her ear.

She pushed him away.

"I've studied everything there is to know about farming, Em. If your poet's farm is anything like my lands, by now he's finished plowing his fields, and he's taking a well-earned break today from putting in his barley and wheat. If he makes a good beer, he should be tending to his hops vines. Shall I go on?"

Her suspicion was still evident. "You read that in a book somewhere."

He put a hand dramatically to his chest. "Are you admitting that I might be knowledgeable enough to read books?"

"I never said you were a fool, Alex."

"No, but the implication is there," he answered, leaning toward her until their foreheads almost touched. "Would I make you swoon if I admitted I studied agriculture the last few years? If I list all the books in my library, will you fall into my arms? Was that how Roswald won your affections?"

She shrugged out from under his arm, and Alex realized they'd attracted attention, two well-dressed members of the nobility entwined in public.

They'd attracted Clifford Roswald's attention, too.

Alex looked down at Emmeline, who was straightening her gown and pulling her cloak about her to hide her magnificent curves. She was trembling.

Hellfire.

"Forgive me, Em, but your old suitor has noticed us."

She couldn't have stiffened any faster if she'd been whipped.

"Alex, this is all your fault!" she hissed.

"Perhaps, but maybe this is a good thing. You

need to see him again after all these years, and I'm frankly curious."

Roswald laid the sleeping child on a blanket, said something to his wife, and began to walk toward them.

"Alex!" Emmeline whispered frantically. "Go away!"

"No. Put your hand in mine, so we look like lovers."

Her mouth dropped open. "Do you think that would actually make me feel better, to pretend there was someone in my life?"

"Em—"

"Be quiet, and don't speak unless I ask you a question."

He was hardly going to follow her orders, but he saw no reason to antagonize her sooner than he had to.

Clifford Roswald stopped before them, wearing a hesitant smile. "Lady Emmeline, 'tis good to see you."

Alex watched the smile that transformed her face into obvious fondness, without a sign of the tension or sorrow she held inside.

"Clifford, what a surprise! Do you live here now?"

He nodded. "My farm is not far outside the village. My wife and I are expecting our fourth," he said proudly.

Clod, Alex thought.

"Congratulations," Emmeline said.

Roswald hesitated, then glanced at Alex. "Are you married now, my lady?"

Emmeline looked wide-eyed at Alex and shook her head. "No! This is Sir Alexander Thornton."

Alex wasn't sure what made him do it, but he took her hand and leaned closer to Roswald. "I'm sure we can trust your old friend, my love. Mr. Roswald, 'tis a secret, but we do hope to make our attachment . . . permanent."

Emmeline stared at Alex. What in God's name was he thinking?

"Now, love, don't look at me like that. I know I promised to say nothing, but you've told me how trustworthy Mr. Roswald is." He squeezed her hand tighter as he turned to Clifford. "Please don't say anything to Blythe. She's rather . . . talkative, and our news would be all about London before we had the chance to tell it. You understand."

News? she thought wildly. She couldn't believe Alex would be so cruel as to imply to Clifford that she had replaced him so easily.

But Clifford gave her an enormous smile, almost as if he were . . . relieved.

"Lady Emmeline, I am so happy for you!"

She stared at him, feeling confused.

"May your life be as blessed as mine has been. Come, I want you to take the noon meal with my family. And that was your sister, Blythe, then? My, how she's matured into a lovely young woman. You must be very proud."

Through a frozen smile, she said, "I am, thank you."

Emmeline barely remembered meeting Clifford's wife, Henrietta, and his children's names escaped her altogether. She was too busy imagining what she'd say if she had Alex alone at that moment. Blythe and Maxwell rejoined them, and Clifford led the way to what he called his favorite tavern. Alex strode along at her side, smiling at everyone, especially her, while she gave him murderous glares whenever she could get away with it.

As they moved through the crowd, she deliberately hung back and Alex stayed at her side.

In a low voice, she said, "What did you mean to accomplish with such a lie?"

"I can't hear you, my love," he answered, sliding his arm into hers and leaning toward her. "Go ahead, whisper your loving thoughts in my ear."

"Loving thoughts? Right now I'd be content to bite your earlobe!"

His eyes took on that wicked gleam that she was beginning to know so well. "Mmm, what a tempting thought. Can I bite you anywhere I want in return?"

She tried to yank her arm away, but he didn't let go. He waved and smiled at Blythe, who was looking back at them curiously.

"You're causing a distraction, Em."

"*I'm* causing a distraction? You practically said we were betrothed! What did you wish to accomplish with such a lie?"

He shrugged as he pulled her along. "I'm not sure. It just seemed amusing. You looked sad, and I'd rather you be anything else, even angry with me."

Emmeline opened her mouth, but could think of nothing to say to such a peculiar thought. Why would he care if she were sad? "But don't you realize that now he thinks I'm getting married?"

"Do you want him to feel guilty, thinking you're a miserable spinster?"

"I—" She stopped in astonishment. "I'm not miserable! And 'tis hardly his fault that I could not marry him."

"Good." He patted her hand. "Then allow him to think that your father hasn't defeated you. After all, I *am* a good catch."

"*You*, a good catch?" she scoffed.

Again, something unknown flickered in his eyes and was gone.

"And no one has defeated me!" she continued.

"Then let us enjoy the day. Your pig farmer seems like a decent sort."

"How do you know he's a pig farmer?" she demanded.

"I don't. But I like pigs; they're good to raise and sell—and eat. Maybe he likes them, too."

Before she could respond, he led her through the doors into a dimly lit tavern, where people pushed and shoved good-naturedly as they moved between the tables. Clifford had commandeered a long table, and was busy pulling up extra benches. He pulled one out for Emmeline, then with a wink made sure Alex sat beside her. His wife was already seated, holding the youngest child asleep in her lap.

It was a strange meal. Blythe chatted amiably with Henrietta, while Maxwell ate and watched them. Clifford and Alex talked about farming, even discussing a disease that had swept the pig population the previous year. She could have easily gaped at both of them, but she found herself mostly watching Alex.

There was no gambling to keep him interested, there were no young ladies to seduce. Yet he seemed to be enjoying himself, discussing farming of all things.

He constantly leaned his arm against hers, asking her opinion, making her appear foolish as she stammered. She knew Clifford must think her flustered with love, for he beamed at them as if he'd made the match himself.

Beneath the table, Alex's hand kept wandering to her thigh. She pushed it away more times than she could count. But always it returned, and he watched her with obvious amusement. She didn't know how many times the barmaid happily refilled his tankard. But as his mood mellowed, his gestures grew expansive, and he constantly bumped against her. She felt like Blythe was staring at her, and she could only imagine what her sister was thinking. Was she hurt? Did Alex mean more to her than she'd admitted?

As the afternoon wore on, the laughing crowd swelled, Clifford's children grew worse behaved, and Alex's wandering hand crept higher up her thigh. Emmeline felt as if she'd reached a limit.

She stood up and smiled at Clifford and his sleepy-eyed wife. "Please excuse me; I'm feeling a little light-headed. I just need some cooler air."

As she skirted benches and tables, she heard Clifford say, "Why don't you go with her, Sir Alexander? Islington can be dangerous at festival time."

Emmeline glanced over her shoulder and saw Blythe and Maxwell giving her curious stares, and Alex, so tall and imposing, following her. She wanted to run.

Behind the tavern, a small garden was laid out around a well. A welcoming bench sat in the sunshine, but she couldn't stop; Alex was bearing down on her, a determined, amused look on his face.

"Emmeline, stop!"

"No!"

He was gaining on her.

"Just talk to me."

She skirted a pair of apple trees. "You have no hold on me, Alex Thornton!"

She gasped as he caught her arm and tugged. She found her back against one of the trees and Alex looming over her. Oh, how he made her weak and sent her thoughts in treacherous directions.

"Stop this foolishness!" she demanded. "Blythe will see."

"The tree is shielding you, love. And I can see who approaches."

Something inside her gave a painful wrench. "Why are you calling me that! Don't you know how much you hurt me—how much this whole day has been a humiliating farce?"

He put his hands on her shoulders, holding her still. "There's nothing humiliating here, Em."

"Don't call me that either!"

He lowered his voice, leaning over her. "You looked so sad when you first saw Roswald that I wanted to give you something else to think about. This was the first idea that occurred to me."

"Well, it was foolish!"

She tried to push against his chest, but he didn't budge. Instead, he trapped her hands with his own. She could feel the rapid beating of his heart beneath her palm.

"I don't think so."

He was so close, she could see that his dark

eyes were depthless, like a pool at the base of a waterfall. Her breathing was labored, and suddenly she was too warm.

"I was able to spend the day at your side, talking to you—" He slid his hands up to cup her face, tilting her head back until her mouth was only inches from his. "—touching you, and now maybe—" His thumbs brushed her trembling lower lip. "—kissing you."

As his mouth covered hers, Emmeline surrendered to every sensation she'd been fighting and closed her eyes. He tasted of ale and wickedness. Her hands slid up his back, feeling the heat of him along every curve of muscle, shamelessly pulling him against her body because she couldn't get close enough. She wanted to lose herself in him, to forget what she was, what she'd become. When her tongue entered his mouth, she felt his knees almost give way and he pressed her hard against the tree trunk.

Chapter 16

"Emmeline."

Alex breathed into her mouth, his teeth nipping at her lower lip, his hand spreading across her ribs. The tips of his fingers brushed the underside of her breast, making her shudder. She wanted him to touch her higher, to ease the ache he'd caused.

"Let us find some place more private," he murmured. "I want to see my ribbon adorn your nakedness."

She was stunned at her own behavior. She was nothing to him but an afternoon's enjoyment, and she was only using *him* to forget.

Emmeline tore her mouth away from his hypnotic kiss and turned her head. "Alex, stop!"

He pressed his mouth against her cheek, his breathing harsh in her ear. "Why is it so easy to forget myself when I'm holding you, Em? Surely 'tis magic you weave about me."

She pushed him away and covered her hot cheeks with her hands. "No magic, but lust, pure and simple. My sister is ignoring you, so I'm convenient, aren't I?"

"That's not true. And I don't care if Blythe ignores me."

His palm flattened against her neck, sliding lower, burning wherever it touched. With the last of her strength, she ducked beneath the tree branch and headed back for the tavern. How could she keep him away from her sister, when she couldn't even stop *herself* from seeing him?

"Well you won't have her, Alex! Playing your games on me will get you nothing."

"Emmeline!"

She opened the door to the tavern and went inside. She found Clifford and his wife gathering up their children.

Clifford smiled at them. "There you are! Lady Emmeline, are you feeling better?"

She nodded, not trusting herself to speak.

"My wife is taking the children to her sister's to rest. I'll show you where the best jongleurs will be singing, and then we'll see the play being performed by the traveling theater troop. There is still so much to do at our little fair!"

Blythe slid her arm through Emmeline's. "Feeling better?"

"Yes."

"I'm glad Alex went out with you. A fair does attract a dangerous sort of man."

She was tempted to let loose with an unladylike snort. Instead, she said, "So tell me, did Maxwell keep you company?"

"Maxwell? Oh, well I mostly talked to Clifford's wife. I must admit, Maxwell is easy to forget. He says so little! I think he misses you when you're gone."

Emmeline rolled her eyes. "What a silly thing to say, Blythe! The man worships you."

"Worships me?" Her eyes widened with shock. "I think you must be mistaken."

"He only talks to me because we're friends, nothing more."

"Maybe he *wants* more."

"Not from me, he doesn't. Give him a chance."

"I give everyone a chance, Emmy. But I can't be the only one working at it."

The afternoon lengthened and Emmeline watched with increasing amazement as Clifford and Alex somehow became—friends. Before she knew it, she was munching meat pasties purchased at a booth, listening to the two of them go on and on about the best ways to rotate crops. She didn't know whether to be offended or merely stunned.

Soon the two men trooped to the next tavern,

where they ignored her protestations on the lateness of the day, and proceeded to become inebriated. Even Maxwell seemed amused by them, and joined in with the drinking, if not the conversation—until they started discussing grapes, and Maxwell was blissfully swept away.

Emmeline heard Blythe sigh. "Dearest, I am sorry this is not enjoyable for you."

"Oh, it's not that, Emmy. In fact, I find it rather . . . amusing."

The three men at their table erupted in boisterous laughter and toasted each other again, having not heard Blythe's comment.

Emmeline shook her head. "How will we ever get them home?"

"I think we are here for the night. Shall I see if there are chambers?"

"We'll go together. Surely there's a reliable boy to take a message home for us. How Humphrey will insist that he should have driven us in the coach!"

Though they found a messenger to dispatch, there were no lodgings to rent. They had dragged the men from inn to inn before Alex remembered that he'd held two rooms for them at the tavern where he'd stabled their horses—just in case.

Standing on the torchlit village green, Emmeline put her hands on her hips and gave him a severe stare, while he looked innocent.

"Well, forgive me for forgetting!" he said,

throwing his arms wide and almost losing his balance.

Maxwell and Clifford snickered, then Clifford sobered enough to stop before Emmeline.

"My lady, now that you've a place to stay, I have to go," he said, taking her hand and bowing over it. He continued in a softer voice. "It did me good to see you happy, Emmeline. Thank you."

What could she say? It had all been Alex's idea, and somehow he'd been right. When she glanced at him, he wore that knowing smile—then hiccupped.

She earnestly wished Clifford well, and was happy she meant it. After he'd left them, Alex and Maxwell slung their arms around each other to sing their way across the village. Emmeline and Blythe fell into step behind, pulling their cloaks about them as the darkness brought with it a remnant of a winter breeze, and the sounds of happy voices began to die away.

Emmeline shivered, then was startled when she heard a strange voice nearby. She whirled about to see another drunken man coming up behind her, and the expression on his face wasn't pleasant.

As he tipped an imaginary hat, she felt Blythe grip her elbow urgently. The man stopped too close to her, reeking of sweat and ale and wearing a sly grin.

"What fine young ladies," he said, with a slur to his voice. "An' me just lookin' for some fun, too."

"We already have plans," Emmeline said cautiously. "Have a good evening, sir." Blythe pulled on her elbow, but she was afraid to turn her back.

The man took her other elbow in a tight grip, and she gasped.

"You can change yer plans," he said.

Before Emmeline could call out, Maxwell appeared out of the darkness at her side, his blond hair mussed, his clothing sadly rumpled.

"Excuse me, sir," he said in a serious, careful voice as if he was trying hard to remember how to speak. "Unhand this lady at once, or I shall be forced to do it for you."

Holding her even more tightly, the drunk laughed and gave Maxwell a push that sent him staggering back a few steps. Maxwell's astonished expression gave way to determination. Just as he was marching toward their assailant, Alex came up from behind them, and without a word, punched the man once in the stomach, then hard across the jaw. He dropped into a heap.

Emmeline stared at the unconscious man, then lifted her gaze to Alex. She saw a burning anger in the darkness of his eyes, a coldness that made her wonder what else he concealed. Then the look vanished, and he gave her a lopsided grin.

"My dear ladies, are you unharmed?"

Blythe nodded as she looked at their assailant. "Is he dead?"

"No, but I doubt he'll arise this night."

"Should we move him?" Emmeline asked.

"Why? Let him awaken in the mud. Shall we go?"

By the time they reached the tavern, Alex and Maxwell were toasting each other's bravery, and in general behaving like fools. Emmeline left them to the cheerfulness of the taproom, while she and her sister followed the chamberlain to their chamber. The room had two narrow pallets for beds, but the sheets were clean, and the fire had been lit earlier, and there were candles on the bedside tables.

The sisters helped each other undress down to their long-sleeved smocks, and while Blythe fell quickly asleep, Emmeline lay on her pallet and stared at the smoke-stained ceiling. She wasn't used to the noise of such a public place, and in the room above them, someone seemed to be dancing.

She tossed and turned for at least an hour, until she heard a soft scratching on her door. Quietly, she crept from the bed and stood listening. The scratching was repeated, then a muffled voice said, "Emmeline?"

She unlocked the door. Opening it just a crack to keep her lack of garments hidden, she peered out and saw Alex, his face stubbled and tired, but his infuriating grin ever present.

"What are you doing here?" she demanded. His doublet and shirt were open at the throat.

There was hair on his chest, and she found that fascinating.

He braced himself with a hand on the door-frame. "I need to talk to you."

"The morning would be a more suitable time," she whispered, turning to see if Blythe had stirred.

The door suddenly bumped against her as he took her hand and drew her into the hall. Embarrassed by the indecency of her garments, she tried to retreat, but he'd already closed the door behind her.

"Alex!" she hissed, crossing her arms over her chest. "I will not stand for this!"

"Maxwell has found someone who knows about vines, so he'll be detained."

She pulled against him, but was no match for his strength as he dragged her through the open door into his chamber.

"And there won't be any privacy on the morrow," he continued, shutting the door and leaning back against it.

Emmeline turned her back on him, feeling that she was almost naked even though her smock covered her from her neck to her toes. But she wore . . . nothing else, not a corset or petticoat. It was certainly indecent—and thrilling.

No. No, it wasn't, she thought desperately, trying not to look at the two pallets, one of which Alex would soon be lying in, wearing . . . what?

She had to get back to her own chamber before

her wicked thoughts grew any worse. "Alex, I am appalled at your behavior. Just tell me what you want and be done with it."

He pushed away from the door unsteadily, and Emmeline had to force herself not to back away from him. He was tall and intimidating, but not in the way of their drunken assailant. He threatened her because she now knew how easily she gave in to the pleasure she felt in his arms.

And they were alone, with no one to disturb them.

He sighed. "I wanted you to know that I regret not seeing your predicament a few hours ago. You trusted me with the safety of yourself and your sister, and if Maxwell hadn't noticed, I might have just kept walking merrily on my way."

"You are too harsh with yourself, Alex. I was about to call out. Trust me, you would have heard me."

One corner of his mouth lifted. "Really? Then you forgive me?"

"There is nothing to forgive. Besides, drunk as he was, that man probably did not need quite the force you demonstrated."

He sobered again and stepped closer. "I could not take a chance, Em. What if it had been one of those men following me?"

"Was it?"

"No."

For the first time, Emmeline realized how seriously he was taking these threats against him.

"Perhaps you need to tell all this to a justice of the peace."

He came another step closer, and she hugged herself even tighter.

"No, Em, for what would I say? I have no clue to their identities, no guess at their motives."

His voice softened, his gaze dropped, and she felt his hand suddenly slide up her arm.

"Alex," she said with a warning in her voice, but she didn't retreat, could barely think with the heat of his skin separated from hers by only fine linen. She had to think of something—anything— else. "Though I did not care for the game you played against Clifford, I did appreciate your kindness to him."

He nodded almost absently, his gaze still on his hand where he rubbed her arm. "It wasn't difficult. He was . . . tolerable."

She licked her lips and tried not to imagine her arm afire where he touched it. "I'm not surprised. I get on well with both of you, so you should be able to tolerate each other."

His hand stopped moving, though he still seemed to have trouble concentrating enough to form words. His gaze flickered up to her eyes. "Why, Em, do you consider me a friend?"

"W-What do you mean?"

"You 'get on well' with me—or so you said. How should I take that?"

She could no longer think, and didn't want to answer his questions. "Alex, why did you really come for me?"

He hesitated, and his eyes returned to hers. "I don't know. I thought about you there, just across the hall, wearing so little."

His gaze dipped down to her chest again, and when she hugged herself tighter, he groaned and closed his eyes.

"You always do that," he said hoarsely, "and instead of hiding yourself from me, it's as if you're presenting your luscious breasts for my admiration."

She inhaled swiftly, feeling embarrassment burn her cheeks even as she dropped her arms to her sides. "Don't say such a thing! I've told you before that you don't have permission to discuss my—me so personally!"

"I want permission."

His words were almost a groan, and made her feel like her world and all she believed were no longer solid around her.

His hand slid up to rest on her shoulder, his thumb gently rubbing her collarbone. His eyes gleamed at her in the low light, intense, hooded, knowledgeable about things of which she was innocent.

And she would remain innocent, she told herself. But his other hand settled on her shoulder, too, and the weight of him felt ... more than pleasant. Suddenly those hands slid down her back, pulling her forward. Without a corset, she could feel every sensuous touch of his fingers. When her breasts brushed his chest, her nipples contracted with a painful pleasure that made her moan.

Oh heavens, how he made her feel! She couldn't look away from his expression, now so intent. As if in a dream, his hands continued their slow slide down her back, following the curves until he cupped her backside in both hands. She gasped as he pulled her up against his hips and ground her against him. She had to catch his shoulders to keep from falling. He took advantage of her swooning weakness by pulling her knee up to his waist. The pressure of him between her thighs, against her most private womanly parts, swept over her like the evening tide. Every part of her burned and ached—especially *there*—and she wanted to rub back against him, his hardness against her softness.

She couldn't hide from him, for he watched every emotion on her face, knew her for the wanton she was. Pulling her even tighter against him, he kissed her hard, slanting his mouth over hers, with none of the gentle teasing he'd shown before. He thrust his tongue into her mouth as he pushed his hips between her legs, and it was incredible and exciting. Their breaths merged, their tongues mated, and she had no will left of her own. Though he still held her hard against him by her knee, his other hand slid up her ribs, hesitating just beneath her breast, his knuckles brushing her curves.

"Emmeline," he breathed against her mouth.

She had no voice, no will to stop him, and worst of all, an incredible desire to feel him touching her. His hand closed on her breast, cupping it firmly but gently. A shudder swept through her. Her skin was so sensitive and aware. Then his fingers moved and caressed, and unimaginable pleasure burned a path from her breasts to the depths of her stomach. He rubbed his thumb over and over her nipple, until she wanted to beg him to stop— and beg him to continue. His tongue swept hers, his hands molded her, and she knew she would gladly give in to whatever he wanted, if only she could feel this just once in her life.

He suddenly released her knee and stepped away, and she reached for him unsteadily. He caught her hand.

"Stand still, love," he murmured as he shrugged his doublet from his broad shoulders.

She had no choice, for surely she would fall with even one step. He unbuttoned his billowing white shirt at the neck and pulled it over his head.

Emmeline's breathing quickened as she stared

amazed at her first sight of man's naked chest. Scattered with dark hair, it gleamed in the firelight and showed curving shadows where his muscles sloped and bulged. Such impressive breadth called to her, and she reached out a hand, then stopped at her own boldness.

"Please touch me, Em," he whispered hoarsely.

But there were sudden footsteps outside the door. Alex stiffened and swore. She wanted to groan her dismay, and it wasn't because they could be caught.

Chapter 17

❦❦❦

"Alex?"
It was Maxwell, stumbling drunkenly against the other side of the wall.

"Which one is our room?" he called plaintively.

Emmeline frantically reached for Alex's shirt and threw it at him. "Dress quickly!" she whispered.

He shook his head. "Ah, love, he won't care that I'm not dressed—but he will care if you're here. We must hide you." He took her shoulders and pushed her toward his pallet. "Quick, slide underneath." He caressed her breast again. "How I wish we could lie there together."

She pushed him away and gaped at the stained wooden floor that looked warped and filthy. "I don't think it's ever been cleaned!"

As the door latch rattled, he said, "What about the draperies?"

Without another word she ran for the chamber's window and slid behind the draperies. She made sure her toes were covered, then held incredibly still, praying the fabric did not outline her breasts. Her hands covered her mouth as she labored to quiet her breathing and hoped it was not cobwebs she felt in her hair.

She heard the door fling wide and Maxwell stumble into the chamber. He gave a brief laugh, said, "Fine evening, eh, Thornton?" then his pallet gave a loud creak.

Emmeline froze, listening to the groan of Alex's pallet, then silence. She didn't know how long she was supposed to wait. But within minutes, she heard both men snoring. She slid from behind the draperies, intending to sneak out as quickly as possible.

But something stopped her. She turned from Maxwell, who lay face down as he snored, to stare at Alex, whose big body almost hung over the edges of the pallet. His chest was still bare, his face in profile as he slept. His dark lashes were long against his cheeks, and his lips looked as soft and full as they felt. He had held her, desired her, and she felt so confused, wanting to attribute the worst motives to him, but knowing she was just as guilty.

She was in danger, not only because she was attracted to him, but because she feared it had become something more, something she couldn't have.

Suddenly he opened his eyes and stared up at her without smiling, his look full of intensity, passion, and something she couldn't recognize. Feeling the sting of tears, she turned and quietly fled the room.

Alex came up on his elbow to watch her leave. In her haste he saw a flash of her ankles before the door shut behind her. What had just happened? Surely it was only the drink that had made him almost ravish Lady Emmeline Prescott, confirmed spinster and guardian to her sister. He lay back.

Hellfire, he could barely remember her sister's name. All he could think about was burying himself inside Emmeline. He ached with the pain of frustration, and for a moment he was tempted to kidnap her from her room, take her to the dark gardens behind the tavern, and *really* take her. He could almost see the moonlight on her pale skin. He would spread his shirt across the grass and she would lie down upon it, her arms reaching for him, her body open to him. She would be heavy-lidded with a desire only he brought out in her. He would stroke his fingers down her inner thigh, part her silken curls, and be the first and only man to touch the core of her, her innocence.

But no. He groaned and covered his face with both hands. He'd had a successful mission today—making her see that Roswald was happy and wanted her to be happy too. It was her first step in coming back to life as a vibrant woman. He needed to let the drink wear off until he was more in control of his impulses.

He flung his arm over his eyes. Even when he was sober, Emmeline Prescott played hell with his impulses. Surely he only felt this way because she was such an unattainable challenge.

In the morning as she dressed, Emmeline kept her back to her sister to hide her worried frown. There was no way to avoid Alex, and she couldn't imagine looking him in the face again after her wanton conduct. Remembering the firelit room, the feel of his hands on her barely clothed body, made her shudder with guilt. How could she enjoy such a thing—and why was she so curious to find out the rest?

Luckily, Blythe distracted her from her thoughts.

"Emmy, something happened yesterday that I don't quite understand. Oh, could you help me button the back of my gown?"

Taking a deep breath, Emmeline approached her sister and was glad not to have to look her in the face. "What is it, dearest?"

"You seemed . . . upset, and it wasn't just meeting up with Mr. Roswald after so many years."

Emmeline took her time with the buttons, telling herself that Blythe was merely curious, not suspicious. Though Emmeline hadn't initiated the deception upon poor Clifford, it weighed on her conscience. Perhaps telling Blythe would ease it.

"Unbeknownst to me, Sir Alexander decided to play a trick upon Clifford. Oh, perhaps 'misled Clifford' is more correct." When the buttons were done, she used her fingers to comb her sister's hair into order.

"Why would he do such a thing? Did he know what Clifford was to you?"

"Yes, he overheard us speaking."

Blythe suddenly whirled about and took Emmeline's hands. "Oh, and this is even more my fault! I once mentioned to Alex that you'd had to turn down a tutor who'd fallen in love with you. Can you forgive me?"

Emmeline felt her own sins magnify next to her sister's. "Blythe, you did nothing wrong; my past is hardly a secret."

"So what did Alex do?"

She gave her a shaky smile. "In front of Clifford, he pretended that we would soon be . . . married."

Blythe's eyes widened, and Emmeline felt her stomach twist as she waited for the worst. But her sister suddenly laughed.

"What a fine amusement, Emmy! I do so enjoy Alex's wit. What did Mr. Roswald think?"

Bewildered, she said, "He thought it wonderful."

"I am not surprised. He must have fond memories of you, to want your happiness after all these years. And now I know why Alex followed you into the garden. More proof to Mr. Roswald of this supposed romantic secret."

Emmeline nodded hesitantly. "You are not upset?"

"Upset?" Blythe smiled as she walked behind Emmeline and used her fingers to comb her sister's hair. "I could not be more pleased with Alex's thoughtfulness. He is becoming a good friend to us, is he not?"

Emmeline could think of nothing to say to that. In the silence, she felt Blythe pull her hair off her neck.

"Emmy, hand me that ribbon."

She lifted the ribbon Alex had bought her off the bed table. "Blythe, I don't think—"

"It will look lovely on you."

It was difficult to swallow as her sister took the ribbon and used it to hold her hair back. As they left the chamber, she tried to return Blythe's smile, but her stomach remained in knots over facing Alex, with the further mortification of having his ribbon entwined in her hair. Would he think she gave her approval of his attentions?

When they reached the taproom, Alex and Maxwell stood up at their table.

"Gentlemen," Blythe said, "have you not ordered our meal? Are you not hungry?"

Maxwell shuddered, and Alex's dark skin paled.

Emmeline felt relieved to be of use. "Dearest, food is beyond our companions at the moment. You and I will eat lightly, I think." Avoiding Alex's gaze, she went to the bar and ordered simple bread and cheese with cider.

When she turned back, it was Alex she saw first, Alex whose dark eyes captured and held her almost as tightly as his arms had. She stumbled to a halt.

"The color of the ribbon goes well with your hair, Lady Emmeline," he said softly.

She opened her mouth, but could think of nothing to say, with the enormity of her passion for him so painfully obvious to herself. Finally, she murmured, "Blythe decided I should wear it this way."

He smiled. "She knows what becomes you."

Blythe looked between the two of them. "Alex, it is not only me, after all. *You* bought the ribbons."

The ball held at the Queen's palace of Whitehall a week later was attended by hundreds, some traveling from their vast estates for the event. It was as if the fear of a looming Spanish invasion, now lifted, had given way to a need for celebration.

Emmeline and Blythe traveled by family barge with their father, and reclined amidst cushions as they waited their turn to dock at the royal palace. A dark, covered walkway led into the palace, but the presence chamber itself was a glorious hall whose walls were gilded in gold, and hung with red and gold tapestries. Such rarities as ostrich eggs and coconut cups were mounted in silver to decorate the room. The rugs that normally covered the floor had been taken away to facilitate dancing.

Emmeline felt excitement bubble inside her. She felt beautiful clothed in a black and white gown that Blythe had had made for her. Her mother's rubies and sapphires hung about her neck and diamonds glittered on her fingers. She had felt foolish, dressing so ostentatiously, but Blythe had adorned her herself, giggling as if they played dress-up with dolls.

It seemed every courtier had donned their finest garments, and the candlelight reflected from shining cloth and jewels. Something good would happen this night, she just knew it. She had been mentioning Maxwell subtly yet often to Blythe, and in a letter, she had told Maxwell outright to ask Blythe to dance.

Now she watched fondly as Blythe was surrounded by young men asking to bring her refreshments, or partner her to dance. Lord Seabrook captured her first, and Emmeline craned her neck to watch her sister amidst the splendor of the dancers, tapping her toe to the beat of the music.

Maxwell Willoughby approached her and bowed. "Lady Emmeline, how lovely you look this night."

"Maxwell!" She gave his hand a squeeze, and bestowed a fond smile on him. "Blythe and I have missed you this past sennight. What kept you from us?"

"I had business in Sussex, my lady, but I thank you for thinking of me." His smile became self-deprecating. "And it is kind of you to say your sister missed me, but I think it not quite the truth."

She waved her hand. "Nonsense. We both enjoyed the day in Islington."

He seemed about to say something else, but only shook his head and smiled. Emmeline felt relieved, because just mentioning the village fair brought back shadowed memories of a nearly naked Alex. She had not seen him during the week, either, and she'd been torn between relief and regret.

"Maxwell, remain here with me. I'm certain Blythe would enjoy a dance with you." She eyed him sternly. "You are going to ask her, aren't you?"

He hesitated.

"Maxwell!"

"I'll try, my lady. It is difficult for me to compete with the gentlemen who gather about her."

"You can do it," she insisted, laying a hand on his arm.

Maxwell covered her hand with his. "I shall do my best."

But dance after dance, Blythe didn't return; she

merely continued to laugh as each dance was claimed before she even left the floor. Emmeline ran out of things to say in the face of Maxwell's growing dejection.

Was she wrong? Would the tentative friendship she felt between Blythe and Maxwell wither rather than flourish?

But no. She sensed *something*, and she had to find a way to give it meaning.

Sighing, she looked out once more into the hall and saw that Blythe was now dancing with Alex. She froze, wondering why she hadn't known he had arrived, why she hadn't felt his presence like a living thing wrapping itself about her?

He didn't look her way as he led her sister through the intricate steps of the dance. The musicians played, the guests laughed and enjoyed themselves, but Emmeline could only stare, remembering Alex's mouth on hers even as that mouth smiled so charmingly at her sister.

But Blythe seemed unaffected, as her gaze wandered about the other dancers and landed only briefly on Alex. Emmeline could not understand why her sister wasn't swooning in his arms, as she would be. But then again, his kiss had meant nothing to Blythe, and that was a great relief.

Tearing her gaze away, she glanced at Maxwell and found that he, too, was staring at the dancing couple. His usual smile was gone, replaced by an intensity of which she had never thought him capable. His eyes were narrowed, unblinking, and she realized that he was angry, even jealous.

"Go to her," she said softly. "Ask her to dance."

But without a word, he stalked away from her and out of the presence chamber.

Emmeline stood alone for a few moments, saddened that her plans were not succeeding. Finally she wandered to where the married and elderly ladies were sitting and took a bench nearby. The evening's promise dwindled away and she sighed.

"Look at him dancing," said a disdainful voice not far from her.

She glanced over her shoulder, then shook her head. It was that dreadful woman again, Lady Boxworth, who had taken such delight in gossiping about Alex at Lady Morley's party.

Emmeline pitied her newest target and didn't feel tempted to listen.

"Who is that he is dancing with?" asked another woman.

"The Prescott girl, Kent's daughter."

Emmeline closed her eyes and barely restrained a groan. Not again. How could she escape without calling attention to herself?

"She is a good match for him, is she not?"

"Too good," said Lady Boxworth. "Last year, perhaps, he might have fancied he could reach such heights, but his masquerade is discovered now. Kent will not suffer him, 'tis certain."

Emmeline kept as still as a hunter's prey, her head averted, feeling guilty and curious at the same time.

"Masquerade?" the other woman said. "I was traveling in the north much of last year, and I fear the gossip did not reach me."

There were titters of laughter and gasps, which quieted when Lady Boxworth spoke.

"You did not hear that Thornton masqueraded as his brother the viscount, undetected, for nearly two years?"

The other woman let out a gasp, echoing Emmeline's. Why had *she* heard nothing of such a scandal? Again, she stared at Alex, while the women continued to talk.

"I know he is a twin," said the other woman, "but to pull off such a deed is arrogant beyond belief! Whyever would his brother allow such a thing?"

"The viscount put his own brother up to the stunt while he was off in Spain spying for England," Lady Boxworth said. "He needed a replacement for himself, so no one would question his whereabouts."

A new, girlish voice said breathlessly, "Then Sir Alexander is a hero!"

"You show your youth, child," Lady Boxworth said in a withering tone. "He wasn't the hero— Lord Thornton was. Sir Alexander should merely have played the part, calling little attention to himself. But a man such as he cannot resist showing his arrogance."

Emmeline stiffened, but she wanted to hear the rest of the story. Truly he *was* a hero, for it could have been dangerous for him.

"Arrogance?" echoed one of the fascinated listeners.

"Yes, indeed," said Lady Boxworth. "Sir Alexander used this pretence to the title to spend vast amounts of his brother's money. He scandalized the court with his affairs with women—" She lowered her voice. *"Married women, as well."*

"Did he ruin his brother?" asked the young girl.

"Thankfully, no."

"Did he perform the viscount's court duties?"

"Yes," Lady Boxworth admitted reluctantly. "But he rose above himself, courting maidens as the viscount, misleading them with his attentions—as if any of these well-born women would marry a mere knight, had they but known. And now, ladies, he's paying for the sins of his arrogance and scandals; he's no longer accepted at the best of homes. His only life was his brother's."

Emmeline's anger heated her veins, and she lifted her head and stared at the cruel women. "Lady Boxworth, you claim Sir Alexander wooed maidens falsely. Did he offer them marriage? Did he make promises he could not keep?"

The old woman's prominent nose rose into the

air. "Thankfully these young women discovered the truth in time."

"Did he make false promises?" Emmeline asked again.

After a brief hesitation, Lady Boxworth coldly said, "No."

"Then I don't see why you feel the need to discredit a man for helping his country."

"And benefiting handsomely from it, I daresay," the woman said quickly.

Emmeline could not respond, because she didn't know all the facts. She merely shook her head at the gossiping women, dismissing them. She turned around and found Alex approaching her, smiling with the ease of a man who didn't know what was being said about him. He bowed to the ladies, and Emmeline wanted to wince.

Then he turned, bowed to her, and held out his hand. "Would you care to dance, Lady Emmeline?"

Chapter 18

Emmeline put her hand in Alex's, happy to be escaping such malicious women, even if it meant subjecting herself to the temptation of his embrace.

"I would enjoy dancing with you, Sir Alexander."

His eyebrows rose, but he said nothing, only led her into the center of the hall.

As they performed the dance steps together, she watched his face, trying to make sense of this new information. She was curious about the two years of his life he'd given up, but she did not know how to raise the subject with a man so private with his true thoughts. She found herself feeling compassion for him, and it softened her. What had it been like to risk his life for his country, then give up the power and wealth to

which he must have become accustomed? Had
he felt the same as she had when she'd given up
Clifford Roswald: lost and frightened of the future? Did men merely hide their feelings beneath
bravado?

His grin turned wolfish. "Ah, you study me so
thoroughly, my lady," he murmured. "I feel
quite . . . ravished."

She wanted to groan. His arrogance only hid
even more arrogance—and salacious thoughts.
"Alex, you really should learn to control your
tongue."

He laughed outright. "Em, you can attest to
how well my tongue obeys me." He lowered his
voice and leaned nearer. "And there are so many
interesting places on your body it wants to delve,
to taste. I want to part your thighs and—"

As she felt her face blush hotly, she was glad
that the dance steps drew her to another man. But
her vivid imagination expounded on Alex's implications until she was breathless and yearning
for the secrets he hinted at.

Yet Lady Boxworth's words rose again in her
mind.

When the dance brought Alex back to Emmeline's arms, he couldn't help staring down at her,
wondering at the subtle change in her. She
seemed pensive, and he wondered if it was because of the intimacies they'd shared—or the ones
he'd just implied.

Or was it due to Maxwell Willoughby? He'd seen Maxwell's hand on her arm, seen her touch him. Feeling a primitive jealousy, Alex had wanted to break off his dance with Blythe and drag Emmeline away.

So she was the next woman he'd danced with. And the only woman here he *wanted* to dance with.

Thankfully, Emmeline spoke before he could dwell on such a ridiculous thought.

"Alex, did you just arrive at the palace?"

"No, I've been here for a time. You just didn't see me." He saw the curiosity in her eyes, watched her bite her full lip to keep from questioning him. "I was with the Queen."

They were swept apart again for several minutes. When they returned together, she repeated, "With the Queen?"

"My, aren't *you* the curious one?"

Emmeline couldn't help it. For a man so looked down upon by much of the nobility, he seemed to have the Queen's attention and companionship. How did he do it? What made him so good with women, even women who knew they should not be attracted to him—like her?

Just dancing with him made most women swoon; why couldn't Maxwell dance like this with Blythe? There must be some secret; maybe all Maxwell needed was guidance.

And who better to teach him than Alex?

A plan began to form in Emmeline's mind, and

she shivered with the daring perfection of it. Could she persuade Alex to teach Maxwell what he knew about courting women?

But how to explain her plan to Alex? She needed privacy, but not enough for him to work his magic on her.

When the dance ended, they bowed to one another.

"Alex, would you lead me to the refreshment table?"

He raised one eyebrow as he eyed her suspiciously. "You don't wish to run from me as quickly as you can?"

"Certainly not. You must be as thirsty as I am."

He inclined his head, then led the way through the milling crowd. At a table laden with sweets, he poured her wine from the elaborate fountain, then sipped his own as he studied her.

Emmeline knew she must be blushing. After all her attempts to get him out of Blythe's life, how could she ask a favor? But she must—for Blythe's sake.

"Emmeline, what is this all about?" he asked softly.

She wet her lips and forced herself to meet his gaze. "I need to speak with you . . . privately."

For a moment he looked incredulous, then his eyes smoldered. "It seems our last private moment was interrupted too quickly for you."

"N-No!" she stammered quickly. "It is . . . nothing like that. I need to ask a"—she lowered her voice—"a favor of you."

Could his smug smile make her face feel any hotter? She wanted to run from him—and yet there were Maxwell and Blythe, two people she knew should be together. She stiffened and tried to meet his gaze coolly.

"It will not require much of you, Alex. Are you willing to hear me out?"

His black eyes regarded her and she stared back. He would not defeat her, she vowed to herself, warming to the challenge of besting him.

"Very well, my lady. Where do you suggest for our little . . . tryst?"

"It is not a tryst," she said crossly, looking toward the high windows. "Do you know how to reach the terrace?"

He grinned and nodded, and she wondered how many secret places in Whitehall he knew about that she did not.

"Very well, I shall meet you out there in a quarter of an hour."

"Must I wait so long?" he murmured.

She resisted the pull of his voice. "I need to speak with you, not lure the rest of the party outside for curiosity's sake."

He heaved a melodramatic sigh. "The minutes will drag like hours."

"For a poet, that is a highly unoriginal phrase, Alex."

He put a hand to his heart and leaned over her. "You wound me, Lady Emmeline."

She backed away. "You'll meet me, then?"

"Of course. How could I resist?"

"Resist your baser impulses, sir, and think only to listen to my request."

He caught her hand before she could escape. "My baser impulses control me when I'm with you, Em."

She could confess to the same sin. She pulled away, trying not to remember the way he'd kissed her, held her, and stroked her. "Fifteen minutes," she whispered, and let the crowd swallow her.

To calm her wayward thoughts, she spent the next few moments discovering Blythe's whereabouts, and then her father's. Neither was looking for her.

She began to walk the length of the chamber, staying near the wall. She wandered through archways and back, hoping to confuse anyone who might see her. Finally, with a last look over her shoulder, she slipped behind a marble column, then out the open doors to the terrace.

The night was overcast and dark, and a slight breeze made bumps stand up along Emmeline's arms. There were torches lit near the palace and guards on duty at the doors, but farther out into the gardens, where the ground dropped away into the next level of terrace, it looked like the end of the earth.

She didn't see Alex. She had not thought of an exact place to meet him, and she now realized she could wander the grounds for days before they found one another.

She walked out toward the stone balustrade, hugging herself against the chill, wondering if she was acting stupidly. Should she have just invited him to the manor and met him in broad daylight? Before her doubts could escalate, he seemed to materialize out of the gloom at her side, his midnight velvet garments concealing him.

She gave a little start of surprise, then sagged against the balustrade with a sigh.

"Expecting someone else?" he asked calmly.

She felt foolish and far too daring than could be good for her. She almost said he might be as good at spying as his brother, but she restrained herself. He had confided none of this to her, and she didn't want to offend him just when she needed something from him.

"I didn't hear you coming, Alex. But thank you for doing so."

"How could I resist when asked so mysteriously?"

He stood too close at her side, and rather than move nervously away, she looked out into the darkness.

She should just ask him the favor; but how to sway him? She could not tell him Maxwell needed help to court Blythe, because surely he would see that as a challenge. She heard him chuckle.

"My lady, did you just need a companion tonight? We could have found a place where even the guards wouldn't find us."

She ignored his implication and decided to charge right in. "Alex, Lord Willoughby needs our help."

Whatever Alex had expected her to say, it wasn't that. "What has he done, gambled away all his money?"

She waved a hand. "Nothing so foolish. He needs a different kind of help, something more . . . personal."

He didn't like the dark sensation that wound through his gut and made him want to bash in Willoughby's face. Emmeline betrayed her fondness for the boy with every smile, and Alex couldn't explain why it bothered him so.

"I know I'm gifted at agriculture, but I can't grow his grapes for him, if that's what you're thinking."

She laughed, then quickly covered her mouth. "Oh, no, 'tis something else. Have you noticed how uneasy Maxwell is with young ladies?"

"He is rather clumsy in his speech. I thought the ladies found that endearing."

"But it bothers Maxwell, and I fear he's quite given up on the idea of courting an appropriate young lady."

Appropriate? What the hell did *that* mean? Did she think Willoughby wasn't moving fast enough for her? Hellfire, it was enough to make him want to shake her—or hold her tight and prove with his mouth that Willoughby wasn't right for her.

"So if he puts his tail between his legs and hies off for Sussex, what does it matter to me?"

Her face was a pale smudge in the darkness. "Alex, do be civil. You—you're very good at charming the ladies. You know what to say, what to do." She took a deep breath. "Do you think you could tutor Maxwell? His shyness would disappear if he but knew what to say, what was expected of him."

He could only stare at her in astonishment. She wanted her newest suitor trained? By *him*? Were there only parts of Alex she tolerated, and these she would graft onto Willoughby and make a new man of him?

His brain was muddled, his chest constricted, and he felt a violent need to slam his fist against the stone balustrade. Never had a woman made him feel so at a loss, so desperate to make her see reason.

All of a sudden he saw himself clearly, and was appalled. Why was he so upset? He could find a way to use this to his advantage, to make Emmeline see that Willoughby would never be the right man for her.

She stepped closer and looked up at him. "Will you do it, Alex?"

"I'm not sure I can, my lady. Such skills might be something a man is born with. No one needed to teach me." He dropped his voice lower, knowing it made her come even nearer.

"But surely you can try?" she pleaded prettily, even putting a hand on his arm.

She should be the one giving lessons, he thought.

All for that fool Willoughby.

He knew in that moment what he would do. "You would need to help me."

A little frown creased her forehead. "But I know nothing of such things."

"Without you, I won't have the first idea of what to teach him. You must be with us every moment, guiding us with your common sense."

"Oh, but I couldn't possibly journey to your lodgings. My presence might be misinterpreted."

"Then Willoughby and I could come to you. Is there a private room where we could work?"

"Well, yes, but—"

"Then that is settled. Now, I am to teach him what, exactly?"

"What to say to young ladies, how to—to—flirt with them." She blurted out the last part quickly, and he knew her blush must be scarlet by now.

"Flirt? I never think of calling it that. I pay women the respect they deserve, treat them the way they want to be treated."

"Well, that might be going too far, Alex."

"Really? Then you do not like things like this?" He caught her hand and brought it up to his mouth, letting his lips learn the smooth feel of her skin. When he didn't release her quickly, he felt a slight tremor run through her hand.

"I—I'm sure other ladies enjoy . . . such things."

Still holding her hand, he glanced up at her. "Does Maxwell do this?"

"No."

"Ah, then this is a skill I can teach."

"Yes, I guess so. Now that you grasp the idea, let us go back inside."

"Wait, my lady, I'm not sure what else I can teach him. What about . . . this?"

He caught her arms and drew her forward to where he leaned on the balustrade. Her full skirts pressed into his legs, and with just a little more pressure, he would feel her hips against his. But there was time for that yet. He leaned down toward her, hearing the catch in her breathing, feeling her hands clutch the fabric covering his chest. Her lips glistened, and it was only through sheer willpower that he turned his head and pressed his mouth to her neck. God, he wanted her, needed her in his bed, and his frustrated desire was maddening.

Her gasp sounded loud in his ear. "Surely this is going too far," she whispered.

He trailed his lips to the edge of the ruff at her throat, then back up. His tongue traced the shell of her ear and she shivered. "But 'tis effective, is it not?"

"But . . . but it's not what a gentleman would do," she answered breathlessly.

"But it's what a *man* would do." He lifted his head and looked down into her eyes, feeling her breath against his mouth, wanting desperately to kiss her. "Very well, so that's not what I'm supposed to teach him. What do you wish of me?"

Her eyes were dazed, and he could almost see her try to rally her thoughts. He wanted to gloat in triumph, to tell her that Willoughby would never make her feel this way. But he would bide his time.

"You're supposed to teach him what to say to a lady," she finally answered, her gaze on his mouth, "how to amuse her."

"Ah. I know quite well how to amuse a lady."

He waited, allowing her imagination to expand on his words.

Chapter 19

Whatever Emmeline imagined made her suddenly push Alex away. There would be no kiss this night, no temptation of her body pressed to his. He was aroused enough that he almost took it from her anyway.

"Alex, this is not amusing. I have requested a favor. Will you help me?"

He hesitated just enough to make her nervous. "I shall help you—but only because you've asked me so nicely. When shall we begin? Shall I talk to Willoughby tonight?"

"Oh, no, I haven't even asked him yet."

"He doesn't know you've come to me for help?"

"I could hardly put such a thought in his mind, and then have you refuse us."

He hated the way she said "us." "Very well, let me know what the two of you decide."

She nodded and slowly backed away.

He forced himself to grin. "You'd better watch what you're doing Em, before you trip."

With a little side step, she just missed a bench, but still she didn't look away from him, as if she were afraid he'd chase her. So he just stared after her until he finally saw her illuminated by the torches near the palace. Then she slipped inside, leaving him to decide how best to work this to his advantage.

Emmeline knew that persuading Maxwell Willoughby to accept help would be almost as difficult as persuading Alex to help. She sent a missive to Maxwell, asking him to come see her on a day when Blythe was out visiting friends. When she finally had him alone, she explained her idea, and though he was mildly offended, he did not summarily dismiss her plan. He admitted that he rather admired Alex's easy ability with women.

So it was settled. Her father left for Kent, and it was almost too simple to persuade Blythe to accompany him to visit friends back home. Except for the servants, Emmeline had the mansion to herself. She immediately issued invitations to both Alex and Maxwell for dinner the following day, a Friday.

Alex was early by half an hour. Emmeline was

informed of his arrival while in the kitchen over-seeing preparations for their meal. The steward beamed as he delivered the news, then disap-peared back into the front of the mansion. Bless him, he was always assuming there was still a man out there for her.

Well, Alex would just have to wait. She was not about to have her plans turned inside out because of him. She didn't want to make small talk, all the while remembering the things they'd done to-gether. Just as she was about to escape up to her chamber by the back staircase, Alex appeared in the kitchen door.

"Lady Emmeline?" he called.

The maids all let out giggling gasps, while Mr. Horatio, the cook, glowered at them. But even he, ever one in control of his domain, had an encour-aging smile for her.

"You see to your guests, my lady," Mr. Horatio said, ushering her forward, ignoring the fact that she was quite unwilling.

Alex grinned at all the women before eyeing Emmeline herself. "I knew I'd find you here. Al-ways working too hard, isn't she, ladies?"

They all bobbed their heads in agreement, and she was forced into a stiff smile. "Sir Alexander, please wait in the parlor. As soon as I finish, I'll—"

But he swept into the room, towering over the servants, smiling so charmingly that Emmeline could see the girls sigh as they gazed up at him.

"Ladies, might I steal Lady Emmeline from you?"

There was really no help for it. She was almost pushed out the door by the cheerful kitchen servants, and then Alex was pulling her to the parlor. When she heard the door close, she whirled to face him.

"Alex, please open the door."

Slowly he walked toward her and she held her ground.

"Now, Em, your father and your sister are gone, am I right?"

"How did you know that?" she demanded, feeling giddiness flutter in her stomach and up into her throat. "Have you been spying on us?"

"Your steward told me when I came in."

"Please don't ask my servants personal questions."

"He volunteered the information."

Alex stepped closer until Emmeline would have to back away or touch him. But he stopped before her, and she arched her neck to look up at him. The air was charged with their breathing, his as rapid as hers, she was amazed to see.

"So we're alone," he murmured.

She was frozen with indecision, wondering what he'd do, wanting—

He suddenly turned away and sprawled on

the settle. "So tell me about your plans for Willoughby's teaching."

The space around her was suddenly so empty. She gripped the back of a chair to keep from falling over. She had wanted to help Maxwell and Blythe, but had not realized how Alex's presence would torture her.

Or had she? Was she unknowingly doing anything she could to be with him?

No, it couldn't be true—she wouldn't *allow* it to be true. She forced herself to smile and sit across from him. "I just want Maxwell to feel at ease in the company of women, to have a fair chance to compete with other men. Anything you feel would be appropriate, I wish you would teach him."

He rested his elbows casually on his knees. "You're trusting me to choose."

She nodded.

"You seem to have much faith in me."

"I certainly have faith in some of the things you're competent at."

"Only competent?" His smile was so knowing that she blushed. "All right, I'll accept competent, although I imagine it is not the first word ascribed to me. I have so much faith in my . . . competence that I propose a wager."

Emmeline shook her head, hiding her trembling hands in her skirt. Where was Maxwell?

This unbearable tension, this feeling of intimate invasion, was becoming more than she could bear. "A lady does not gamble, Alex. Regardless, I don't see what we could possibly wager on."

"I wager on a lot of things you might never imagine," he said slowly. "But I don't propose we use money. I'll wager that I can turn Maxwell Willoughby into the most sought-after gentleman in all of England."

She blinked at him for a moment, wondering if he jested.

"This is foolish," she finally said. "He does not need to be the most sought-after gentleman in all of England. It only matters to—to one woman," she finished, relieved that she had not said Blythe's name. He would go storming from her home if he knew he was training his competition.

Although Alex's posture didn't change, he almost seemed to stiffen. "And who is the woman?"

She smiled brightly. "Whomever Maxwell chooses."

They both heard a sudden knock echo through the front hall, then the steward's footsteps. They continued to stare at each other, until Alex finally said, "After you've seen a demonstration, we can discuss the wager."

"Demonstration?" she whispered, knowing Maxwell must have entered the mansion by now. "Behave yourself. And there will be no wager!"

Alex watched Willoughby being shown into the parlor. The other man bowed toward him, a little stiffly, perhaps, but when his gaze landed on Emmeline, his smile relaxed.

Hellfire.

"Lady Emmeline, Sir Alexander," Willoughby said politely.

Alex grinned. "Since I'm to be your teacher, you might as well call me Alex. And I'll call you Max."

Willoughby cleared his throat. "Although no one calls me by that name, it would not bother me to have you do so."

"I think we can start right there, Max," Alex said, standing up.

"I thought we might have dinner first," Emmeline interrupted.

"In a moment, my lady. Max, the first thing you must do is lose this stiff attitude of yours."

Alex heard the groan Emmeline tried to suppress, and watched Willoughby blink at him silently.

"When people or situations take you off guard," Alex continued, warming to his task, "like my calling you by a different name, don't act uncertain or hesitant."

"I didn't mean to imply—"

"Just relax into it. If you don't know what you're going to say, just smile or laugh while you're thinking, instead of stiffening."

"And is this how you deal with every situation?" Emmeline asked, her probing eyes seeing more than he meant to show her.

"It is quite natural for me not to take anything people say to heart. Why would I allow them that kind of advantage over me? Max, make a joke of things when you need to."

"I already have a sense of humor," Willoughby said mildly, "though I admit to not always using it. But I am not here to have you rebuild me in your image, Alex."

Instead of being offended, Alex found himself rather impressed. "Nicely done. I think we can make this work. Now, my lady, you mentioned food?"

Emmeline looked between them with obvious confusion, then she shrugged and turned toward the dining chamber. Alex stepped quickly to walk at her side, and found that Willoughby was already on her other side. Damn, the man wasn't as foolish as Alex had surmised. Together, they led Emmeline into the next room.

Alex let the lessons go as he studied Willoughby's ease of conversation with Emmeline. There hardly seemed to be a problem in this area, so did she want Willoughby to be more confident in other areas? He couldn't stop his thoughts from dwelling darkly on this, and didn't realize the others were looking at him.

"Alex?" Emmeline said.

He glanced at her. "Yes?"

"You've hardly eaten a thing. Is something wrong?"

He smiled. "I just broke my fast at a late hour this morn, my lady. Do forgive my lack of appetite. Max, are you ready to begin?"

They returned to the parlor, and with amusement, he watched Emmeline nervously look out into the hallway. She didn't quite have the nerve to shut the doors, though.

"Emmeline, don't hide yourself in a corner," Alex said, trying not to laugh. "Do come here with Max and me. You'll be an integral part of our lessons."

"Me?" she managed, coming toward them.

He couldn't help taking in the whole lovely picture she made, from her hair pulled up tight beneath her French headdress, down to her corseted waist, which only made her full breasts and curvaceous hips all the more appealing. When she looked like that, he could not imagine why another man had not snatched her up in a mouthful.

But not Willoughby, of course.

"Yes, Emmeline," he continued, "it will be impossible for me to show Max the lessons I'm trying to teach without someone to demonstrate on."

He watched with satisfaction as the scarlet coloring began in her cheeks and traveled all the way down her neck to disappear under her ruff.

"What an improper suggestion!"

Willoughby looked between them in a be-mused fashion.

"Lady Emmeline," Alex said, as if affronted, "surely you misunderstand me. I will teach no les-sons I think improper for public viewing. Did you expect such a thing of me?"

"No!" she replied too quickly.

He saw the glance she shot at Willoughby, and his gut tightened. So she didn't want her latest conquest to know she was attracted to Alex?

"Max, let's pretend that Emmeline is a lady I've just been introduced to."

He swept into a deep bow before her, extending one leg. She gave a quick curtsy, then Alex caught her hand.

"While still bowing," he continued, "reach for her hand and kiss it. Linger for a bit."

Alex brought Emmeline's hand to his lips and held it there.

Willoughby cleared his throat. "Surely bowing is enough?"

Though she tugged, Alex didn't release her, and spoke against her sweet-smelling skin. "A kiss, Max," he murmured, pleased to feel her tremble. "And linger. Even meet her eyes again."

He looked up her arm and found her gazing at him wide-eyed.

"Emmeline, does this work?" he asked, lifting his head ever so slightly, letting his breath warm her hand. Her hesitation fed his victory.

"I—I suppose 'twould not be *too* improper."

He released her and stepped back. "Your turn, Max."

Emmeline gathered her composure as she watched Maxwell take her hand. He kissed it, even lingered, but . . . it was not the same. Over his head she looked up at Alex, who was staring at her in obvious triumph. Oh, why did he have to know that his kiss affected her more than Maxwell's?

Maxwell released her and stepped back. "What if a woman does not freely give me her hand?"

Emmeline knew he was imagining Blythe's rejection.

"Then you take it," Alex said. "A woman does not always know what is best for her."

Glaring, she fisted her hands on her hips. "I beg your pardon?"

He held up both hands and laughed. "Perhaps my choice of words was poor. Let us say, 'A woman does not always know her own mind.'"

She shook her head.

"'A woman does not always know how she feels about you until you show her'?" he asked, his voice softening.

Emmeline swallowed heavily. "Still not accurate, but not so insulting."

"Thank you, my lady."

"Shall we move on to another topic?" she asked, knowing Maxwell watched them with curious eyes.

Alex studied her thoughtfully, his brow furrowed, and even had the audacity to walk about, perusing her from all sides.

"What are you doing?" she finally demanded.

"Deciding what to teach next. My lady, it is not as if I ever deliberately think of the way I relate to a woman. It comes very naturally to me."

Emmeline suppressed an unladylike snort.

He held up a hand. "I have it! Max, it's often about how you look at a woman, as well as what you say. A woman wants to know she's the center of your thoughts—at the moment, anyway—and she should be able to read that on your face. Look deeply into her eyes and don't look away. Emmeline?"

He caught up her hand again, pressing his lips to the back of it.

"You already demonstrated this," she said tightly.

"We must reinforce the lesson," he murmured, then looked up at her with laughing eyes.

But the laughter died and he stared at her as he slowly straightened to his full height. She looked into those black, mysterious depths, transfixed by the intensity and the banked emotion he usually kept hidden.

Then it was all suddenly gone, as if it had never existed.

He grinned at a wide-eyed Maxwell. "Do you see what I mean?"

Emmeline felt like slumping into a chair, as if she were a puppet with her strings cut.

Maxwell shook his head. "I could hardly stare in silence at a woman, Alex. I'd be laughed out of the room."

"I admit, there's a trick to knowing exactly how long is enough. But you could be complimenting the style of her gown meanwhile, or the color of her eyes. Women love compliments, don't they, Emmeline?"

"Uh . . . of course, provided it's tastefully done and not to the extreme."

"Just don't look away, Max," Alex said.

"What if the women looks away first?" Maxwell asked.

"Then use the tone of your voice and your compliments to woo her attention. Practice the things you'll say. Ask her what she enjoys. Don't brag about yourself, unless she asks you first. Now, would you like to practice on Emmeline?"

Maxwell wiped a hand across his face and gave a tired sigh. "Before I make a fool of myself, I think I need to practice in private. Thank you for your help, Alex."

"That can't be all," she said quickly. "Aren't there more things to tell Maxwell about?"

"I did have a few others in mind," Alex said.

"Then could we meet another time?" Maxwell asked. "I have an appointment with a vintner who wishes to sample my wine."

Emmeline handed him his hat and gloves. "If we meet two days from now, will that give you enough time?"

She almost felt sorry for him as he sighed—but not quite. She was doing this for *his* benefit, after all.

"Lady Emmeline, you have been too kind. I cannot ask—"

"But you can, and I insist. Noon again, on Monday? Our cook will make another wonderful dinner."

He finally smiled at her. "You are persuasive, my lady. I shall be here." He turned to look at Alex. "And thank you for playing the tutor so well. Would you care to ride into town with me?"

To Emmeline's surprise, Alex shook his head. "No, I have to discuss our next lessons with my assistant. A good day to you."

Maxwell gave Alex a speculative look, nodded politely to Emmeline, and left the room. She kept her back to Alex, wishing she could have begged Maxwell to stay. But then she would have had to admit she didn't want to be alone with Alex.

Chapter 20

Emmeline was not about to play the coward. Straightening her shoulders, she turned around and confronted Alex.

"More of your secret tricks?" she asked coolly.

"They aren't tricks, Em," he said softly. "I'm not lying when I tell a woman she interests me, or show it with my attention to her. Women fascinate me—*you* fascinate me."

What could she say to that? When he acted serious, it played havoc with her emotional control. She wanted to run into his arms, to ask why she couldn't be the only woman who fascinated him.

"I haven't forgotten our wager," he said. "Now do you believe I can make Max a sought-after gentleman?"

"I know you'll try, especially if there's money involved."

He walked closer, until she was forced to back up step by step.

"I already told you, I don't want money."

Her back hit the paneled wall. "Then what do you want?"

She made herself ask it boldly, even as he braced his hands on either side of her shoulders, trapping her. Her breath shuddered in and out of her lungs, and heat shot from her breasts deep into her belly.

"I want a kiss," he whispered, leaning his head down, and his black hair fell about his cheekbones.

"Why do you keep wanting to kiss me?"

"Because I like it—I like *you*. You arouse me, Em."

She closed her eyes, pressing her hands against the wall instead of his chest. "Surely other women arouse you," she said, hating how her voice shook.

"Yes, but since I met you, I—"

With what sounded like a moan, he closed the last inches between them and kissed her. His body pressed hers into the wall, his mouth opened and slanted over hers, willing a response she gladly gave. His tongue stroked hers; his teeth nibbled her lower lip. All the while he pressed urgently against her, as if he would fall if she did not hold him up. She thrilled to the hard length of his body touching her everywhere.

Emmeline was the first to break the kiss. She

turned away and felt his head lean against hers as his breath came in deep gasps. Was he truly as affected as she was? Did he desire her honestly, or only because she was not so easily attainable?

She wanted to laugh—not attainable? She responded to his every touch with an indecency that bordered on sinful. There was something about Alex, ever laughing, ever hiding what he was feeling. If only she understood him.

"Please, any of the servants could see us."

He lifted his head and straightened, but continued to keep her against the wall. "Perhaps the wager shouldn't just be a kiss, which until now I've taken freely, but rather a kiss freely given by you."

"Oh Alex," she whispered, feeling sorrow and guilt seep through her. "Why do you do this to me? What about Blythe?"

"Blythe who?"

He rubbed a stray curl of her hair between his fingers, then covered her mouth when she opened it in outrage.

"I barely remember her name, Emmeline."

His hoarse words should not thrill her, but they did.

"I may have originally come here to see her, but no longer. She is . . . not you."

His hands moved up her shoulders and behind her neck, and the laces on her ruff were suddenly loose. When the neckpiece fell to the floor, she stared at his hands as they worked the little buttons down the thin material of her bodice. He was shaking, which moved her as much as a declaration of feelings.

He spread the top of her bodice and looked down on the valley of her heavily corseted bosom. He took a sharp breath, and she watched in stunned amazement when his fingers dipped between her breasts. She moaned.

"Beautiful," he whispered, then bent his head and placed a kiss there.

It was heaven and the torture of hell all at the same moment to have his mouth on her skin, to imagine her clothing gone and his mouth even lower.

But oh God, she was standing in full view of anyone who walked into the room, with Alex's head at her breasts.

And he had just declared that he only wanted her to satisfy a physical need. He didn't love her.

Rallying her courage, she ran her fingers through his soft hair and whispered, "Is this a proposal, Alex?" knowing it wasn't, knowing that was for the best. He was too wild, too unsettled for someone as simple as she.

He froze, and in disappointment she pushed him away and pulled her bodice together, barely able to work the buttons. When she looked over her shoulder he had one hand braced against the wall, his head hung low.

"That is as good an answer as any," she said. "You must go."

"I know." He lifted his head and his dark eyes smoldered. "Em, I have no plans to marry anyone."

"Why?"

He simply shook his head. "I have no answer to give you that would make sense. But I'll be back to tutor Max on Monday."

She nodded wordlessly, then sank into a chair as he strode from the room. Sorrow tightened her chest. If he didn't want to marry her, then the reason that he no longer came to see Blythe was because her sister would not give in to his seduction, as Emmeline had done. She wanted to feel guilty—but she couldn't. Her feelings for him overwhelmed her, and the more she discovered about him, the more he dominated her thoughts. He wasn't at all what he showed the world.

On Monday Alex stood before Kent Hall, feeling renewed of purpose. He had spent the weekend wrestling with his desire for Emmeline, trying to drink and gamble away the indecision that wracked him. What was wrong with him? Shouldn't her mention of marriage send him fleeing London, or at least into the arms of another woman?

But he hadn't had another woman since he'd

met Emmeline Prescott. He was shocked to realize it had been two months now. Had he ever in his adulthood gone that long without taking a willing woman to bed?

When he was finished with the project that was Emmeline, she would live her life free of the past and its sadness. He would find a new mistress, and life would go back to the way it was before he'd been the viscount, before his life had upended.

He felt confident that he had everything under control.

He greeted Emmeline, and Willoughby arrived soon after. Alex's brows rose as Willoughby swept into a bow and kissed Emmeline's hand with gusto. There was an unexplainable knot of tension in Alex's stomach, until Willoughby looked deeply into her eyes—and the two of them convulsed with laughter.

His relief was like a sudden rush of pleasure. She didn't laugh when *he* looked at her. "Nicely done, Max. Emmeline, do you wish to eat before resuming our work?"

She did, and he magnanimously allowed Willoughby to escort her into the dining chamber. While they were waiting for the first course, Alex said, "Max, tomorrow night is Lady Rutherford's card party. We can practice today's lesson there."

Willoughby's smile was not quite confident. "And what would today's lesson be?"

"Touching."

Out of the corner of his eye, Alex saw Emmeline flinch, even as she kept her gaze on her plate.

Willoughby's face flushed. "I assure you, I do not wish to lose a lady's respect by something so improper."

Alex laughed. "I'm not suggesting you *grope* the girl in question. But you must learn to take advantage of a situation's opportunities."

"As in?"

"The table is a good place to start. Emmeline?"

She jumped as if Alex had announced to Willoughby how much he'd already touched *her*. Ah, how fond he was of her and her sweet innocence—even as he wanted to take it away, too.

"Emmeline, do be good enough to drop your napkin, and then reach to pick it up. Max, pay attention."

While glancing at him in obvious bewilderment, she did as he'd asked. Alex reached for the cloth as well, and they bumped heads and brushed fingers. She straightened, clutching the napkin in her lap.

"Did you see that, Max?" Alex asked.

"Well, I saw you bump into her."

"I also brushed my fingers along hers, and I smiled at her when we were but inches apart."

"Surely that means nothing," Maxwell scoffed.

Emmeline prayed that Alex would not ask what she had felt, for just the touch of his fingers had made her heart answer with a faster beat. Even when she knew she was being manipulated, she could only bask in the warmth of his apologetic smile, and overlook how contrived it all was.

Alex shook his head. "Max, my young friend, you have much to learn. Every touch means something. Look for every opportunity, even if it's only your leg brushing her skirt. Come back to the parlor and I'll show you."

Though Alex's methods were suspect, she knew everything he said was right, because it all worked on her.

She was so gullible, so foolish.

· Yet these lessons *had* to help Maxwell, and she could not throw such an opportunity away. So she followed the two men back to the parlor, feeling her pace lag with reluctance. When she stepped through the doorway, Alex was waiting.

"Come, Emmeline, I have so many more demonstrations in mind."

For another hour she endured his onslaught, feeling aroused and angry and near tears. He demonstrated how to brush against a woman when he passed by, how to take her arm so she wouldn't stumble down the stairs. Her skin, her very awareness, was attuned to him, and she despised her weakness even as she allowed it free rein. If all this was an act on his part, why was he so successful at it? Why did everything seem so real?

And then he wanted to dance with her, and he put his lessons in gazing and touching all together in one devastating package. Maxwell was so oblivious to what was happening that he happily pounded out the beat to a dance on a table. He seemed to approve every soulful look Alex bestowed on her as he clung to her waist just a moment longer than the dance required.

"Enough," she finally cried, breaking from Alex's hold, her breath coming hard from exertion—or so she told herself.

He smiled at her. "Then you're ready for Max's turn at the dance?"

"No! I need—fresh air," she stammered, giving Maxwell an apologetic look before taking his arm. She led Blythe's suitor out the tall, windowed doors leading into the gardens, knowing that Alex followed because she could feel his movement like a part of her.

"Why, this is a perfect idea," he said, coming to stand beside her on the terrace.

She glanced warily at him. "What do you mean?"

"What a fine way to again demonstrate the art of touching."

He was gazing at a meadow on the side of the mansion, where archery targets had been set up.

"Many of your lady friends practice archery, do they not?" he asked, walking toward the grass.

Emmeline had no choice but to trail behind the

two men, for Maxwell seemed intrigued—or at least, amused by the possibilities.

"Come, Alex," he said, "surely there is not a way to court a young lady on an archery field!"

Alex grinned back at him. "There is *always* a way. You must use ingenuity to find it. Emmeline, do you shoot?"

"A bit," she murmured skeptically.

"Good. Do come here, then, and show me your form."

She inhaled and glared at him.

"I mean your archery form, my lady. Max, she takes such easy offense, does she not?"

Maxwell's grunt was noncommittal.

Emmeline lifted the bow she had been using that morning, but before she could even take the correct stance, Alex was at her back, his hands on her arms. Stunned, she wondered what to say, how to make him stop without Maxwell realizing how much Alex affected her.

But Alex didn't seem to be feeling the same things. "Max," he called, "see how I lift her elbow to the correct height, how I lean close, how I allow my breath to lightly fan her neck?"

Maxwell chuckled and Emmeline forced herself to do the same, trying desperately to control her blush and the shivering that made her arms seem not her own.

She almost kissed Maxwell when he strode toward them. "I can do this, Alex. Let me try."

Alex's grip tightened, and she heard his quickly inhaled breath. She glanced over her shoulder at him and saw not playfulness, but unguarded anger in his eyes.

Anger?

Then Maxwell stepped between them, and he guided her left hand to lift the bow, and her right hand to pull back the string.

"Just a bit farther, my lady," he said in an almost apologetic voice.

Suddenly the back of his hand touched her breast, and he jumped away from her as if she'd burned him.

"Oh, my lady, forgive my clumsiness!" he cried, looking mortified.

Flustered, Emmeline glanced at Alex, ready for his amused laughter. Instead his narrowed gaze pinned Maxwell like a sword. Was he angry that another man had touched her?

"Willoughby, you've gone too quickly to the advanced lesson," Alex said in a low voice unlike his own.

She gaped at him, wondering if he was actually jealous—over her? She didn't know if she was giddy at the possibility or frightened. She was held motionless, trapped by the mysterious depths of his gaze.

Maxwell blathered on, obviously unaware of the emotions raging around him.

"Your friendship has meant so much to me,

my lady, but how will I ever look upon you again?"

"It was merely an accident," she said quickly, needing to end their lesson. Watching Alex, she felt like she was trying to stop a rising storm.

"I should go," Maxwell said. "I can't believe I—"

"Willoughby, you're not using my lessons enough," Alex said slowly.

She watched with awe as he seemed to lock every emotion behind an effortless mask of friendliness. He was much more complicated than the face he showed the world. What did he hide, and why did she desperately want to understand it all?

"But tomorrow night you will," Alex continued. "You will practice touching at Lady Rutherford's card party."

Maxwell's face faded to the color of an uncooked pastry. "Alex, I cannot—I wouldn't know where to begin, what to say."

"You will wait for a woman to play the spinet, and you will sit beside her, helping her to turn the pages of the music. And you will touch her."

"Alex!" Emmeline cried. "What are you doing?"

"It will work," he said patiently, never taking his gaze from her. "You'll see."

Maxwell stuttered through his good-byes, and

soon she and Alex were alone. The emotions raging through her were only for him. He could manipulate her very heartbeat and the blood that pulsed through her veins.

And the way he looked at her now, his amusement gone, his intensity making him seem like a stranger—

Without a word, she dashed around him at a dead run for the house, knowing she was not capable of resisting him anymore. He caught her arm, pulling her about to face him.

"Em, what did you think you were doing?"

"I?" she cried, aghast. "I've only done everything you wanted me to do."

"Then why did you let him touch you like that?" he demanded, gripping her by both arms now.

"*Let* him?"

"Very well, I'll be more blunt. You *leaned* into his hand."

"I did not!" How could he even suggest such a thing? Anger clouded the last of her good judgment. "Why are you acting like this over a simple accident?"

He opened his mouth, frustration raging across his face.

"Do you not understand?" he asked in a hoarse voice. "No one can touch you but me."

The kiss Alex gave her was demanding and

possessive, and Emmeline felt tears of frustration fall down her cheeks. She finally pushed him away and wiped her hand across her mouth.

"Stop this!" she cried. "Our encounters cannot always end thus. You don't mean any of it!"

With a sob, she turned and ran from him, ignoring his call, not stopping until she slammed the door to her chamber and leaned against it, holding the stitch in her side.

And still the tears came. How had he done it? He was destroying all her defenses against him. She'd been wrong about love, wrong about everything she'd ever experienced with her poet. None of it compared to even one touch from Alex—a man too hurt by his own problems to commit to a woman.

Oh, she'd spent nights reminding herself of his past scandals, of the women he must have seduced. But some foolish part of her was convinced there was a different Alex hidden inside him, one who was hurting, who covered it all with scandal and flirting and wagering. Her feelings for him frightened her, because Alex was not the kind of man who fell in love. He pursued her for the adventure, for amusement.

Her plan to be content as the maiden aunt no longer seemed enough—and it was all Alex Thornton's fault. Did he even understand what he did, how he made her feel like a desirable woman? Yet what would it get her but seduced, or even left with a child and no husband? Had he truly only turned to her because she was more available than her sister?

Wiping away her tears, she gave a reluctant laugh. To think she had never thought to feel this torn by desire. She would have gone to her grave not knowing this painful pleasure, the wonder of being the only thing one man looked at.

But she hadn't found it with a man who would marry her.

That night at the Rooster, Alex sat at a corner table and finished his fourth tankard of beer, ignoring the tumult of voices raised in a drunken song. But he couldn't drink away the jealousy that ate at him, jealousy he'd never felt in his life over a woman. Why had he showed Emmeline his emotions? Now she *knew* he was jealous, and would think she had a hold over him. If he wasn't careful, he was still going to have to leave London for a while—taking some future mistress, of course.

Because there would be a mistress, he thought, looking dejectedly at the tavern maids. He would not make a fool of himself over a noble maiden he couldn't have; he'd done that enough while posing as Spencer. He still remembered when he'd first visited Lady Margaret, daughter of a duke, after his true identity had been discovered. They had danced and flirted and kissed for months, and she was the first person he was actually relieved to reveal himself to. But what he'd thought had been feminine interest on her part had been only a lusting for power and wealth. Her father expected a brilliant match, she told him coolly, and she expected no less for herself.

Women like Lady Margaret—and Emmeline— were for men with titles and power. Though Emmeline desired him, she had already learned long ago that desire didn't matter. She would be a dutiful daughter and marry as her father told her to.

Chapter 21

Lady Rutherford's card party was going to be a sedate, relaxed affair, Emmeline realized, as she came through the doorway. At her side was Blythe, who had arrived home in time for the event. On the coach ride over she'd told Emmeline about the people she'd seen in Kent, the parties she'd attended, but all the while Emmeline had gotten the impression that Blythe was almost relieved to be back in London.

Guilt swamped Emmeline as her sister rushed forward happily to a table occupied by her female friends. She hoped Blythe wasn't looking for Alex, because how could she tell her that Alex wasn't interested in her anymore? Blythe would want to know how she knew, and Emmeline would have to say—*because he's trying to seduce me!*

Blythe waved her over and Emmeline shook

267

her head, pointing to the refreshment table. She stood there alone a moment, sipping wine handed to her by a servant, until Maxwell joined her.

Perspiration shone on his forehead, and his normally pristine appearance seemed hastily put together.

"Maxwell?" she said uncertainly.

He seemed to force a grin. "A good evening to you, Lady Emmeline."

Before she could say another word, he burst out, "I cannot do this."

She slumped with disappointment. "Oh, Maxwell, what am I to do with you? You *know* Alex is right."

"Yes, but I feel so foolish. Surely I will be the joke of the party."

"Never. You are a well-respected man. So let us see who's at the spinet."

They both turned and saw that Blythe had just taken the bench, and was now looking through the sheet music.

"How perfect!" Emmeline said, though she could see him swallow and tug at the high ruff beneath his chin. "Go ahead, Maxwell."

"But . . . surely her friends will help her."

"Then you'd best sit beside her before they do."

She turned him about by the shoulders and gave him a little push toward the spinet. He stumbled, then straightened and walked determinedly to the instrument. Blythe looked up and smiled at him, easing Emmeline's nerves.

Maxwell took Blythe's hand and bowed over it, pressing a kiss that made Blythe blush. Emmeline could barely contain her glee. Maxwell spoke to her sister, leaning over, and suddenly Blythe was making room for him on the bench.

Emmeline could have clapped and shouted her praise. Oh, good for Maxwell!

She didn't want to spy on them, so she turned her back and looked out over the room. Little tables were scattered about, and already people were engrossed in card games, while servants wandered about with wine and food.

At the table behind her, a man said, "Did you hear? Viscount Thornton has returned to London. I just spoke with him tonight."

Emmeline barely stopped herself from rudely interrupting for details. Alex's brother was back from the Isle of Wight? She could not wait to see the man Alex had successfully impersonated for almost two years. Were their personalities as alike as their faces?

And then she saw him speaking to their hostess, Lady Rutherford. She studied him thoughtfully, amazed at their identical looks, then looking deeper for their differences. He held himself with a formal, straight bearing, where Alex always seemed casually relaxed. As he spoke his expression was serious, and the smile he finally showed seemed restrained. This was not a man who freely gave in to his emotions.

And then Lady Rutherford was leading him toward Emmeline, and she saw for herself that the banked wickedness in Alex's eyes was absent in his brother's.

And she missed it. In Alex there was always the promise of wildness and unpredictability.

"Lady Emmeline?" Lady Rutherford said. "I would like to introduce you to Lord Thornton."

Emmeline curtsied deeply, then looked up into the interested eyes of Alex's brother.

"Lady Emmeline," he said, "I asked for this introduction because I had to meet the woman that my . . . mother spoke so much of. I understand she and your mother were friends."

"Yes, my lord. And how is your mother doing?"

"Quite well, thank you. We had a pleasant visit together."

Oh, he was nothing like Alex, so formal, so polite.

"Congratulations on the birth of your child, Lord Thornton. I understand it was a boy? And your wife is well?"

"Thank you, yes. She was not up to traveling yet, but I'm sure she can't wait to meet you."

Emmeline tried not to frown. "But . . . why? I am merely a friend of your broth—mother."

"I guess it was because of the message my brother asked me to relay to you." His smile was full of chagrin. "Regretfully I cannot say it in so public a place. It is a rather private request."

She didn't know what to say as Lord Thornton took her arm. What could Alex have said to him?

Before she knew it they were in a small library, where a fire was rapidly becoming only embers. She turned in confusion to Lord Thornton, and found him closing the door. He leaned back against it, watching her.

"My lord," she began cautiously, "what could Alex have needed to say that he could not say himself?"

Instead of speaking, he reached for both her hands. He suddenly yanked her against him, and wicked amusement spilled from his eyes. She only had a moment to breathe, "Alex," before he kissed her.

As always, his passion threatened to overwhelm her, but Emmeline fought the pleasure stealing over her by pushing him away.

"Alex Thornton!" she gasped.

The courtly bow he gave her was exaggerated with a flourish. "My lady."

"I didn't even guess—I didn't see—"

"No one ever does," he said, still laughing.

But she was uneasy at his laughter, at . . . something.

"I have not met your brother, but you were very successful at not portraying yourself. I can see why you fooled so many people."

"Not just 'so many people.' I fool everyone."

"Even your mother?"

"Well, no. But you, Em, you believed it."

And though he smiled at her, made a joke of it all, she felt a sympathetic chill move through her. Somehow, she knew he had wanted her *not* to be fooled, to know him anywhere. And she'd failed.

She didn't think that he even knew it had been some sort of a test. She suddenly realized that Alex used laughter when anything cut too deep to his emotions. So many things made sense now.

Emmeline forced a smile, but all she felt was sadness. Living as his brother must have changed him in ways he didn't want to face. Instead of seeing himself as but a man doing a job, he must have thought of himself as somehow less than Spencer. Had such feelings always been a part of him?

She wanted to reassure him, to tell him she knew everything, but it was not her place. Such rights belonged to a wife, not the current object of his fancy. So she had to distract him, while inside her throat ached with unshed tears.

"Alex, I need to ask your forbearance."

"Over what?"

"Maxwell and Blythe. I know you've claimed that you are finished courting her—"

"I never *courted* her."

"—but please, give them this chance at happiness. They are perfect for each other. You've helped Maxwell, and forgive me for not telling you the full truth, but I thought you would feel I was pushing you out of Blythe's life."

Alex knew he stared foolishly down at her, his mouth open, but for once he was at a loss. He blurted, "But I thought you wanted Max for yourself."

Her eyes went wide. "For myself? Maxwell is a dear friend, that is all. No, it is *Blythe* I am concerned for."

Alex could neither understand nor explain his relief, and he had never thought to feel such confusion. "But . . . what about your dreams for yourself, Em? What about *your* life?"

Though she laughed, he saw the pain she always kept buried. And for the first time, a woman's pain hurt him.

"Oh, Alex, surely you see that I have made my peace with my life? I know my future, and I gladly accept it. I will be happy living with Blythe's family. And I want her to be happy, to choose the sort of stable man who will complement her high spirits. We do well together, my sister and I. I can help raise her children, and be her companion in our old age. What more could I want?"

Alex saw that she had convinced herself that she meant it.

"Go back to your sister, then," he said, smiling at her. "I will not interfere between her and Max."

The light in her face could have blinded him. "Truly, Alex? Oh, thank you! You do not know how I have worried. I shall see you at the party, won't I? We can play cards together, and I can see if you play just as well as you use your mouth."

Her face flamed scarlet as she realized what she'd said.

"Oh! I meant how you talk, not how you—you—" She ran from the room.

Alex was left alone, staring after her, reflecting on a strange ache in his chest. His smile faded as he went to the window and looked unseeingly outside.

How had he not noticed it? Not only had Emmeline given up on her own life, she thought to live through her sister. All his kisses and passion had done nothing to make her see that she was a desirable woman, that any marriageable man would be happy to have her.

But it wouldn't be someone like him. He certainly didn't need to be with her—he didn't *need* any woman.

But Emmeline needed someone to show her that her life was not to be led in the service of her sister. He wouldn't let her give up that easily.

When Emmeline returned to the card party, she fanned herself as she gazed about the room. Would she always make a fool of herself around Alex?

She was distracted by the sight of Maxwell and Blythe, still sitting at the spinet, but seeming to be in turmoil. Then she saw that Maxwell's sleeve was caught on the shoulder trim of Blythe's gown. Emmeline could have groaned. The dear man must have tried to follow Alex's orders, and only succeeded at embarrassing himself further. This would certainly not help his confidence.

She had to make things right between them, before Maxwell was discouraged forever. She took a step forward, then felt a hand suddenly clasp her shoulder.

"No, Em, stay here."

Alex stood at her back, his words gentle but firm.

"Let me go! Surely you see that all my plans could be ruined right here!" She looked frantically toward the spinet, but two men had stopped before her to talk, blocking her view.

She knew Alex leaned toward her, because his words were close to her ear. "It's time to trust them. Your sister is a grown woman, Maxwell a man. You can't live their lives for them—you can't live *through* them."

The last was said so softly she almost thought she had imagined it. But surely he was wrong. How could she risk seeing Blythe unhappy—as unhappy as she'd been when she was forced to give up Clifford?

"But Alex—"

"Just look," he whispered, pointing over her shoulder toward the spinet.

The men had gone, and she had a clear view of Maxwell and Blythe—laughing. He was leaning close to her, fingering a spot at her shoulder that had perhaps torn. But he wasn't blushing; he didn't seem to be stuttering. Could it be—

And then Lord Seabrook approached, obviously asking Blythe to partner with him. He led her away, and Emmeline groaned, feeling a total failure. But just before she turned away in defeat, Maxwell looked at her—

And smiled. He mouthed the words "Thank you," crossed his arms at his chest, and watched Blythe walk away.

To Emmeline's amazement, Blythe looked back at Maxwell and smiled.

"There," Alex said. "You have done your sisterly duty. Now I think it's time you proved your proficiency at cards."

She turned to face him, gazing up at the scandalous man who'd become a friend. "I am quite good at cards."

"You are quite good at many things, and I have yet to discover them all."

She wasn't sure she knew what that meant, but perhaps she could find out. She laughed and followed him to a table.

* * *

Over the next few days, Maxwell came alive as a suitor. He sent Blythe gifts and flowers and even visited every day. Many times Emmeline came upon them in the parlor or the garden, their heads bent together in conversation as if Maxwell's stuttering had never existed.

She realized with satisfaction that although Alex's tutoring had helped, it was Maxwell's true, more confident self that Blythe seemed interested in. But her other suitors were still a part of her life, and Emmeline had to remind herself that she had interfered enough.

She had not seen Alex since the card party five days before and told herself it was for the best. When he sent a missive asking to see her, she ignored it. She had no illusions that Alex wanted more from her than merely satisfying his physical needs.

But she couldn't help the curiosity that kept her awake at night. She couldn't stop herself from wondering about the man who'd masqueraded so successfully as his brother. Surely that meant he'd had much practice. Before his ruse for the good of the country, why would he have pretended to be Spencer?

As if Emmeline's thoughts had magically produced him, she saw Alex the next day.

She had agreed to go boating with Blythe and Maxwell, and sat on a cushion at one end of the boat. At the far end, beyond the two servants rowing, Blythe reclined amidst dozens of pillows, with Maxwell seated at her side. Netting hung from a canopy about the two of them to keep out the insects, and it might as well have blocked their voices, because Emmeline could hear nothing but low murmurs and occasional laughter. They sat properly apart, so she had little cause to watch them.

Instead, she pushed her canopy back a bit, so she could lift her face to the sun. The lazy rocking of the boat relaxed her, soothed her.

"Lady Emmeline, Lady Blythe!" a voice called out across the water.

Alex.

Emmeline opened her eyes with a snap. She expected to find him on the shore, but he was in another boat.

She calmly lifted a hand, even though her heart seemed to bounce about in her chest. As he turned his back to row, she admired the way his white shirt clung damply to his back, revealing muscles that she had pressed her palms against. She remembered every caress, every kiss. Her body heated clear to the depths of her stomach as he approached.

And kept approaching. Surely he would turn away from them, she thought uneasily.

But when he continued to row, she called, "Alex, you're getting too close."

He didn't turn around. Behind her, their oarsmen began to row harder, but it would be too late. She heard Blythe gasp, and Maxwell call out a warning. Without thinking, Emmeline stood as if she could push the boat aside.

At the last moment Alex glanced at them, steered his boat suddenly sideways, then caught Emmeline about the hips as he passed. She cried out, finding herself dumped at his feet, the boat rocking precariously enough to splash her. Coming up on her knees, she gripped the edge and looked back at Blythe's boat. Because it was larger and more stable, it merely swayed in the current. She heard the merry peal of Blythe's laughter as the boats drifted apart.

Emmeline turned and found herself kneeling between Alex's knees. All thoughts of a lecture on safety fled her mind as her gaze drifted up his thighs, past his powerful hands on the oars, to the width of his chest. His face loomed over her, dark and mesmerizing.

"My, what a lovely position you find yourself in, Em," he murmured.

Though she tried to stop herself, her gaze fell back to his thighs, and she remembered being held tightly to his hips, feeling the powerful evidence of his desire for her.

He groaned. "Exactly what I was thinking."

She quickly sat on the bench behind her and straightened her back. "If you really knew what I was thinking, you'd be apologizing profusely. You quite endangered us all."

He heaved a dramatic sigh and began to row away from Kent Hall.

"Alex, what are you doing?"

"Your servants told me you were boating. It seemed a perfect time to tell you of my fantasy."

Emmeline's throat tightened and a sudden wicked feeling swirled through her belly. "What fantasy?"

Alex rested his elbows on the oars, allowing the current to guide them. "Do you remember when I found you drunk at the Paris Gardens?"

"I was not inebriated," she sniffed.

He leaned closer and his voice lowered. "Then do you remember caressing me with your eyes and your hands?"

Emmeline was too stunned to move. That had been almost two months ago, before they'd even kissed. "I couldn't . . . I didn't—"

"You could and you did, love. In fact, you told me I was 'sinfully handsome.'"

She should be embarrassed, for that day's memories were vague at best. But since then, her actions had only proven the powerful emotions she felt in his presence. She watched his mouth, remembered his kiss.

"And why are you telling me this now?" she whispered.

He lifted one hand from the oar and reached for the hem of her skirt. She watched wide-eyed as he slowly revealed her slippers, then her ankles.

"Because while you were busy trying to seduce me with your eyes—"

"Alex!"

"—I was fantasizing about seducing you in that wherry."

She opened her mouth, but nothing came out. Goose flesh rose on every part of her body.

"Do you want me to tell you what I was thinking?"

He took her foot in his hand and slid off her slipper, never breaking their shared gaze. Gently he rubbed his thumbs into the arch, and she couldn't stifle a moan.

"Tell me." She watched with fascination as a breeze lifted his black hair away from his face.

"You wore a man's shirt," he said softly, "and when you leaned back I could see your breasts through the fabric."

She could feel her nipples harden, and with each rapid breath, they brushed against her smock. Between her thighs, her muscles were tight and damp, and the ache was maddening. With half-closed eyes, she watched Alex pull her skirt back over her foot, then place her foot directly between his thighs, resting against the hard ridge of his erection. With a gasp, she gripped the bench beneath her.

His voice grew hoarse. "When I saw you like that under the sun, I could do nothing to appease my hunger, for not only were you drunk, you were dressed as a boy."

She laughed, then experimentally wiggled her toes. It pleased her when she heard his breath suddenly leave his lungs.

"So I had to content myself with my imagination," he continued after a moment.

"And is it as wicked as you are?"

He grinned. "Even more so."

"And what did you imagine?" She felt his hands beneath her skirt, sliding from her ankle up to her calf. His fingers traced patterns across her skin and made her squirm.

"I imagined a tree like that one—"

He nodded toward the southern bank of the Thames, where a grove of trees grew at the water's edge. One particularly large willow tree bent low over the river, with its branches dragging in the current.

"—And in my mind," he continued, almost in a whisper now, "I rowed you beneath its branches, into our own private bower."

When his hand left her leg, she almost gave voice to her disappointment until she watched him row toward his mysterious tree. Her heart picked up pace, and her trembling increased as the first branches swept over the bow of the boat. Alex reached over to guide the branches around her, then around him. The leaves silently slid back into the water, like a curtain over a bright window. The sunlight faded, and the current ceased its tugging in their little shallow pool by the roots of the willow tree.

For a moment they just stared at each other, connected only by her foot between his thighs.

"What happened next?" she asked softly.

Chapter 22

Alex rose up above her and Emmeline leaned back, her elbows on the next bench.

"You were wearing much less clothing that day," he said. "I imagined parting your thighs and settling between them."

He slid one hand up her calf, then along her inner thigh. Her breath came in gasps at the exquisite sensations he left in the wake of his touch. She willingly spread her legs, wanting his touch *there*, at the private center of her desperate yearning.

But just before he lowered his body onto hers, a frog leapt from the muddy riverbank and landed on Emmeline's chest. With a shriek, she tried to sit up, rocking the boat. Alex lost his balance and tumbled over the side.

The frog, too, jumped overboard and swam leisurely toward shore. Alex came up on his hands and knees in two feet of muddy water, coughing and spitting. Aghast, she gaped at him until he lifted his gaze to hers. His face was spotted with mud, and his hair dripped with it.

She covered her mouth, but couldn't quite smother a giggle. With a growl he rose up menacingly and she cried out, but he only dove into the clear water on the other side of the boat. Laughter overwhelmed her as she sagged back against the bench. He emerged a moment later, wet but clean, stood up in the shallow water, and stepped into the boat. She clutched the sides until he sat opposite her and the rocking ceased.

They eyed one another.

Alex sighed. "I don't suppose we can begin again."

Though she still trembled, she had her reckless emotions back under control. "I think we should leave such fanciful thoughts to your imagination, where they belong."

"They need to be acted out by the light of day," he grumbled, gripping the oars, "or by moonlight in your bedchamber."

"But then something much more dangerous than a frog might interrupt us."

"And what dreaded creature should I fear? A house cat?"

"My father," she murmured, her amusement dying. What would Alex's reaction be if they were discovered in a compromising position?

As they both ducked beneath the willow branches, she felt a need to lighten the mood.

"How did you know there would be a perfect tree nearby today?"

He pushed the wet hair back off his face. "Because I've been searching for it, hoping for the right opportunity. One day I'll have to tell you about my fantasy of the two of us naked in a garden."

"Really?" she murmured, shocked yet secretly thrilled.

Alex appeared again the next day, during a wet, foggy afternoon. When the steward came to her chamber to announce him, Emmeline sternly quelled her pleasure and anticipation.

She had to resist his charm and remember her future. She could not let him jeopardize it.

But oh, she'd never imagined how wonderful it would feel to know he truly came to see her, not her sister. He was the unknown—yet he was Alex.

She hurried to meet him, almost tripping down the stairs in her haste. He was there in the hall, his dark hair wet and unruly, his smile so wicked it made her weak with memories.

"Lady Emmeline, I've taken the liberty of having your horse saddled. Do come for a ride with me."

She remained on the last marble step, not daring to come closer for fear she'd show how eager she was.

"Alex, the weather is not cooperating, and it is close to supper. Can we not speak here?"

He looked about them as if dozens of people lingered to eavesdrop. "No. Come outside with me, my lady. The day shall yet turn lovely. And I promise you a meal worthy of kings."

She told herself not to, even as the steward brought her cloak. She fastened it about her neck, her speculative gaze on Alex. What did he want?

Outside, the groom helped her mount. When she wheeled her horse about, Alex was already in his saddle, and he nodded toward the gate and London beyond.

What did he want with her, and why was she making it so easy for him?

They approached the double gates riding side by side, while the fog wet her hair despite her hood. Everything about them was hidden, as if only she and Alex existed in the world. She relaxed and began to enjoy the odd intimacy.

On the Strand, Emmeline's horse suddenly reared up. With a cry, she caught the pommel before sliding off. Hands reached out of the fog, dragging Alex from his saddle. When a club bashed him over the head, she screamed, then felt herself being pulled down into the mist.

* * *

Alex awoke to soft hands touching his head and face, even as he felt his body vibrate with the motion of a moving coach. A smell that was all Emmeline, a refined hint of roses and some other mysterious fragrance, wafted about him. He felt pressure on his chest, heard the rustle of silk skirts, and opened his eyes.

Ah, she was close, her face inches above him in the gloom, her hands holding a cloth to his temple. Her changeable eyes were wide and moist and so concerned.

"Alex?"

He gave her a lazy smile, then grimaced. "So is this your attempt to get me alone?"

"This is serious!" she whispered, looking toward the closed door of the coach. "We've been captured!"

"So I see." He almost straightened up from his slumped position, but thought better of it when he realized Emmeline was practically lying across his lap as she dabbed at his head. "I take it that I'm bleeding."

She bit her lip and held up the cloth that she had obviously torn from her own underskirts. There wasn't much blood, though his head was pounding enough to ring a church bell. He deliberately winced, then watched in satisfaction as she leaned even closer.

"Does it hurt much, Alex?"

"Not if you'll continue your tender ministrations," he murmured, heaving a sigh and leaning into her hand.

"Oh, you!" she suddenly cried, throwing the cloth at his chest and sitting back into the corner of the bench. A dim lantern hung just above her head, barely piercing the darkness.

He laughed as he sat up and waited for the dizziness to pass. "How long have I been unconscious?"

She crossed her arms over her chest, but her glare was already fading. "Close to an hour, I imagine."

"And we've been in the coach the whole time?"

She nodded. "The windows and doors are barred shut from the outside."

He tested her claim with his own strength. The door didn't budge, though cracks of daylight teased them.

"'Tis those men, isn't it?" she said softly. "The ones who attacked you before?"

He glanced over his shoulder to smile at her. "How do you know it's not a suitor, jealous of my attentions toward you?"

Her eyes glinted with anger. "That isn't amusing, Alex. We're in danger here."

"Not if they're who you think they are," he said lightly, though tension tightened his body. "They have yet to do any dirty deed well."

"But you haven't caught them, have you."

He shrugged, then sat back opposite her and stretched out his legs.

Emmeline straightened, glancing between him and the door. "Well?"

"Well what?"

"Why aren't you trying to escape?"

"I've already tried, and it seems impossible. All we can do is wait until they confront us."

"Or kill us!"

"If that's what they wanted, they'd have done it by now. They want something of me." Hellfire, she was angry, not even afraid.

But he was. For the first time in his life, he felt afraid—because he'd put her in danger. He'd ignored the threats, pretended that these foolish criminals weren't capable of carrying out their promises. How would he live with himself if she came to harm because of him?

Huddled in her corner, Emmeline tried not to glare at Alex. He was right—there was no sense in beating futilely at the coach, though the impulse to do just that almost had her squirming.

But how could he be so relaxed? Why did that damnable smile never leave his face?

And why did he have to keep watching her from beneath lowered eyelids, making her forget the danger, forget everything but his mouth on hers, his hands touching her, cupping her—

She had to distract herself. "Alex, the noise has died away, so we must have left London."

"I know. We can only wait and see what their intentions are."

"Then . . . distract me!"

He was off his bench and over her so fast that she gave a little gasp, even as she stopped him with a hand on his chest.

"Not like that!"

He leaned even harder against her, his body overwhelming, the heat in his eyes stunning her. They were in horrible danger, and the first thing he thought about was . . . *that*?

"Then shall I compose poetry for you, fair Emmeline?" he murmured, his lips so close to her upturned face. "I'm sure I could think of something for the occasion. We could call it 'The Seduction of Emmeline.'"

"Alex!"

"'A proud, noble beauty, above reproach; lost her innocence while traveling in a—'"

"Stop!" she cried. In a weak voice, she continued, "Tell me . . . tell me about when your brother was spying against Spain."

He blinked, and though he didn't move, she could sense everything freezing inside him. After a moment, he gave her a bland smile and slid back onto his bench. His ability to control his expression always amazed her.

"So you've been talking to people about me."

"Not deliberately. I overheard a conversation."

"I can only imagine," he said dryly. "How long have you known?"

"A fortnight."

He said softly, "Why didn't you say something before now?"

She felt another dreaded blush steal over her. "If you'll remember, whenever we've been alone, you haven't given me much chance to . . . talk."

His narrowed gaze roamed down her body, and she wished she had not reminded him.

Quickly, she said, "But I'd like to talk now."

"Very well. Ask your questions."

"I don't have any questions yet, because I don't know what happened. Won't you tell me?"

She held her breath, waiting, until he finally nodded.

"It is quite simple, really. The Queen asked my brother to run off to Spain and pose as a Spaniard, all for the sake of our good England. And I was to stay behind, posing as Spencer, though occasionally I came to town as myself just for appearances. I was much better suited to playing the nobleman than the spy; my command of the Spanish language would fool no one, you see."

Emmeline watched him, barely daring to breathe, knowing that even as he made light of his situation, there was a lingering bitterness he thought hidden from her. "Did the plan succeed?"

"Oh yes, Spencer returned quite the hero, England was saved, and I was released from the drudgery of estate management."

"Perhaps your brother had all the glory, but your efforts were just as noble," she said softly.

He laughed. "Emmeline, how kind you are, but the danger was all Spencer's. I had nothing more dangerous than three mistresses and too much money to spend."

She ignored her painful spasm of jealousy. "But without you, Spencer couldn't have succeeded as a spy for so long. It was over a year, wasn't it? Questions would have been asked, threatening his life. You prevented that."

The coach rumbled over another hole in the road, and she held onto her bench lest she be tossed into Alex's lap.

As the silence continued, she asked, "What was it like, pretending to be someone else for so long?"

He hesitated, then said simply, "I almost forgot who I was."

She forced away the sting of tears, knowing he'd hate her sympathy. His smile spread wide, and he leaned forward to rub one finger over her skirt-covered knee.

"I'm teasing, of course. Can you imagine me as a viscount, with all those responsibilities, all that money to manage? I had to give Spencer some of my personality, for how else could I repay him for such a sacrifice?"

"Hence the mistresses," she said dryly. "The naked statue given to Queen Elizabeth."

He laughed. "You know about that, do you?"

She studied him, knowing that perhaps there was a deeper reason he felt the need to add his own behavior to Alex's. Hadn't he said before that no one ever recognized him? Which meant that somehow he wanted desperately to be seen for himself.

"Oh please, do not think Spencer was ever a saint," Alex continued. "He cut a swath through London that I had a hard time following. After Roselyn left him—"

"She left him?" she interrupted, intrigued.

He shook his head. "Too long a story. But suffice it to say, my brother set quite the example. And I continued it, giving him more of a personality than he deserved."

"But surely there's more to the life of a viscount than women and scandal."

"Sad to say, but yes, the drudgery did take up a good part of my day."

"What drudgery?"

"The estates, of course, the many people who depended on the Thornton name for their livelihood."

"I heard of no mass starvation from the Thornton households," she said in a teasing voice.

She knew he wanted to withhold a smile, but couldn't.

"True. I didn't quite manage to ruin everything."

"Ruin everything? I seem to recall a comment my father made a year or so ago. He was quite grudging in his praise of how well the Thornton estates were managed. And it wasn't Spencer managing them, but you."

He remained still, watching her. "And how would you know if I had employed a very capable steward?"

"I'm sure you had one, for you cannot be everywhere at once. But your conversation with Clifford about farming—it was not the talk of a man uninterested, uninvolved. I seem to recall . . ." She lifted his hand from her knee and turned it over, spreading his fingers wide. ". . . calluses." She ran her finger over the hard bumps at the base of each finger. "You did not get these from dancing."

She stared at his large hand resting in hers, afraid to look up and meet his eyes. There was such a discrepancy between what Alex truly was, and what he showed the world. Why? Why did playing his brother seem to damage him somehow? And did he lodge away from Thornton manor because he couldn't bear to watch his brother take back what had given Alex so much pride?

She was afraid if she looked into his eyes right now, she'd gladly surrender to his embrace, melt against this man she was growing to care too much for. And then it would truly be "The Seduction of Emmeline."

"We've been traveling too long," Alex finally said, his hoarse voice making her shiver.

She let go of his hand.

He turned away toward the door and threw his shoulder against it repeatedly, until she began to shudder with each painful-sounding hit.

"Alex, stop. This won't work—"

But the door suddenly flung wide, and Alex leaned out to catch it before it could bang against the side of the coach. Emmeline smothered a cry as he seemed to hang precariously out over the moving landscape.

Cold air rushed in and swirled about them. The sun had set, and the growing darkness made the retreating fog seem ever more ethereal. It hugged the hollows in the farm fields, and obscured where the road ended at their side.

Emmeline grabbed Alex's doublet and hauled him back inside.

He sat back and held the door partially closed as he glanced at Emmeline. "Thank you. We'll wait a few moments to make sure they didn't hear us."

"Wait for what? The next time they stop, we'll burst out at them and—"

"Be shot or stabbed for our effort? I don't think so. There are at least two men holding us prisoner, and you're not up to the fight. So we'll go now."

"Now?" she echoed, her voice a high-pitched squeak. "But . . . we can't even see where the ground is. We'll break our necks."

"I saw a grassy embankment. We'll be all right."

"But Alex—"

"Would you rather wait here and see what they have in mind for you?" he asked bluntly.

"But 'tis *you* they're after," she protested.

"And you'll be the added treat."

After only a brief hesitation, she leaned forward and opened the door herself. She stared transfixed at the fog-covered ground that moved past, the brisk air swirling, rushing about her. Before she could gather her courage, she felt his arms about her waist, then her feet leaving the floor, heard "What the hell," and then they were flying out into the night.

Chapter 23

$\sim\!\!\sim\!\!\sim\!\!\circlearrowright\!\circlearrowleft\!\sim\!\!\sim\!\!\sim$

Alex twisted his body in mid-air, landing beneath Emmeline on a mossy hill. The air was
knocked out of him, but he held onto her; they
fell, tumbling over and over until they came to a
sudden halt against a field of small, sharp stones,
then lay still, gasping for breath, Emmeline
sprawled across his chest. In the sudden silence
he heard the gurgling of water nearby, and a shrill
chorus of insects.

While he lay there, trying to decide if he'd bro-
ken anything, she lifted her head. In the twilight
he could see that her hair had come down, and
hung in long, curling waves about them. This was
how she would look in bed, riding him.

He groaned and tried to banish the vivid im-
ages his lust brought to mind.

"Oh Alex, are you hurt?" she whispered.

He felt her hands move almost frantically across his chest, pressing.

"If you allow me to sit up, I'll be better able to tell you."

She slid off him hastily, and he regretted not pretending a small injury. With a sigh he sat up, feeling only a twinge in his lower back. He moved his neck, bent his arms and legs, but everything seemed unbroken.

"I'm fine, Em. How do you feel?"

She sat back on her heels. "Except for the terror of finding myself flying, I have survived intact." She hesitated. "I know you broke my fall."

"Accidentally, I assure you."

"Thank you, Alex."

He waited for tears, her worries, even the possibility that she was terrified of the outdoors. Instead, her spirits seemed to be lifting as she looked about them with shining eyes.

"Where do you think we are? Do you think they heard us and are even now circling back? Should we—"

"Wait, wait," he said, getting slowly to his knees. "One question at a time—after I've had a drink."

He leaned over the shallow stream and dipped his cupped hands. He drank in the cool sweetness, amazed to find how thirsty he actually was. Out of the corner of his eye, he saw Emmeline attempting to imitate him, but her hair and the ruff at her throat kept getting in the way.

"Here, allow me to help," he said, moving behind her. His spread knees pressed into her lower legs. Carefully he untied the strings and removed her ruff, and she gave a little sigh and rolled her head about. Then he pulled her hair back and held the heavy, silky mass in both hands while she bent over the stream. He closed his eyes, but could not stop his thoughts of pulling her skirts up and thrusting inside her from behind. By the time she had satisfied her thirst, he was feverish with wanting her.

She straightened up and her back bumped into his chest. She would move soon, he knew she would. He remained frozen, enjoying the possibilities, with his hands tangled in her hair. They were alone, where no one would interrupt them.

"You were going to answer my questions," she said softly.

"Hmmm," he murmured, pressing his face into her hair and breathing deeply. It was torture—yet he waded in gladly.

"I asked if they could be coming back."

But she didn't move. He let her hair cascade down as he settled his hands on her shoulders. He marshaled his thoughts, tried to concentrate on their predicament. But all he could manage was, "I don't hear anything."

"Perhaps we should hide?" she whispered.

She seemed to sway beneath his hands and her

head tipped to the side. The length of her hair slid back to reveal her delicate neck. The darkness lulled him into oblivion, and he wanted to press his mouth to the sweet curve of her skin.

But she had recently brought his conscience back to life, and it didn't look to be abandoning him now.

"You're right," he said with a sigh, coming to sit beside her. "We'll need to find a safe place to camp, and try to start a fire."

She laughed suddenly and he glanced at her in surprise.

"Did you intend all along to steal me away?" she teased.

He saw the shine of her eyes, and his respect for her courage grew.

"Of course that was my plan. Remember 'The Seduction of Emmeline'? How perfect that my nemeses did the deed for me."

"You can't mean the seduction," she said, giggling at her own joke.

"No," he said, lowering his voice. "'Tis an honor I claim all my own."

As silence grew, Emmeline found she could not stop looking at Alex. In the growing darkness he appeared even more dangerous, with the shadow of stubble on his face, and the wicked gleam she so adored in his eyes. But there was a seriousness there as well that was unfamiliar to her.

She frightened herself, because the danger of

their situation had retreated, and only the excitement of being alone with him remained. She couldn't stop the thrill of adventure that made her shiver. She'd never been away from London alone with a man—especially not a man like Alex, with mysterious depths he was only just beginning to reveal.

In the next hour, he surprised her yet again. She watched in amazement as he cleared the brush from the base of tall hedges that blocked them from the road. He cut branches for them to sit on with a knife he kept in his boot. When she returned with kindling, he grinned and produced flint and steel from a pouch at his waist as if by magic. Soon they were sitting side by side just above the bank of the creek, with thick hedges at their backs, and a cheery fire at their feet.

Their silence was rather comforting, and Emmeline thought that Alex was the one person she'd want to be stranded with. Being alone with him had its own danger, but he made her feel safe from everything else.

Then her stomach growled loudly.

She groaned and hugged herself. "Forgive me, Alex; I can wait until tomorrow to eat. But I guess my stomach can't forget that you were going to offer me a meal worthy of kings."

From that same pouch, he removed a bulging

wallet. "Did you think I meant at the finest inn in London? I am much more original than that—and 'tis a good thing, too, for here is our evening repast."

Smiling, she watched as he shook out a napkin over the grass. On it he placed lumpy cheese, flattened bread, some rather crushed strawberries, and two apples. Their eyes met over their feast, and Emmeline experienced such a feeling of sweet contentment, of—rightness. She hoped she wasn't falling in love. But tonight, she would not think about how disastrous such a thing would be with Alex Thornton.

"Ah, sir, how you do woo me," she said, pulling off a chunk of bread.

"Such high praise." Grinning, he tossed some berries in his mouth, and licked the juice from his fingers.

Emmeline felt her smile die away, replaced by a deep longing. What was wrong with her? Why was she so foolish as to wish that she could understand Alex? He'd seemed jealous over Maxwell's friendship to her—he'd said no one could touch her but him. He would have considered it an "honor" to seduce her, as if he hadn't done such a thing to other women.

She was afraid to hope, but could not help it—could he have feelings for her that he didn't recognize? Why else would he want to spend time with her? Why else would he show only her the competent man that he truly was?

But he'd tried to be honest when he'd said he wouldn't marry. She should listen to him.

Dazedly, she put a berry in her mouth and chewed. Alex watched her as if eating food were something new and fascinating. There was a drop of strawberry juice on the corner of his lip, and she wanted to lick it with her tongue. His smile died, as if he read her mind and was willing to complete "The Seduction of Emmeline."

She was willing, too, regardless of the risk.

To distract them, she said, "Tell me more about what it's like to be a twin."

He merely blinked at her, then looked down to wrap bread about a small piece of cheese. He popped it into his mouth, and after he'd swallowed, his guarded gaze rose to meet hers.

"Where do these questions come from, Em?"

She shrugged and picked apart her bread. "When you posed as your brother the other night, you seemed so good at it. I couldn't help thinking that you had done such a thing long before Queen Elizabeth asked it of you."

He leaned back on one elbow at her side, staring into the fire. Endless minutes passed before he spoke, and she'd begun to think he wouldn't answer.

"It was natural, I guess, for Spencer and me to

play at being each other. The servants began it first, by confusing our identities so often. By the age of eight, we learned that trouble could be avoided by blaming the other brother."

"Was that not cruel?"

He shrugged. "We both thought it was funny to see who could get the other in the most trouble. As long as we did nothing bad enough to involve our parents, the servants were content to deal with us themselves."

She tried to understand. "But wouldn't the innocent brother protest with the truth?"

"And risk being unable to get his revenge the same way? No, it was too good a scheme." Alex's fond smile faded. "As we grew older, I sometimes took his place when it was necessary to display the 'heir.'"

She hesitated. "That must have been difficult."

"I hadn't thought so at first. Then it became uncomfortable, and I began to resist Spence's requests for help."

"Why was it uncomfortable?"

"I'm not sure."

He bit into his apple, and she was patient while he chewed it. When he didn't offer more, she softly said, "Sometimes I feel like I'm always behind Blythe, in the shadows, I guess."

"How ridiculous." He tossed the apple aside and propped himself higher on his hand, so that they faced one another. "If you are, 'tis only because you put yourself there."

"Did I?" she asked boldly, studying him, wanting to see that this connection between them was more than physical, that there was much they shared. "Why would I do that?"

He was watching her lips now, and she fought the urge to wet them with her tongue.

"You're trying to distract me," he said.

"From what?" Her voice was breathless as her desires cavorted madly throughout her body, making her feel hot and flustered and aching with the want of his touch.

He cocked his head to the side and reached up to cup her cheek. "I seem to remember that you still owe me a kiss."

She looked at his mouth. "Why?"

"For turning Max into a much sought-after gentleman."

She couldn't think, could barely quote his words back to him. "The terms of the wager have certainly not been met. I think you said you could turn him into the most sought-after gentleman in all of England."

His thumb rubbed across her bottom lip, parting it from the other. "But is he sought after by Blythe?"

She blinked slowly, lazily, leaning toward him. "Perhaps," she whispered, then shuddered as his finger touched her tongue.

He suddenly released her and lay back on the embankment to look up at her. "I'm waiting."

"This is hardly an appropriate time or place," she murmured, bracing herself on one arm as she leaned above him. Her hair slid over her shoulder to pool across his chest, and for a moment, she could have sworn he was stunned. He might not love her, but he desired her, and she felt powerful in the night, with the stars above her and Alex vulnerable below her.

"This is the perfect time and place," he said hoarsely. "Aren't you always saying someone might see us?"

She had no other answer than to lean even nearer, bracing her arm on the other side of his body. She saw how rapidly he breathed, how intently he watched her face. He showed a raw desire that made her feel truly a woman.

She had learned much from him, and she used her knowledge well. With her mouth mere inches from his, she paused, letting her breath touch his face while she stared into his dark eyes. There was still so much he kept hidden, so much she wanted to understand.

But she understood the power that crackled between them. It was mutual desire. She leaned even closer, and when her hair slid against his face, he gasped.

Her body answered on its own, tightening deep

inside until she wanted to press her thighs together to stop the ache.

"Alex," she whispered, then lightly touched her mouth to his.

She felt him trembling as he lay there and allowed her the lead. She kissed him gently, her lips slightly parted as they tested the smooth shape of his. When she tasted the corner of his mouth with her tongue, she felt him shudder.

In one uncontrollable moment, they both turned their heads and deepened the kiss. She gladly opened her mouth to him, rasping her tongue against his, tasting everything he was and wanting more. Nothing mattered but being as close to him as she could, giving everything up to this man who more and more meant everything to her.

Emmeline lifted her head. "It's time for poetry. Finish 'The Seduction of Emmeline.'"

"Finish . . ." he whispered, his eyes widening.

She kissed him again, more confident with each intimacy. She rested her hand on the side of his face, feeling harsh stubble and smooth skin. "I think a stanza beneath the stars would be appropriate." She moaned softly as her chest pressed to his.

His big hand cupped her head and brought their mouths together again. She found herself rolled sideways until Alex was above her. The feel of him pressing her down was more exciting than she ever could have imagined. His leg parted her thighs, and then his body slid between them. Though they were still separated by all their garments, the pressure of him in such an intimate place made her cry out and shudder beneath him. His moist kisses covered her face, her neck, and lower. He fumbled with a button on her bodice, and she heard the slight tear of the delicate fabric. It mattered not a whit to her.

But it must have to him. He suddenly stilled, his head at her breasts. Slowly, his gaze met hers.

Chapter 24

For just a moment longer, Alex allowed himself the sight of Emmeline, her eyes glittering with passion in the firelight, her hair a tumbled glory about her face. Everything in him strained to press deeper between her thighs. He wanted their clothes off, to see her nudity shine beneath the stars.

But she was innocent, a virgin, and he'd ripped her gown in his haste to have her.

"No," he said, somehow finding the strength to roll off her and into a sitting position, his hands dangling between his bent knees.

"No?" She came up on her elbows, bewildered hurt in her expression.

"You deserve better than a damp, muddy hillside, Em. I won't have this be your first memory of intimacy. You're frightened and overwhelmed, and surely only clinging to me out of desperation."

"I'm not frightened, Alex, and please don't imply that I would offer myself to any man who rescued me."

"I didn't mean—"

"Yes, you did, and I wish to know why. Why don't you think you would be the man I'd choose in *any* situation?"

"Go to sleep, Emmeline," he said tightly, not wanting to hear another word of her ridiculous notions. "Pull your cloak about you."

"If you don't wish to discuss this now, fine, but there will be another day."

He looked away, before her disheveled appearance made him forget his nobility. He lay down on his side, his back to Em, and hugged his arms against the chill. For a few minutes, all he heard was the crackling of the fire, the distant sound of crickets, and the rapid pounding of his own heart.

"I'm cold, Alex," she said matter-of-factly. "I'm going to put more wood on the fire."

"No, we can't risk our camp being seen in the distance." He sighed loudly. "Just—lean up against my back."

He heard the rustle of her garments, then felt the press of her body from her shoulder to her hip. Her shivering didn't stop.

"Alex—"

"Very well!" He rolled over and found her watching him. "Roll away from me."

"Alex—"

"Stop questioning everything I ask and just do it." He knew he sounded grumpy and rude, but wasn't about to soften, not when he knew the torture he was about to face.

And it *was* torture. He lifted the cloak, then reluctantly curled his body about hers, tucking his thighs behind hers, sliding his arm about her waist. Almost immediately her shivering lessened, and she gave a relieved sigh.

Alex closed his eyes and tried to pretend he wasn't feeling what he was feeling. Then in puzzlement he moved his hand at her waist and felt the hardness of her boned corset.

"Emmeline? How can you possibly be comfortable in this?"

"I see no other choice," she said stiffly.

"At least loosen it."

There was a pause, and he barely heard her soft voice. "I can't do it by myself."

More and more, he was regretting his noble behavior. She would have had all of her garments off by now. Mumbling angrily beneath his breath, he reached between them and began to unbutton her gown.

Though she stiffened, she said nothing, even when he loosened the laces of her corset. When the garment didn't immediately sag open, he gritted his teeth and worked the laces apart, touching the smooth skin of her back with each tug.

When he could feel at least two inches of flesh between the laces, he heard her inhale deeply and release a satisfied sigh.

"Thank you, Alex. Good night."

He almost gave her a real reason to be satisfied, but instead he pulled her rather hard against him and did his best to sleep.

It didn't go well. He felt every movement, heard every sound she made. He knew when she slipped into sleep by her deep breathing, and the way she relaxed and cuddled back into him. And all through it, his erection throbbed between them.

Night dragged on endlessly, and finally in the early morning, Alex slept a few hours. When he awoke well before dawn, Emmeline was facing him, her head pressed to his chest, her arms twined about him against the cold. For some strange reason, he imagined waking up in her arms every morning.

He told himself it would be boring, that her charms would fade for him. But he found himself kissing the top of her head just before gently shaking her awake.

She moaned and burrowed even tighter against him, nestling her warm face against his neck. He steeled himself against her softness and pushed her away. When she opened her eyes she seemed puzzled, until reality flooded back.

"Alex, come back here; it's not even light yet."

He'd heard that from more than one mistress, and he chuckled.

"What is it?" she asked suspiciously.

"Nothing. But we need to start back the way we came. Wouldn't you like to break your fast at a comfortable inn? And wouldn't you like to get there without my enemies finding us?"

Without another grumble, she stood up and the cloak dropped to the ground. She clutched at her gown as it sagged off her shoulders. Alex felt his mouth go dry even as she presented her back.

"Could you lace me up, please?"

Where was his prim Emmeline, guardian of her sister's virtue? Just last night, she had wanted to give hers away.

And he had refused. God, he was a fool.

After two hours of walking, which tore holes in Emmeline's town slippers, they reached a small but clean inn north of London. Alex made a lame excuse to the proprietor about their coach breaking down, while Emmeline tried not to look guilty.

After all, what did she have to feel guilty about? She'd been captured and had barely managed to escape.

And she'd wantonly offered herself to Alex Thornton. She was acting just like every other woman he knew.

But she hadn't been able to stop herself.

Alex secured a private room for their meal, then whispered in her ear that he was dangerously low on funds. Luckily she had enough coins in the purse at her waist.

It seemed to take forever, but soon there was hot porridge and apple cider and warm bread spread out before them. Emmeline had only taken one spoonful of porridge, when the door was suddenly thrown open and two plainly dressed men blocked the entrance.

Even as their faces struck a chord in her memory, Alex surged to his feet and stepped before her. She couldn't help leaning sideways to see.

In the sudden silence, she said, "You're the men who attacked Alex at the Rooster."

They pushed the door shut behind them, and the affronted anger in their faces was proof of the truth.

Alex said, "You obviously know who I am, but I am at a loss as to why you've been pursuing me."

It seemed almost comic when the taller kidnapper pulled the hat from his head as he said, "I'm Kenneth Langston, and this is my brother Harold. Do you recognize our name, Thornton? Because you've dishonored it."

"Then I don't owe you money?"

The younger brother spat on the floor at Alex's feet, while Kenneth said, "Money will not solve your problem. Our family's honor is at risk, and we won't allow that."

"Enough with the riddles and the stalking," Alex said. "Just tell me what I've supposedly done."

"You have dishonored our innocent sister, and now you're going to marry her."

Nausea swept through Emmeline, and she gripped the edge of the table until slivers pricked her fingers. She desperately wanted him to deny it.

Instead, he asked, "What is your sister's name?"

"Elizabeth."

"Common enough," he said with a shake of his head. "Gentlemen, since her face does not come to mind, I won't know the truth until I see her."

Emmeline closed her eyes as disappointment suffused her. She'd thought his mistresses were willing and experienced. Surely he did not regularly seek to ruin maidens.

Or had she imagined she was the only one, somehow special to him?

She didn't know what to believe anymore, only that she'd thought she could be the one to change him. Instead there was another girl out there who must have thought the same thing.

The two brothers stepped forward menacingly. "You're coming to Lincolnshire with us, to face our family and the law—and then our pastor."

"I think not," Alex said lightly. "I'll meet the girl in London."

"You've already met," said Harold as his hand settled on the hilt of his sword.

"I'm not convinced of that."

Alex widened his stance, blocking her from them. Then she heard the door slam open. She peered beneath Alex's bent arm and saw Edmund Blackwell filling almost every bit of the doorframe.

"Alex, you couldn't share a meal with the common folk, now could—" He broke off when he saw their visitors.

"Your sword!" Alex shouted.

Emmeline was suddenly pushed into the corner. She turned to see Alex pull the knife from his boot as the Langston brothers drew their swords with a sharp scrape of metal on metal. The four men came together, then fell through the door and into the main taproom of the inn.

With a cheer, four other patrons joined the fight that degenerated into a brawl. Emmeline stood in the doorway and clutched the frame, trying to keep Alex in her sight. When he finally came up for air, she heaved a sigh.

Puzzled, he looked about him. "Edmund, where did the Langston brothers go?"

Edmund shook two men off him and stood up. "I don't know."

Somehow, in the confusion of the crowd, the Langstons had fled.

* * *

Only after Edmund had handed over a sub-stantial amount of money were they allowed to retire once more to their private dining chamber. Emmeline stared down at her food, but didn't feel hungry anymore.

"What are you doing here?" Alex asked, hand-ing Edmund a tankard of cider. "I've wondered where you were—you've been gone almost a month."

"Did you even send a missive tracking me down?" Edmund asked darkly.

"Well . . . I've been distracted."

Both men turned to look at her, and she glared at them.

Edmund drained half his tankard, then rubbed his forehead. He looked tired for such a short fight.

"I did successfully journey to Cumberland," he began slowly. "In fact, I just paid the innkeeper with your money."

"So I assumed," Alex said as he accepted a heavy pouch from his friend. "My thanks for this."

He reached into the pouch, then laid a few coins on the table before Emmeline.

She stared from the coins to him in outrage. "What is this for?"

"You paid for the meal," he answered, giving her a befuddled look before he turned back to his friend. "Edmund, what have you been doing all this time?"

Emmeline hugged herself and stared at the two men without caring what they said. Alex kept glancing at her, his face impassive, but she knew him well enough now to see the worry.

Edmund looked down. "I took my time, I'll admit. And then when I returned to London, Elizabeth would no longer see me."

Elizabeth? Emmeline thought.

"Those men were the Langston brothers," Edmund continued. "I recently started following them, though I did not connect them to you. Did they admit that they're the ones who've been hounding you?"

"Yes."

"Did they tell you why?"

"They said I'd seduced their sister Elizabeth, and that they were going to make me marry her." He hesitated. "I knew immediately that they meant *your* Elizabeth, but I didn't admit it. I would never implicate you."

Emmeline gaped at him, realizing how easily he'd lied to the Langstons.

"Don't you see, Alex, this wager has gone too far!" Edmund said.

There was a horrible silence as she fought to understand their words. *Wager?*

"Edmund—" Alex began.

"They mistook you for me," Edmund said heavily. He gave Emmeline an apologetic glance. "Forgive me for saying such crude things in front of you, Lady Emmeline, but you deserve to know what kind of man I am." He glanced back at Alex. "I let it go too far. What was supposed to be a kiss ended in . . . seduction. What I don't understand is why they think you're me. If Elizabeth told them this much, why didn't she explain it all?"

Emmeline slumped down heavily in the chair, trying to work through her confusion. Shouldn't she be relieved that the culprit wasn't Alex? But how could she feel better, when he practically admitted it could have been him? And what was this wager that played with women's lives?

"I'll insist that Elizabeth talk to me," Edmund was saying. "She shouldn't bear any dishonor for my actions."

"Are you ready to marry her?" Alex asked.

"If that is what she wants."

Alex nodded, then turned to look at Emmeline intently. She returned his stare with a coolness that surprised her.

"Edmund, would you mind waiting out in the taproom? Em and I need to talk."

Edmund bowed toward her but didn't quite meet her eyes. Alex closed the door behind him and leaned back against it, watching her.

When she didn't speak, he said, "I don't supposed you're relieved to know it wasn't I who compromised the girl?"

She slowly stood up. "But it could have been, couldn't it?"

"I don't make it a habit to seduce maidens."

"Then what is this wager?"

Was Alex actually blushing?

With a grim voice, he said, "Edmund and I had grown rather bored. A scandal was expected of me—hell, I expected it of myself—so we proposed a private wager. We each picked out the target for the other."

"Target?" she whispered, feeling her throat squeeze tightly around the word.

"It was only a kiss," he insisted. "We bet on who could be the first to kiss a maiden. For him I picked out Lady Elizabeth, and for me he chose . . ."

His words died away and Emmeline finished for him. "Blythe."

He nodded slowly. "Yes."

A fury like she'd never experienced began to bubble in her veins. "You deliberately toyed with my sister's affections, all for a kiss."

"I only did what any other man there was trying to do, and that was to get to know her."

"For a selfish purpose!" she shot back, advancing on him. "She is looking for a man to spend her life with, and you were someone she considered, because she was flattered by your attentions. But all you wanted was a kiss! Or was it more?"

"Em—"

"Edmund did not stop with a kiss, so surely you, the great master of scoundrels, would not have stopped there, either."

"I promise you, I was not interested in her like that. I don't need to compromise young girls when there are so many women who *want* to be compromised!"

Emmeline, feeling her face drain of blood, swayed with dizziness. "You mean women like me," she whispered, her wide eyes fixed on him.

Chapter 25

❧ ❧

Alex's face paled. "I didn't mean you, Emme-line. You must believe me."

"Sweet God, how you must be laughing at me."

"Em—"

He tried to take her hand, but she backed away from him.

"I even offered myself to you! You hardly needed to *try* to compromise me."

"You weren't part of the wager," he said, stepping toward her. "In fact, you stood in the way of it. And I was intrigued, damn it."

"Then why didn't you change the wager to me?"

His silence was her answer.

"You wanted to, didn't you?" she said, forcing a laugh even as everything in her seemed to die. "I was much easier than my sister."

"If that's all it was, I could have ended the wager long ago. I had already kissed your sister, but I didn't tell Edmund."

"Then it must be because you wanted to finish what you started."

"No, because I wanted to be with you!"

She covered her mouth with her hand, feeling tears well in her eyes and fall down her cheeks. "Don't! Don't lie to make this easier on yourself."

Alex took hold of her shoulders and pulled her closer. "I am not lying."

She looked up into the face of a man who could seduce women as a game. Just when she saw a better side of him, he revealed a new low. Everything everyone said about him was true, and she had foolishly thought only she understood him. But he'd been using her and her sister as an amusing diversion.

In trying to protect her sister from hurt, she had opened herself up to despair and humiliation. She couldn't look at him anymore.

"Let me go," she whispered.

For a moment she almost wished he'd disobey her, so she could slap him. But he released her.

"Where are you going?" he asked.

"Edmund can escort me home." She couldn't look back at him. "I don't ever want to see you again."

The door slammed shut and Alex flinched. In his mind he saw Emmeline's face again—her shock and disappointment turning into horror—and he felt sick inside.

How had a foolish game ended up causing so much harm? Why had he not seen what the repercussions would be?

Because he was a selfish fool, who thought only of his own pleasure. He had never imagined the desperation of needing to explain himself. He had wanted Emmeline's understanding—only to find that it was too late.

He told himself it was better this way. What did he think would come of this, after all? Now he could pay off his debts, go back to his mistress, and live the life he was good at.

Then why did the coming days seem so bleak, so—lonely? How had he come to depend on Emmeline's presence?

A sennight passed, and Emmeline began to breathe easier. Her father and the servants kept quiet about her adventure with Alex, and her reputation remained intact. Blythe didn't need her anymore; she had more suitors than ever, and Maxwell was a frequent visitor. Emmeline tried to make her life as it used to be, even attending meetings at Whitehall.

But every night she sobbed alone in her room until her chest ached. Surely she could cry away the emptiness she felt. How could she miss Alex so desperately, after he'd made a fool of her?

Eight days had passed since she'd last seen him, and that night she sat alone in her chamber, looking out the window over the gardens toward the Thames. Her throat was raw from crying. In the distance she could see the wherries ferrying passengers by lantern light.

She heard a knock at the door and ignored it, so whoever it was would think she was asleep. But the door creaked open.

"Emmy?"

She quickly wiped the tears from her face and donned a stiff smile before facing Blythe. "Why dearest, you should be in bed. 'Tis late."

Blythe held a candle that illuminated her concern. "You've said more than once that you don't want to talk, but I just can't pass by your chamber and hear you crying and do nothing. Emmy, please, talk to me!"

Emmeline shook her head as she stood up. "There's nothing to say. I've made a fool of myself and I just need to recover from it. 'Tis anger causing these tears."

"I don't believe you," Blythe said softly, coming forward to take Emmeline's hand. "You miss him."

She bit her lip, surprised that she even had tears left to flood her eyes. "I refuse to miss him. He is not worthy of that."

"You don't mean that. I agree that the wager was an inconsiderate thing to do, but I was not hurt by it."

But I was, Emmeline thought. She hadn't told her sister everything, how Alex had tried to seduce her, and how she'd nearly given in. She would never be able to put her humiliation into words.

"You're too close to see it clearly," Blythe continued. "Alex wanted to be with *you*, not me. Everything he did was meant to give you a reason to see him. You cannot fault him for that."

"You don't understand men like him," Emmeline said. "There was only one reason he wanted to be near me."

"I don't believe that. It's been months, Emmy. He could have found what you're implying quite easily, with any of his old mistresses. But he didn't."

"How could you know such a thing?" she demanded, aghast that she was having such a conversation with her innocent sister.

"I asked Maxwell to find out for me."

"What!"

"I privately told him that I thought Alex was interested in you, and he agreed. Then he went off to speak to Alex's acquaintances. Believe me, Maxwell can be very circumspect. He said that Alex has not acted like himself for many months. The places he used to frequent, well, he just has not had time to visit them. He's been too busy—with you."

Emmeline opened her mouth, but could think

of nothing to say. Could Blythe be right? Yet it was so painful to hope.

"Dearest, I will think about what you said." Emmeline squeezed the girl's hand and let go, attempting a smile. "I don't know if I can get used to you being so grown up and wise."

Blythe kissed her cheek and walked to the door. "If I am so, then it is all because of you, Emmy. Sleep well."

Early the next day, Emmeline's maid handed her a missive from Alex's mother. She stared at the parchment in surprise, then felt foreboding when she was told the coachman was waiting for an answer. She hadn't known that Lady Thornton had returned from Wight. The last letter she'd received from the countess had mentioned no travel plans. What could she have to say—unless something had happened to Alex?

She quickly broke open the wax seal and read the letter. It was not Alex who was in trouble—it was his brother, Spencer. The viscount had escorted his mother back to London after her visit with her grandson, and last evening he had disappeared, leaving his horse to return home without him. Lady Thornton said Alex suspected the Langston brothers again, and she thought Emmeline would want to know.

Emmeline felt not a moment of doubt about what she would do.

She was going to Alex.

She ran up to her chamber to dress. In the flurry of activity she felt strangely removed, even amazed. What else could her certainty mean, except that she must be in love with him?

She had always thought that love would come to her like shooting stars, or the greatest orchestration of music. Instead, during the mundane task of fastening her cloak, she knew with a certainty that being with Alex was all that mattered, that she loved him. All she could think about was the Alex who had dreamed of modernization instead of dissipation when he'd played the viscount, the Alex who felt he always came in second in his family. Later, she would deal with discovering whether he loved her in return.

Emmeline barely remembered the coach ride to Thornton Manor. She jumped out before the coach had quite stopped and raced up the steps in the rain, flinging open the door instead of knocking. A surprised servant fell back, and Emmeline barreled past him, saying, "Where is Sir Alexander?"

"In the withdrawing chamber, my lady," the servant answered. "May I take your—"

But she pushed open the door and came to a stop at the threshold. Lady Thornton, at the window, but gave her a welcoming smile. Alex and Edmund were hunched over a paper-strewn desk. Neither saw her.

"Damn, but you should have tried to get to Elizabeth sooner," Alex was saying.

"I visited every day, but she refused to see me!" Edmund protested.

"You could have climbed into her chamber at night."

"And make her think that I didn't want to marry her honorably by the light of day? But why take Spencer?"

"Because they think he's me! Haven't they proven their stupidity over and over again? Just let me explain my plan."

Emmeline sank into a chair beside the door and simply watched Alex. He looked tired, with dark circles beneath his eyes, as if he'd spent the week as sleepless as she had. Yet his voice was cool and precise as he explained his plan to invade the Langston household with a score of men. He showed no desperation, only the confidence of an intelligent man who knew without a doubt that he would succeed at whatever he did.

Emmeline could only watch, feeling the enormity of her love for him swell in her chest. The jokes he reserved for when things were too emotionally confusing were gone—he was serious and focused. Would it always be like this? Would she always find a new, deeper Alex to love?

As she contemplated her feelings, a man who looked just like Alex walked into the withdrawing room. As she looked up, he smiled down at her and took off his rain-spattered cloak.

It was Spencer, alive and unharmed!

He held a finger to his lips, a devilish glint in his eye reminiscent of Alex. She could only gape as relief made her sag back in the chair. He casually strolled toward the two men still pondering their plans at the desk. With his hands behind his back, he studied them.

Alex was talking to Edmund. "I'll go in the main door, so they'll be confused. After all, they think they have me. I want you to enter through the back, and try to keep hidden until you see that I need you."

Spencer cleared his throat. "And what would you like me to do?"

"You go around to the—" Alex broke off and swiftly straightened. "Spence!"

Lady Thornton let out a glad cry and rushed to hug her son. Emmeline saw the deep relief Alex quickly covered, and the easygoing grin that replaced it. Before her eyes he turned back into scandalous Alex Thornton.

He clasped Spencer's hand. "Well, I'm glad I don't have to exert myself. It's been so long, I was certain I'd forgotten how to use a sword."

Lady Thornton dabbed at her eyes, even as she kept Spencer's arm about her shoulders. "Tell us how you escaped, my son."

"'Tis hardly a tale worth telling," Spencer answered, as he accepted a goblet of wine from Edmund. "Of course they wouldn't believe me when I said I wasn't you. They were inept and didn't think to post a guard after they'd tied me up and left me in a room. It was rather easy to get away after that."

As the three men congratulated each other, Lady Thornton called out, "Lady Emmeline! Please come join us."

Emmeline rose to her feet as the men turned to stare at her. Alex's black eyes seemed to light from within for a moment, then his smile faded.

"Lady Emmeline," he said, nodding too courteously to her. "Forgive me for not greeting you earlier."

"I did not want to disturb you," she said, coming forward. "But now you could introduce me to your brother."

He seemed to blink at her in surprise, then did as she asked. "Spence, this is Lady Emmeline Prescott. Lady Emmeline, my brother, Lord Thornton."

"My lord," she said, curtsying, all the while keeping her gaze locked with Alex's. "I'm glad to see you have returned safely home."

"How did you know about the kidnapping?" Alex asked.

"Lady Thornton sent me a missive."

He glanced sharply at his mother, who merely smiled innocently at him and said, "Now that she's here, she can enjoy a celebratory dinner with us. Would you stay, Lady Emmeline?"

Alex said, "I'm sure she won't want—"

"I would enjoy that," Emmeline interrupted.

He studied her as she allowed Spencer to lead her into the dining chamber. Let him think what he would. She didn't know what she meant to do about Alex Thornton yet, but she was not about to let him go easily.

Chapter 26

After a pleasant reunion meal, where Alex stared at her so much she had trouble remembering how to eat, Emmeline accepted his offer to escort her home. Lady Thornton approached her, and to Emmeline's amazement, kissed both of her cheeks and whispered, "Courage, dear one."

Soon Emmeline and Alex were alone in the coach, leaving the Thornton estate for the busy streets of London. She said nothing, but just allowed Alex to sit at her side in silence, listening to the soft patter of rain on the roof. She had no plan—she could hardly blurt out her love for him, knowing that he would reject any such sentiment.

"I still don't know why you came," he finally said. "You said you never wanted to see me again."

"I changed my mind."

"I can't change what I did, or explain it in better terms."

"I don't expect you to."

"Then what *do* you want of me?"

Your love, she thought desperately, knowing it wasn't what he wanted to hear. But all she said was, "Maybe I came because I thought you might need me."

He smiled. "According to you, I needed you for only one thing."

"I'm reconsidering that."

He stretched his long legs out in the casual, uncaring sprawl he was so good at. "Why?"

"I had thought that you might need some support while your brother was missing." Hesitantly, she laid her hand on top of his. "It must have brought up all the worries you felt when he was gone so long helping the government."

He pulled away. "Worries? What worries did I have, Emmeline? I had all my brother's wealth and all his power. Maybe I didn't even want him to return."

"You don't truly mean that."

"Don't I? Don't you think there were moments when I was only him, not myself? I looked in a mirror and saw him. I looked at his friends, and to them I was him." He paused. "Maybe some part of me didn't want to give that up."

His sudden despair made her ache for him.

Without looking at her, he said hoarsely, "I'm

afraid there was some part of me that didn't want Spencer to return. Maybe I only needed to rescue him today out of guilt, or some old loyalty that became meaningless long ago. When he was gone so long, I never even looked into where he was!"

"You couldn't, not without risking his life."

"You don't know that—*I* don't know that. Maybe I *wanted* him to be dead."

Emmeline rose up on her knees on the bench and leaned against his chest, framing his face in her hands. "Don't do this to yourself. You may have envied your brother, but you wouldn't wish him dead. I *know* you."

"You *don't* know me, Em."

She kissed him hard on the mouth, putting all her love there in hopes that he'd recognize it for what it was. "I want to know everything about you, good and bad. I want you to let me in."

She kissed him again, softly, gently, and moaned when his hand cupped her head.

"Em—"

"No, don't talk." She reached behind him and unrolled the curtain, then did the same on the other side, muting the light in the coach. When she came back to him he was watching her, the despair receding from his face and passion taking its place. She didn't want him thinking, only feeling, and maybe that was really the way to communicate her love to him.

Staring into his eyes, she spread his doublet

wide and let her hands run down his chest, her thumbs brushing over his nipples as he'd done to her. He shuddered and whispered her name.

Oh, this was heady, this sensation of knowing she could affect him the way he'd affected her. She pushed him lower onto the bench, then straddled him, pushing her skirts to the sides. Pulling him toward her chest, she removed his doublet, then remained still as he spread kisses down her neck and against her gown. He quickly unbuttoned her bodice even as she unbuttoned his shirt. He held her upright and she sat directly on his lap, with only his loose breeches separating them. Instinctively she wanted to rub against the hard ridge of him there.

He suddenly froze, his dark, wicked eyes staring at her breasts covered only by her thin smock. "No corset?"

She shook her head. "When I received your mother's letter, I had no time to dress properly."

"My lucky day," he murmured, as he pooled the gown at her waist.

She slid his shirt over his head. The broad expanse of his chest was fascinating, and she trailed her fingers through the scattering of hair about his nipples.

Alex slowly pulled her smock down and her breasts were revealed in the dim light. The rumbling of the carriage over rutted streets made them bounce, and she wanted to cover them. But he groaned and buried his face between them, his arms around her body as he held her tightly.

"Em, you're so beautiful," he whispered in a husky voice.

For the first time, she truly believed him. He held her breasts with both hands, looking at each as if he didn't know which to choose. She savored the rough skin of his palms and the admiration in his eyes. As he bent his head and leaned her back in his lap, he locked his gaze to hers and they stared at one another as he opened his mouth to her breast. She knew his touch would feel wondrous, but the searing pleasure that rocked through her as he drew her nipple into his mouth made her cry out and convulse against him. He pressed his erection hard between her legs, sucking on her nipple. When she didn't think she could take such wild pleasure for another moment, he moved to her other breast, this time licking gently as if she were a sweet he'd not treated himself to in a long time. She clutched his shoulders and held on as he ran his hands down her back and beneath her skirts. She groaned and pressed herself even harder against him.

The touch of his hands on her bare buttocks was a wicked shock. He squeezed her, rubbing her hips against his. She was lost in what he did to her, in the rise of hot desire that had her yearning for what only he could give her. What was this terrible need that raced through her body, centering between her thighs?

Suddenly she found herself rolled over on her back on the seat. Looking into her eyes, he seemed to flinch.

"What is it?" she whispered.

"I'm getting wet," he said with a lazy grin. "There's a leak in the roof."

He leaned aside, and a few raindrops splattered across her breasts. She caught her breath at the cool sensation, then almost choked when he bent and licked each drop off, following the winding path of water between her breasts and even to the very peaks. For an endless moment, he suckled one nipple and caressed the other with knowing fingers, until she was squirming beneath him.

"I need to see you," he said, sliding her out of the rain. He knelt down on the coach floor between her thighs.

Her face hot, she whispered, "Really? Are you certain?"

He gave a deep laugh, even as he rolled her skirts up and bunched them with her bodice. She was naked to him above the waist and below, and she tried to clutch her thighs together, but he stopped her.

"No, love, let me look upon your beauty. How wondrous you look with your hair tumbling about your breasts and that flush on your cheeks." He sat back on his heels, running his palms in slow circles up her inner thighs then spreading her legs wider.

She couldn't stop shaking with the incredible sensations he evoked, even as she covered her face in embarrassment. But she peeked between her fingers as he bent his head. She felt the gentle kiss he placed between her thighs like bolt of lightning. Her hips lifted off the bench in a spasm as she cried out his name.

She should beg him to stop, but she was mindless with the rising surge of pleasure that rocked through her. She felt his hot breath a moment before his tongue swept over her, parting her.

"I knew you'd taste like the sweetest wine," he said hoarsely, even as his fingers spread her wider.

She couldn't speak, couldn't think as he bent his head and licked her again. He suckled the most sensitive nub of flesh into his mouth, and the pleasure roared through her in waves that buffeted her body and shuddered across her skin in a final release unlike anything she'd imagined. She was mindless and aware at the same time. Even as she sagged in his arms, she thought, *This is what brings women and men together. This is why women risk everything for love.* And she would, too.

Moments later, the coach slowed and they heard the coachman call out to the gatekeeper.

"Oh, sweet heaven," she whispered, sitting upright on the bench. "We're home."

Alex groaned and laughed at the same time, dropping his head to her shoulder for a moment. "Ah, how I wanted to join you in such bliss."

"I—"

"No, you mustn't worry, love. Here, let's get you assembled."

Together they tugged up her smock and gown, and pulled her skirts down about her legs. She buttoned her bodice while watching him slide his shirt over his head and tuck it back in his breeches. He looked down at himself, then back up at her with a grin.

"What?" she asked in confusion as she did her best to pin up her hair.

"You've made me damp in a rather inconvenient place."

She didn't understand until he tied up one of the curtains and she saw the wet stain across his breeches. She gasped. "That's from . . . me? From when I . . ."

He kissed her quickly. "That's your body preparing for me—and nothing could excite me more."

"But you didn't—we didn't—"

He slipped on his doublet and collapsed beside her. "Believe me, I know. But I didn't want your first time to be in a leaky coach."

She stared at him, wishing she could ask what

this all meant to him, hoping he knew what it meant to her.

When the coachman threw open the door and helped her down, she looked back up at him.

"I can't come out," he said with regret in his voice.

"I know." She blinked the rain out of her eyes and asked, "Will you come to visit me?"

He grinned. "Nothing could keep me away."

The coachman closed the door, then climbed up above to take up the reins. As they headed back for the gate, Emmeline linked her hands behind her back and went around the mansion, avoiding the front entrance. Her legs felt wobbly and she was getting wet—but she needed to think.

Heading down the sloping gravel path toward the Thames, she breathed deeply of the spring flowers and tried to plan what to do next. She couldn't keep giving in to Alex, or "The Seduction of Emmeline" would turn into "The Ruination of Emmeline." How could she convince him they belonged together, that he'd be happy married to her?

She felt a hand on her arm and she turned, expecting her sister. Instead she looked up into the faces of the Langston brothers. Stunned, she opened her mouth to scream, and they stuffed a gag in instead.

After Alex had changed, he and Edmund rode their horses to Langston House to confront Lady

Elizabeth and her brothers once and for all. A maidservant graciously showed them into the great hall, with its old black-beamed ceiling and stone walls. When the girl reappeared, her plump face had taken on a decidedly hesitant demeanor.

"My lady is not feeling well, my lords. She requests that you visit another day."

"That won't do," Edmund said, walking toward the door the girl had just come from.

Alex stayed at his side, brushing off the maid's distress. "We won't harm your mistress, girl, we just need to speak with her."

A woman was trying to escape out the glass doors into the garden when they entered the room.

"Elizabeth!" Edmund called, running to catch her arm and haul her back inside.

"Let me go!"

Her pink cheeks were flushed, and blond tendrils of hair framed her lovely face. Alex could see why Edmund had allowed himself to be swept away.

"All we need you to do is answer our questions," Edmund said gruffly. "I know I've wronged you—and I promise to make it right—but that is no reason to send your brothers after my friend. And only you could have told them such a thing. Why did you do it?"

She pulled away from him and stood with her head held high. "I had no choice!" she said coldly.

"I had already dishonored myself. The only way I could atone to my family was by offering them a husband more suitable to them."

Edmund's face reddened. "I was good enough to pleasure you, but not to marry?"

She whirled to face him. "That is a crude thing to say!"

"But 'tis the truth, isn't it?"

Alex stepped between them. "You both have much to discuss, but right now we need to tell your brothers the truth. Where are they?"

Lady Elizabeth stiffened. "I don't know."

"You're lying," Alex said flatly, advancing on her. She backed up step by step. "I have done nothing to you, but you've made sure your brothers stalked me, robbed me, and kidnapped me. Last night they took my brother in my place. I will have this done, my lady, and it won't be in marriage to you! Tell me where they are!" he shouted.

She looked away. "I don't know what they mean to do. All I heard them say was that they planned to hurt you in any way that they could until you agreed to marry me."

"In any way that they . . ." Alex's words faded as a chill of foreboding seeped through him. There was only one real way to hurt him now. *Hellfire.* "Edmund, they're after Emmeline." He grabbed the stunned girl by the shoulders. "Where have they taken her?"

"I don't know what you're talking about!" she cried, her wide eyes frightened.

Edmund gripped him from behind. "I believe her, Alex. Let her go and listen to me."

Alex was stunned by the blind rage that had seized him. But he released her and she ran out of the room.

"I just left her at Kent Hall," he said slowly. "I didn't even see her to the door. All I could think about was my problems with Spencer."

"Before we jump to conclusions, let's see if she's at home."

Thankfully, Kent Hall was nearby and Alex's galloping horse covered the distance in only minutes. But his fears were confirmed when a servant told him that Emmeline had not returned from her morning visit to see him.

Frantic now, he ran behind the house into the gardens, calling her name. No one answered, and a chilling bleakness overcame him.

Edmund caught up with him. "Alex, she's not here. We must think about where they would take her."

"Edmund, what if they—"

"I don't think they'd hurt Emmeline. They just want our attention. I'm assuming they wouldn't take her to your brother's home, nor to Langston House and risk tainting their sister with another scandal. Where, then, could they have gone?"

Alex had never felt so irrational. He wanted

only to pound their faces into a bloody mess. But he forced himself to consider what the Langston brothers' purpose could be. "Well, if they want to hurt me, they'll want me to know about it. So where could they wait, knowing I'd come?"

At the same moment, they both said, "The Rooster."

Chapter 27

Running up the rickety stairs to his lodgings over the Rooster, Alex was afraid to imagine what he'd see. Out of breath, he flung open the door to find the Langston brothers pacing, and Emmeline gagged and tied to a chair before the hearth. The great fools, they hadn't even been watching for him. The brothers fell back to guard her, their swords up.

Alex brought his pistol up and aimed.

Kenneth, the older brother, stared aghast at the weapon. "You have no honor!"

"Honor!" Alex said, knowing Edmund entered behind him. "What honor is there in kidnapping an innocent woman?"

"What honor is there in hurting our sister?"

Edmund stepped to his side. "He didn't do it. She's been lying to you, so she could make a wealthy marriage. We just spoke with her."

The two men exchanged glances, as if they knew what their sister might be capable of but hadn't thought it through.

"We don't believe you!" said the younger brother wildly. "You deserve to suffer as you've made *her* suffer."

"Harold—" began Kenneth.

"No! They're lying! We tried to take away his reputation, his money, to humble him as he's humbled our sister. Well, it's time for you to suffer, Thornton! If this girl means so much to you, then you can watch her be humiliated. We're going to compromise her!"

Alex gave an obvious glance at his gun. "I seem to have the power to stop you."

"Cease this foolishness!" Edmund commanded. "You will listen to me. It wasn't Alex who compromised your sister, but me. I'm here, ready to marry her or whatever she'd like, but you will let my friends go free while we discuss this like gentlemen."

"I still want to shoot one of them," Alex said darkly.

"If they don't put down their swords, you can."

But the Langston brothers weren't quite that foolish. They let Edmund take their swords and lead them out of the room. Kenneth looked abashed, and Harold was sulky. Alex dropped to his knees to remove Emmeline's gag before starting on the ropes.

She moistened her lips before speaking. "So is it all finally settled?"

"We spoke to Lady Elizabeth and got her to admit the truth. Frankly, Edmund should refuse to marry her, after the lies *she's* told."

When he had her hands free, he rubbed them gently. "Are you all right? Did they hurt you?"

She shook her head and smiled. "I am fine. Your deeds were quite heroic this day. Maybe you should write a poem about it."

"'The Rescue of Emmeline'?" he asked, feeling a strange warmth flow through him as he watched her sweet face.

This wasn't just relief; he was feeling something else, something that made him want to remain at her side always. She had become more important to him than his own life. He had spent years protecting himself against this kind of pain, yet somehow she had slipped past his wall of defenses.

Men like the Marquess of Kent didn't give their daughters to scandalous younger brothers. And he'd already seen how dutiful Emmeline was to her family. He wouldn't set himself up for disappointment—nor did he want her to once again feel the pain of her father's disapproval.

He kissed Emmeline's forehead before helping

her to her feet. She smiled up at him, and he had to turn away.

Emmeline felt her chest constrict. Alex couldn't even meet her eyes. He was doing it again, retreating from her and the emotions she inspired in him. Soon he'd be joking as if nothing had happened. But the look on his face when she'd been in danger—he *had* to be in love with her!

As he led her down the back stairs to his horse outside, she just kept looking at him with all the love she felt shining from her eyes. He mounted his horse, then lifted her up to ride across his lap, never looking into her face.

She leaned back against his chest and let the afternoon sun bathe them in warmth. He and she were so alike in many ways, both resigning themselves to life without happiness, as if there were a limited supply.

But no more. She deserved a good life, a good marriage, and she'd find that only with Alex. She had to discover the courage to make it happen, especially knowing she had to face her father. Once again, he would try to tell her a man wasn't good enough for her.

But this time she was truly in love, and she would fight for her happiness.

That evening, Emmeline stood outside her father's private withdrawing room and tried to steady her breathing. She knocked on the door and pushed it open when he bade her to enter.

"Father?"

He sat behind his massive desk, parchment and account books spread out before him. When he saw that it was her, he only harrumphed and looked back down.

"I am busy, Emmeline. Can we discuss whatever it is in the morning?"

"This is important, Father—it can't wait."

Though she seated herself on a bench before his desk, her father didn't look up.

"Then speak your mind, girl, but be to the point."

"Very well, then," she said, straightening her back with defiance. She took a deep breath. "I am in love with Sir Alexander Thornton, and I wish to marry him."

Her father didn't move, and the room was so quiet she could hear the last embers crackling in the hearth.

"Did you hear me, Father? I am in love with—"

"I heard you." He gave her a piercing stare she couldn't read, and sat back with his hands linked across his stomach. "You've done it again, Emmeline. You've chosen a man who is not possibly suited to your station."

"I disagree. His brother is a viscount, his father was well respected. Sir Alexander has estates in the north to keep us in sufficient wealth."

"You are the daughter of a marquess," he said, his voice only slightly louder. "You could marry a duke!"

"But a duke doesn't want me, and a knight does."

"Then why isn't he here begging for your hand?"

"Because he doesn't think you'd accept him," she said, hoping she wasn't lying.

"Then he was right; I won't." He gave her a patronizing smile, as if everything would be fine just because he'd said so. "Now, put aside this foolishness, Emmeline. There will be other men."

"For Blythe, perhaps, Father, but not for me," she said, her desperation rising. "I am in love with Alex, and I want to marry him."

"I forbid it."

Without thinking her words through, she said, "I might be carrying his child."

Her father slammed his fists on his desk as he vaulted to his feet. "He attacked you!"

Emmeline stood as well, facing him with her chin high. "He did not attack me! I love him! Now, do you want a scandal that will shake all of England, or will you quietly allow me to marry him?"

He wiped a hand down his face. "Emmeline, how could you risk such a thing? We have a good life here. You take care of your sister—surely you love her. And you practically have your own households to manage."

"They're *your* households," she answered, a sick suspicion permeating her mind. Perhaps he had deliberately kept her with him so he wouldn't have to take care of Blythe. Did she run his households so well that he only used her as a glorified steward? Had he *deliberately* given only Blythe's suitors encouragement?

"How could you do this, Emmeline?" he asked, his voice still cajoling. "I have given you a man's education; I have given you every freedom you could want."

"Except the freedom to marry, to choose my own husband," she said coldly.

"But how will we manage without you? You are the very image of your mother, and it does me such good to look upon you."

The image of her mother?

All her guilt vanished as if it had never existed, replaced by pity for her father and her own stupidity. In a sad way, she was grateful he had stopped her from marrying Clifford Roswald, but he wouldn't succeed this time. She saw now that her father's manipulations, his subtle implications that she would never make a desirable wife, were all a selfish means to keep her with him as a servant. And she had responded by living through her sister—but no more . . . it was time to make her own dreams come true.

"Father, if you refuse to give me your blessing to marry—and I don't need your permission—I will bring a scandal down upon this family such as you've never seen."

"You would do that to your sister?" he asked in a cold voice.

"My sister wants me to be happy, and she approves of Alex."

"Then you give me no choice. Has he asked you to marry him?"

"Not yet."

"Then he will be made to. I will demand an audience at Thornton Manor first thing in the morning. Thornton will marry you immediately."

Emmeline saw all her plans coming to fruition, even as her relationship with her father died of disillusionment. His disappointment was obviously so great he could hardly look at her.

But it was only Alex that concerned her. She was forcing him into something he had not said he wanted—and she could only pray she was doing the right thing.

By dawn, Emmeline's doubts had escalated into full-blown fears. What if Alex refused to marry her?

She just wished that Blythe were home to discuss it. Emmeline had returned from her "adventure" with the Langstons yesterday, only to find a note from her sister that she'd gone to their country home to visit a friend who needed her.

So Emmeline rode in the coach beside her father to Thornton Manor, while the sun was still low in the sky. He didn't speak to her, and she had nothing to say to him.

Once at the manor, her father pounded on the door until a wide-eyed maidservant opened it.

"I am the Marquess of Kent, and I demand an audience with the viscount!"

Emmeline wanted to groan. As the maidservant scurried away, she whispered, "Father, can't we just quietly talk to Alex? There is no need for his whole family to know like this!"

"Are you protecting that scoundrel even now?" he demanded.

Another voice said, "That scoundrel is my brother."

Spencer Thornton descended the wide marble staircase with his mother at his side. Lady Thornton smiled encouragingly at Emmeline, who could only hope the lady would forgive her.

Her father nodded in Spencer's direction. "Lord Thornton, we have much to discuss about the disgraceful conduct of your brother."

"Then perhaps he should be here to answer your charges. Mother?" he asked, turning aside.

Lady Thornton nodded. "I have already sent for him."

"Still abed, I see," said the marquess with a sneer in his voice.

Can this get any worse? Emmeline thought as they all left the hall.

Alex came down the stairs, shrugging into his doublet, wondering what the hell was going on. Emmeline and her father were both here? He picked up his pace, glad that seeing her face would be the start of his day. He followed the group as they all entered the withdrawing room, and heard his mother call for wine and cakes.

"Someone wanted me?" he said, watching in surprise as everyone turned to face him.

On seeing Emmeline, he felt a peacefulness settle over him. What would it be like to see her every morning?

But his mother and brother looked serious, Emmeline's eyes were pleading, and her father looked like a thundercloud.

"Alexander Thornton," the marquess said, giving him a cold, dismissive stare. "You have abused the trust shown to you by my family."

"I have?" he asked, lifting a brow as he turned to stare at Emmeline.

"Alex—" she began, but her father motioned her to silence.

"I wish I could have you horsewhipped, instead of giving you the privilege of marrying Emmeline."

Stunned, Alex repeated, "Marrying Emmeline?"

"Do not dare to try to squirm your way out of it!"

"May I ask what brought this about?" he said mildly.

"As if you didn't know!" the marquess said with disgust in his voice. "You have seduced my daughter, and even now she could be with child."

Alex heard his mother gasp, but he himself could only stare at Emmeline in amazement. She gave him a wide-eyed shake of her head, then covered her face with her hands for a moment.

"Father," she said in a tremulous voice, "I asked you to allow me to deal with this."

"No, it's all right," Alex said. Emmeline must have initiated this scene; how else would anyone know what had happened between them? He had wanted her to have her own life, but he'd never thought she would choose him. Yet she had. A few months ago he would have been horrified, but now he felt strangely . . . relieved.

"I will obtain a special license," the marquess continued. "And you *will* marry her."

"Of course I will." Alex smiled reassuringly at his mother and brother, both of whom stared at him in shock.

Then he turned to Emmeline. He took her hands in his and kissed both of them. Looking deeply into her eyes, he felt bathed in a warmth that made him feel newly reborn. It was good that they'd be together, that she'd be waiting for him each night.

She would become used to his schedule; things wouldn't be so different. And he didn't have to find the words he'd never had to say before.

He almost wanted to laugh. He never would have thought that his biggest scandal would be being manipulated by an innocent virgin.

But Emmeline was studying him worriedly.

Her father stepped between them. "There is nothing more to be said. She is coming home with me to prepare for the wedding, but I will send a messenger with the details."

Alex looked at the marquess, knowing the man wasn't capable of true fatherly concern. "I'll abide by your wishes—for now."

Emmeline left at her father's side without looking back at him. He heard the echo of the front door slamming, then the suffocating silence of his family. He turned and smiled at them.

"Well. It seems I'm to be married."

"I'm not sure what to say," Spencer said. "I don't know Lady Emmeline."

"I do," said their mother, frowning at Alex. "She is a good girl, and it is a shame to see her humiliated in such a way."

"I didn't mean to hurt her, *Madre*," Alex said. "And I certainly wouldn't have humiliated her as her father did."

"Well, I am pleased you are taking responsibility for your actions, Alexander. And I approve of your choice of young ladies."

"Did it look like I did the choosing?" Alex asked, forcing a laugh.

"I think you chose months ago, though you may not have known it."

"That is absurd!"

She shrugged and spread her hands. "There is no more need to talk. I have a wedding to prepare for. Just tell me—is she with child?"

"No," Alex said shortly.

Spencer gave him an incredulous stare. "So certain, are you?"

"Positive."

Spencer nodded. "All right. I'll send a message to Roselyn, but it's too soon for the baby to travel. Such a shame. She'd want to see *you* married. Surely hell is freezing over as we speak."

Alex rolled his eyes and started to walk out of the room.

"Wait!" Spencer called. "I didn't mean to offend you."

"Of course you did."

"Very well, I did. But before this whole marriage . . . erupted, I wanted to tell you about some important news I received this morning. And I wanted *Madre* to hear it, too."

"Go ahead," Alex said warily.

"I've been looking into the improvements you made to our Cumberland estates while I was in Spain, and wanted to tell you how impressed I was—"

"Didn't think I could make a success of things, did you?"

"I've always known you're more than capable, Alex. And now it seems other people know, too."

"What do you mean?" Alex asked, wishing his mother didn't look so intrigued and hopeful. He was getting tired of always disappointing her.

"The Cumberland town councils elected you to represent them in the House of Commons."

Stunned, Alex accepted his mother's hug, and let Spencer pump his hand. "But why? I wasn't acting like me—I was acting like you."

"Apparently you were knowledgeable enough to impress everyone. I've heard from various people how diligent you were in the House of Lords—even when your eyes were bloodshot."

Alex nodded slowly, amazed at how good it felt to have a purpose in his life. And then he realized that the first person he wanted to tell was Emmeline.

After their mother left to spread the good news, Spencer's grin faded. "Can I just say one more thing? 'Tis about Lady Emmeline."

"Spence, I know what I'm doing."

"I'm sure you do, but you'll want to hear this. Years ago, I danced a time or two with your betrothed."

Alex laughed. "My 'betrothed.' I never thought I'd hear that. Don't worry—I am not a jealous man."

Spencer only raised an eyebrow. "After we danced, her father drew me aside and told me that Emmeline was ill and not expected to live long."

Alex gaped at his brother. "She's as healthy as any woman I know!"

"I see that. I just thought you might find it interesting."

"When exactly did this happen?"

"About seven years ago."

Alex ran a hand through his hair in frustration. "This is too much of a coincidence."

"What do you mean?" Spencer asked.

"That was the exact time she thought she was in love with a tutor. Her father forbade her to marry."

"Could it have been because she was ill?"

"No, she told me her father didn't approve of Roswald, that he wasn't good enough for her. Of course I'm sure he's said the same thing about me."

Spencer grinned. "Well, you certainly aren't good enough for her."

"I know," Alex said as he shrugged. "I think her father was trying to hold on to her. She keeps his books like a steward, and she's practically Blythe's mother. Kent never had to worry about a thing with Emmeline in charge."

"If that's true, it's quite sad."

"Oh, it's true," he said grimly. "Why else would

not a single man court her? But I don't think I can tell Emmeline. She'd be devastated."

Spencer nodded. "No need to start a marriage with a devastated bride."

"After the wedding," Alex continued, "I'll have a talk with my father by marriage. I'll make it clear that if he doesn't leave Emmeline and me alone to begin our new life, I'll reveal his lies to the world."

Spencer clapped him on the shoulder and left the room. Alex stood still, remembering Emmeline's passion in the coach, her plea that he make love to her. And then he thought of her alone in bed later tonight, waiting for him.

Chapter 28

❦

That night, Emmeline stared wide-eyed up at the shadows cast by firelight on her bed-chamber ceiling. The scene at Thornton Manor kept playing over and over in her mind.

Alex hadn't seemed angry—or had he merely hidden it well? She'd known not to expect declarations of love, yet she couldn't help feeling vaguely disappointed.

But she had chosen this plan, and it had worked: Alex was going to marry her. She didn't care about where they would live or any other detail—she was going to be married to the man she loved, and she would make him so happy, he would *have* to love her.

Emmeline had sent a missive telling Blythe about the wedding, and hoped her sister would return in time. She prayed her brothers would be there as well, but she couldn't know if her letters would reach them.

She must have finally dozed off, because suddenly she awoke and knew she wasn't alone. She felt the press of a male body along her side. The fire had gone out and she could see nothing, but she didn't need to see to know that it was Alex, even as he drew the blankets away from her. Her heart swelled to bursting.

She whispered his name and turned into him, wrapping her arms about him. He was naked, his skin warm everywhere it touched hers—which were only her feet and her hands. Yet her smock began a slow slide up her legs as he pulled it.

It felt so right to lie in bed at his side. Surely every night would be like this. He must love her, he *must*. But she waited for the words in vain.

Instead, he spoke to her with his body, overwhelming her with a passion she had never imagined could exist between two people. He pulled the smock over her head, and she lay naked and embarrassed, praying he would touch her.

Instead he whispered, "I want to see you. Is there a candle on the table?"

"Yes, but Alex—"

"Just wait."

He left the bed, and after a moment a candle flared to life as he lit it in the last embers of the fire. She stared at his body as he walked toward her, in awe at the elegant way his muscles moved. He was broad through the shoulders and lean through his hips; his penis was erect and full. The thought of it inside her made her shudder wickedly. Would he let her kiss it?

She realized he was staring down at her, and she lay back on the pillow and let him look. He grinned at her, then found even more candles, until the bed was surrounded in a romantic glow.

On his hands and knees, he crawled onto the bed and over her body, dropping kisses as he passed. His lips praised her feet and the backs of her knees, the inside of her thighs, and her hipbones. He dipped his tongue into her naval, then licked a long path up and around her breasts, even as she prayed he would kiss their peaks again. But he teased her, coming ever nearer with his teeth and tongue, until she wanted to put her breast into his mouth.

Finally his tongue swirled about her nipple and she cried out. She quickly clapped her hand over her mouth as Alex laughed softly against her breast. That felt almost as erotic as his tongue. Then he was kissing her and licking her and touching her everywhere, whispering impassioned words of her beauty. He came up to her mouth and kissed her, lowering his body on top of hers. Every inch of his skin burned her with a heat she gladly welcomed. She wanted him a part of her always, and she wrapped her arms about him.

Feeling hesitant, she bent her knee and slid her foot along his leg. His hips settled deeper between her thighs, where the hard length of his erection teased her.

He groaned into her mouth and stroked her tongue with his. She slid her hands down his face and neck, then over the strong muscles of his shoulders. His back was warm and hard, so smooth. She brushed her fingers over his nipples. Between her legs, his erection pulsed against her.

"Em, I can't wait," he whispered hoarsely.

"Don't wait. Just tell me what to do."

"Bend your other knee, and I promise I'll be as gentle as I can."

He braced himself above her, and she felt him probe between her thighs. With a shudder, he slid a small ways into her, then out.

"Is something wrong?" she asked, desperate to experience again what he'd made her feel in the coach.

"The first time will hurt you."

"I know. But please—"

She tilted her hips up toward him, and was rewarded as he slid in deeper. With a groan he thrust all the way inside her, and a small pain stung her, then faded away.

"Are you all right?" he asked, bending to kiss her mouth. "Because you feel wondrous."

"I am more than all right. Make me come alive again, Alex."

He began a slow slide in and out of her, and every brush of his hips against hers made her long for completion. Rounding his back, he bent and licked her nipples until the ache between her thighs ravaged her mind and her will. There was only Alex and her, his body joined to hers, his soul a part of hers. The spasm of pleasure she'd longed for jolted through her, and with a groan, he buried himself deep inside her and shuddered as the same pleasure took him.

Afterward, Alex braced himself above her, not wanting to move for fear he'd never again find the perfection that he'd discovered in her embrace. The candlelight glowed across her skin as she lay looking up at him, wide-eyed and sated. But there was more, because she smiled tremulously, and in her eyes warmth and trust shone through like he'd never seen before.

And it was all for him. He was overwhelmed, amazed, and grateful.

She had orchestrated their betrothal—but did she love him?

He came down by her side, pulling her into his arms. As he stroked her back, he smiled and whispered, "So who is the father of your child?"

She groaned and pressed her face into his neck. "I'm not with child."

"I know. But now that I've given you a demonstration of how babies are made, you won't make that mistake again, will you?"

She laughed and lay back against her pillow to look up at him. Slowly her smile died, and she reached up to brush his hair back from his forehead.

"Alex, we should talk."

"No."

"Don't you want to know why I—"

"You chose me, and that's all I need to know, Em." ·

"Then you aren't angry?"

He leaned down to kiss her mouth. "Do I taste angry?" He took her hand and brought it to his hard penis. "Do I feel angry?"

Wearing an intrigued expression, she explored him with her hands. He allowed it, though her every touch made him want to thrust inside her, as if they hadn't just shaken the bed with their lovemaking.

Keeping a tight hold on him, she glanced at his face. "Am I allowed to kiss you as you've kissed me?"

He stared at her, and desire blotted out his every rational thought. "Do anything you please," he said hoarsely.

She pushed herself up onto her knees and sat back to look at him. Though her blush never diminished, she explored his body with hands soft as silk. She pressed delicate kisses along his chest and thighs, and her hair trailed after her in an erotic wake. She lingered above his hips and looked up at him.

"May I do anything here?"

He sucked in a breath and could only nod. How had he ever imagined innocence to be boring? Then she took him into her mouth and a moan escaped him. He lasted only a minute before he pulled her knee across to straddle him.

"Alex?"

"Just hold on."

He thrust up inside her, and she threw her head back and smiled, catching onto the motion quickly. Her breasts were like ripe fruit that he eagerly captured. He reached between her legs to stroke her, and it was only moments before they both climaxed again.

She fell down shuddering against his chest. He rolled her to the side and held her and was glad that in only two days' time he'd never have to leave her bed.

He kissed her cheek, and she smiled, but didn't open her eyes. "I must go," he whispered, nibbling her lower lip.

"Hmmm."

He looked at her—sweet and warm and soon to be his wife. He tucked the blankets around her, wondering if tonight they'd made a babe, and trying to imagine himself a father.

It was a strange feeling, one that made him

want to distance himself from the overwhelming nature of it. Emmeline opened her eyes and looked up at him, and he said the first stupid thing that came to mind.

"Well, if we have to marry, at least now there's a reason for it."

She blinked at him, and he cursed himself for a fool and got out of bed before he made it worse. She never said another word, even when he stood on the windowsill and blew her a kiss good-bye.

Emmeline spent a restless night. Oh, she didn't worry about Alex's foolish words, because she knew he didn't mean them. She even found it reassuring that their lovemaking meant so much to him that he had to joke about it to cover his feelings.

But all the next day, she pondered her unease, even while she chose one of her newer gowns as her wedding garment. The servants bustled about her, preparing a feast, though her father hadn't ordered one. They were thrilled for her, and Emmeline was touched.

But something was wrong. On the drive to the church the following morning, she felt nauseated and shaky, and altogether unlike herself. Had she made a dreadful mistake, manipulating Alex's life just as her father had manipulated hers?

They arrived at the church and Humphrey, her beloved coachman, opened the door and beamed up at her, prouder than her own father, who sat silently at her side with his face turned away. She looked up to see Alex waiting at the church door, resplendent in gold and white garments that glittered in the sun.

And Emmeline couldn't do it. She wouldn't force him to marry her. She ignored Humphrey's hand, jumped out of the coach and started to run. It was the only thing she could think of to make Alex declare himself. Panic engulfed her, and she wondered if she'd just made the worst decision of her life. Would he follow her?

Alex felt utterly ridiculous gaping at Emmeline as she ran down the street. Her lovely peach gown rippled behind her feet. He heard his mother's horrified gasp, saw Spencer shaking his head in sympathy. For a moment, all he could think was how this had happened to his brother—how could it happen to him, too?

"Emmeline!" he yelled, setting off after her. "Damnit, I even wrote a poem for the ceremony! You have to come back!"

He dodged people on the street, ignored the jeers and the shouts. He heard a coach behind him and looked over his shoulder to see Humphrey determinedly following him.

The more Emmeline ran, the more heartsick he felt. A bitter darkness would enshroud his life without her in it.

He put on a burst of speed, and caught her by

the elbow; she whirled toward him. He expected to see remorse on her face, but instead she looked wide-eyed and hopeful. He saw the crowd they'd drawn, saw Humphrey practically vault from the driver's box to hold the coach door open.

He took her by the shoulders.

"Em, what are you doing? Don't you want to marry me?"

Amazingly, she smiled. "Of course I do. You've changed me in so many ways, helped me to realize that I have a life just as valuable as Blythe's or anyone else's. I deserve happiness, just as you do. And we can be happy with one another, I *know* it. But I need more. I love you, Alex."

She took a deep breath, and her smile became almost blinding in its soft beauty as she gazed up at him with luminous, shining eyes. He was speechless at the magnitude of what he felt for her, the relief and joy of knowing that she wanted to be married to him.

Suddenly, Emmeline put her hands on her hips and frowned up at him. "Well?"

And he knew then that he could no longer lie to her or himself. He loved her—how could he not have known it? Why had he been a coward by not announcing it to the whole world?

He took her face in his hands and smiled down at her. "I love you, Em."

A resounding cheer rose up around them.

"You are everything that is brave and good," he continued, using his thumb to wipe the tear that fell from her eye. "You stood up to your father for me, something I still find amazing. You would help anyone—your sister, Max, even me, though I little deserve it. Long ago something inside me changed, made me think the kind of man I was wasn't as important as the power and wealth I lacked. Every woman before you only confirmed this in my eyes. For it was the money they wanted, not me."

She pressed herself against him, hugging him around the waist.

"I thought only power counted," he said. "Did I tell you I was just elected to the House of Commons?"

"Oh, Alex, how wonderful!"

"But don't you see, it doesn't matter! I'm the same man, regardless of what I do. I've found myself again by loving you."

She pulled his head down and kissed him. "Alex, you're not saying you'll refuse the appointment, are you?"

"Well, of course not." He grinned. "I just hope I can sometimes keep my mind on business, and not always on you."

"Don't change, Alex," she whispered. "But let's make our scandals smaller from now on."

With a laugh, he swung her up in his arms, and

into the waiting coach. As it rolled down the street, they leaned out the windows and waved to the excited crowd that followed them.

When they pulled up to the church they were still hanging from the coach indecorously, and the reception of some of the nobility was a trifle cool.

But Alex didn't care. He was in a hurry to marry the woman he loved, to begin their life together. He lifted her out of the coach and carried her all the way up the stairs, while she clung to his shoulders and laughed. At the top, he saw Spencer grinning, and his mother tearfully blowing her nose in a handkerchief.

Emmeline tugged on his hand. "So Alex, once we're married, can I see the naked statue of you?"

He almost stumbled as he laughed. It would be a good life.

•

Epilogue

The wedding feast was an event Emmeline would never forget. Crowds of people were waiting for them at Kent Hall. She was touched that so many wished them well. Two of her three brothers had even reached London in time.

But Edmund found her and Alex first, and they drew him aside.

"What happened with the Langstons?" Alex asked.

Edmund shrugged. "I will follow you to the altar in a week. I can only hope that someday we can be as happy as the two of you are."

Alex frowned. "Edmund—"

Edmund laughed and stepped away. "This is your day—enjoy it! Congratulations to both of you."

"Emmy!"

Emmeline whirled about to see Blythe running toward her, dragging Maxwell behind her. The two sisters embraced.

"I missed the ceremony," Blythe said, pulling back to smile into Emmeline's face, "but I'm so glad I'm here for the celebration—and there's so much to celebrate!" She looped her arm through Maxwell's and pulled him up to her side. "We're married! Maxwell had the banns read in his home parish without telling me!"

Emmeline gaped at her sister, and saw Alex unsuccessfully hiding a smile. Maxwell blushed, but withstood her stare with a new pride.

"Isn't this what you wanted?" Blythe asked.

"Oh, dearest, please tell me this is not because of my manipulations. Can you forgive me?"

"Only if you can forgive me for manipulating you."

"What do you mean?"

Blythe smiled up at Maxwell, and the love in their eyes made Emmeline feel at peace.

"I suspected almost from the beginning that you and Alex were meant for each other," Blythe said. "So I made sure he stayed around enough to find out." She clasped Emmeline's hands. "Oh Emmy, you are the bravest person I know. Where I ran away to marry, you stood up to Father and made it happen. Now it's my turn to be brave. It's time to go tell Father."

Emmeline stared after her sister for a moment,

wondering how her father would take another daughter's disobedience, but deciding it didn't matter. She looked up into her husband's eyes. "I was never that courageous at her age."

"It's a good thing, too," Alex said, leaning down to kiss her nose. "Otherwise you'd be married to the tutor turned pig farmer."

"I did marry a pig farmer, or so you've told me."

"Pig farmer or member of Parliament—does it matter?" he asked, demolishing her with that wicked grin she so loved.

"I don't care what you do, Alex, as long as you do it with me."

He slung an arm around her shoulders and began pulling her through the crowd. "Is that an invitation?"

"Alex!" she cried, feeling a flush blaze across her face, even as she watched the laughter of her family and friends.

"They won't miss us. We can come back later."

And then Alex was kissing her, and promising his love forever. "I've begun a new poem, Em. It's called 'The Marriage of Emmeline.' Let's start on the first stanza."

"Alex, please, no more poems!"